The Flying Saucer Mystery

The Silver Dragonfly Series

Book 1

*A Teen, Science Fiction
Adventure Mystery*

By
Dennis R. Durbin

ISBN 13: 978-1-949809-19-0
ISBN 10: 1-949809-19-6

Library of Congress Catalog Card Number: 2018963272

Dedication

IN MEMORY OF MY PARENTS
Who provided loving care and encouragement all their lives.
Charles Ray Durbin, 1923 – 2005
Vyvyne Brooks Durbin, 1923 – 1988

THE SILVER DRAGONFLY SERIES IS DEDICATED
TO MY FAMILY
My Wife, Linda Durbin
My Son, Daniel Durbin
My Daughter, Deanna Durbin
And
My Brother, Donald Durbin
Dennis R. Durbin

Contents

Author's Note

From the beginning of time, most of those who criticize "School" (otherwise known as formal training outside the home by non-family professionals) have NEVER been able to come up with any feasible or practical alternative method to the lecture classroom.

What ideas have been proposed are either vastly too expensive (1 teacher per student), monumentally inappropriate (". . .let's run it like military boot camp!") or horribly misguided ("We don't need testing—just let them enjoy themselves and be kids!").

This book, the first in a series of four, follows the lives of two high school students as they progress through high school, college and beyond using the EDucational REVolution theory. That is, "It's not WHAT you know but HOW FAST you can find the answer!"

There is a more effective method of learning. . .and this book is the key.

Prologue

"General! General Lacey, sir!" the Space Force Technical Sergeant called excitedly. "I'm getting that signal again, the one we couldn't identify before!"

"Can we triangulate it this time and find out where the signal comes from, Sergeant?" General Lacey called out as he ran over to the radar console. "Is the tracking software ready to record?"

"Yes sir, it's ready. I'm tracking it right now, General."

The sergeant studied his radar instrument screen.

"It's definitely inside our borders, sir. . ." he paused, "in the West or Midwest, west of the Mississippi, eastern edge of the Rockies. . .wait a minute! . . .wait a minute! . . .It's farther west than I first thought. . .right. . .about. . .here!" And he put his finger on the spot.

"Good work, Sergeant!" the general said approvingly. "Now, where is 'here?'"

"Just let me zoom in closer, and we'll find out, sir."

The sergeant zoomed the computer screen into its smallest area map and read the name out loud.

"The last trace was in. . .Echo Canyon." Both men looked at each other. "General, isn't that where we estimated that big meteor hit, only we never found an impact crater?"

General Lacey was silent for a few moments, then replied softly, "Yes, it is, Sergeant, yes it is." The general paused briefly before continuing slowly. "The thing is. . .what if it wasn't a meteor you tracked? What if it was something that wouldn't leave a crater? What, if it was. . . something else?" They both stared at the spot on the screen marked Echo Canyon.

Overview—The Flying Saucer Mystery

The Mystery in Echo Canyon is about two high school students living through the 21st Century re-structuring of Education via the EDucational REVolution (the EDREV). The greater freedom given to students includes homework assignments far from school. One of these includes an unexpected encounter with a flying saucer and the students fight to evade capture. As a result of their actions, the United States captures the unmanned saucer and learns how it works. The President of the United States awards both students scholarships to the Space Academy in Colorado Springs, Colorado.

As the two youngest officers, Dan and Jolene are chosen by a computer to test fly the saucer HAL. During that time, they save the life of an F-22 Raptor Fighter Pilot when his escape capsule doesn't open in time and are contacted by the Saurian planetary supercomputer they name "CHARLIE." Using the saucer with help from Charlie, they fly around the moon and finally introduce Charlie to the President of the United States and Space Force General Lacey.

Chapter 1
INTRODUCTION

Daniel Jackson became alert as the ball was kicked towards his goal. He was tired after playing almost two hours of spaceball on the field at Ridgeway High School. His muscles ached, and his right knee was really sore where he had been hit several times by the ball or accidentally kicked by other players.

That'll teach me to always block with my right side! Dan thought in frustration. He shifted his weight to his left foot.

The cheerleaders were doing their best to excite the crowd into making more noise. This was tougher in spaceball than other American sports since the ball changed hands so quickly. The cheerleaders were only supposed to cheer when their team was on offense, but sometimes both sets of cheerleaders were cheering at the same time doing the same cheer!

Dan enjoyed playing spaceball, a game that combined the best of American football and basketball, European soccer with a little English rugby thrown in. From football came the concept of different points for different scores, throwing the ball and defensive and offensive formations. Soccer's contribution was continuous play and the scoring nets at each end of the field. Rugby contributed running and passing the ball plus tackling your opponents to get the ball, and basketball-inspired passing back and forth in any direction any number of times. All in all, the popularity of spaceball had almost eclipsed its parent games.

The play was coming from the left side of the field, and Dan moved closer to that side. Suddenly, one of his defenders tripped, and that gave the other team a one-person advantage. The other team quickly passed the ball back and forth and advanced it down the field as Dan moved back to the left and got ready to block. At the last second, the ball was kicked all the way across the field to a lone forward who had a clear shot at Dan's goal from his right side.

Dan was way out of position, and he knew it.

Desperately he ran to his right just as the opponent kicked the ball towards the corner of the net.

Dan leaped high into the air and barely deflected the ball with his fingertips. The ball struck the top bar behind him, bounced straight up into the air, came back down to hit the bar again. . .and bounced out of bounds behind the net.

"Save!" yelled one of the referees. "Out of bounds shot, green!"

As Dan picked himself up off the grass, he wondered if he had really hurt his knee this time. His knee continued hurting as he limped over to the referee to get the ball.

Coach Riley noticed Dan was limping and substituted another goalie to take Dan's place. Dan was his best goalie, but this game was almost over anyway.

"Great save, Dan!" Bill Johnson shouted to him as he ran up. "I don't know how you do that so often. Coach told me to take your place for a while."

"Thanks, Bill." Grateful for a chance to just sit on the bench, Dan asked Coach Riley for a cold pack for his knee. The coach told him they were out of cold packs. Again!

"Sorry, Dan," the coach said. "I'll try to get some more before the next season starts," he promised. The game ended a few minutes later as Dan watched from the bench. Dan's team won by a score of 15 to 9.

Thank heavens for small favors! Dan thought as he limped into the school's locker room to change. *At least I've got six weeks to heal before the next season starts.*

Dan was an athletically built high school student a couple of inches above average height. He had blonde hair, bright blue eyes, and a very winning personality. Not only was Dan talented in sports, but he was also one of the best trumpet players in the school. He played in the symphonic and jazz bands, but his real interest was competition marching band. Dan loved the marching competitions where his "Marching Rebels" got to compete, then mix with other band students after the show. Dan also had an outstanding record in academics, usually ranking in the top thirty in his class. He enjoyed camping out and was a junior leader in the Campers of America organization. Dan had spent a sizable portion of his life outside camping, sleeping and "surviving" in the wilderness. He always attended church services but sang in the choir only when he couldn't get out of it.

Although Dan didn't realize it, school athletics had changed dramatically during his lifetime. Before the Educational Revolution, most high schools just had one "varsity" team in each sport. After the Educational Revolution in the early 21st Century, however, entire high schools, as well as athletic conferences, were sometimes consolidated into just one building. These consolidated schools, like the one centered at Ridgeway High School in the northwest Chicago suburbs, developed several teams in each sport. These teams competed against each other on an internal basis and only after each school determined a "champion" team would that team play against other schools. This new system cut athletic transportation costs by over 70% and made "away" games special and rare enough that a lot more people attended.

At first, many coaches and parents had been afraid athletics might suffer due to the EdRev consolidation of schools. In fact, the exact opposite occurred! Before the EdRev, many students didn't go out for sports because they knew they would sit on the bench all season or simply never make "the team." After the consolidation, however, more students joined because they knew multiple teams meant they would really get to play. In fact, most schools were able to field multiple teams in many sports, not just the popular ones.

The consolidation that many felt would hurt school athletics had the exact opposite effect. Student participation in athletics more than doubled after the EdRev.

"Great job, Dan!" several of his teammates said as they changed clothes.

"Thanks, guys, but it's easy when you keep the ball at the other end of the field most of the time."

"We know that, but we didn't want you to get too bored."

"Right!" Dan answered. "I really believe that, John!"

Dan grimaced as his knee twinged again. He knew accidents and injuries, and rough landings still happened even when you were playing against your best friends. Dan had thought about quitting spaceball, but he kept playing because his dad had played spaceball in college and he wanted to please his dad.

After he showered and changed clothes, Dan eased himself onto his personal floater and gingerly drove home. [Think of a personal floater as a small, two-person airborne anti-gravity motorcycle with fail-safe controls and energy shield against weather.] Home for Dan was a large Geodesic

Dome Cluster with the main 50-foot dome on the top of a small hill. This dome was connected to a 30-foot dome that served as the floater garage with an office and recreation room overhead. The bedrooms and large bathroom were all safely underground in the basement of the main dome, and the living room, dining room, kitchen, second bathroom, and guestroom were on the first floor. The main dome's second floor was an 800 square foot open loft used for reading, music or whatever. Dan thought it was a great spot for parties. The third dome was actually a 25-foot screen dome with lawn furniture and a small pool inside. The three domes were connected in a triangular pattern with a garden area in the central space.

With his floater safely put away, Dan got a cold pack for his knee and settled in to work on his academic assignments. He knew EdRev schoolwork didn't take as much time as attending lecture classes every day at school used to take, and he was glad he could work as fast as he wanted. His computer also gave him the freedom to choose which of the four Core subjects to work on first and how much time to spend on each subject. Dan thought he'd better check his overall progress before starting.

One of the neatest things about school, and a direct result of the EdRev was the fact schoolwork could be mostly done at home on the computer. This "work at home" idea was great for both advanced and slower students since they could go at their own speed. Another change allowed students to check their grade status on "Centerpoint" software at any time. Of course, since their parents could also check on their grades daily, periodic "report cards" had become a thing of the past.

"Status," Dan said out loud, waited for the screen to clear, then said, "CORE subjects." *It seemed no matter how fast your computer ran, you still had to wait,* Dan thought.

OK, now let's see where I am, he thought when the 'CORE' screen opened.

"Math," he said out loud, and the screen read. . .*1.9 years above norm.*

"Language,". . .*1.4 years above norm.*

"Science,". . . *1.5 years above norm*

"Social Science,". . . *2.0 years above norm.*

"Norm" was the timeline used as the recommended or "normal" rate of learning. If you were above the norm, you were considered to be ahead of the learning curve timeline and received advantages. These "advantages" were things like not attending school every day, not staying in classes all day plus a much greater choice of Encore classes. If you were close to the norm, you worked on a school computer four hours a day for two to three days a week with teachers present to give extra help. (Attending school now meant working on a computer workstation and not going from classroom to classroom to listen to boring lectures!) If you were below the norm, you had the more traditional five days a week school for about seven hours a day. However, this time was also spent mostly on the computer or in small group instruction much better suited for individualized help than old-style lecture classes used to be. Every student had an Individualized Learning Plan, and the more a student achieved at home, the less time they had to spend at school!

Not a bad report! Dan thought with satisfaction, *and since I am more than one year above norm in all four CORE areas, I only need to check in at school once this week. Great! I think I'll work on Language first since that is my "lowest" grade.* Theoretically, Dan had to check in at school only once this week, but that seldom happened. Band class met almost every day, but it was right before the school diner opened. Dan, as well as most of the other students, liked to spend time "hanging out" in the diner, so attending band class was not a hardship. (The school diner had replaced more traditional teenage "hangout" places, like the burger joints, the pizza places, the laser combat arcades and so on.) Band class was fun, and Dan was beginning to enjoy playing trumpet more than he liked playing spaceball. At least, you seldom got hurt playing trumpet even during competition marching season! What Dan didn't miss at all were the lecture type classes students used to suffer through when all students were forced to sit in mandatory classes and "learn" at the same speed. Dan remembered those lecture classes well since the EdRev change didn't happen until he was in second grade. As Dan started work on his Core subject Language, he thought, *there must be a way I can get out of spaceball next season! I've just got to find some reason Dad will accept.*

Jolene Fisher brushed her long straight hair as she thought about which boys she could ask to be her partner for the musical tryouts.

Jolene was a little taller than average for a high school girl, and her long hair was somewhere between blonde and auburn, depending on the light. She had a slim build that was due more to dancing than athletics and a very strong personality that set her apart from other girls. Her interests include playing flute in band (piccolo in marching band,) singing in the school choir and her church choir, dancing, theater and drama, and new clothes. Jolene was a very finicky dresser, and one of the most admired girls in school. This was due not only to her stunning appearance but her academic achievement and "wonder woman" personality.

Jolene knew this musical had a lot of dancing, and she needed a partner who could dance, sing, and who was also strong enough to toss and catch her.

I know some of the tosses are high, she thought, *and some of the dances are difficult, and I want to feel safe.*

I also want a partner who is not a jerk!

Most of the boys who dance and sing well are so obnoxious I'd probably knock them silly the first time they grabbed me wrong or touched me where they shouldn't! Some of them probably didn't know that girls are different than boys yet anyway, she thought scornfully!

All the boys except Dan. Jolene sighed deeply. No matter how hard she tried not to, her thoughts always came back to Dan. Dan was the perfect gentleman. He could sing, he could dance, and the thought of him holding her while they were dancing was exciting. Jolene knew her crush on Dan started when he stopped some bullies from picking on her back in early elementary school. She saw him every day in band and watched him in the school diner. His friends were all nice, but none of them danced and sang the way he did. His strong baritone/bass voice sounded nice in church services, and she had tried several times to get him to sing regularly in the choir.

She also knew how smart Dan was, even though he went to great lengths to hide it.

Jolene had peeked at his records while she was assigned to help in the office. Dan was 23rd out of 907 students in his "class." That was important to Jolene. She was 12th out of 1012 in her "class," and she was determined to stay in the top twenty-five scholars.

It must be Dan, she decided firmly. *I know he doesn't date much yet, but I wonder if he has discovered girls are different from boys? If not,* she thought with anticipation, *I can let him know exactly what pleases me! He has lots of friends, and I'll bet some of them will be glad to help me.*

Now. . .am I really ready to 'Press my first guy let alone 'Pin' him, she thought to herself? Jolene pondered that idea for a while, then put her hairbrush aside and opened her flute case. She twisted the head joint carefully onto the body, then twisted the foot joint so her right little finger could reach the low C and Bb keys comfortably and started practicing.

The tragedy had occurred about 35 Earth-years ago. Over centuries, an intelligent species had risen to create a civilization. They had gone from muscle power to machine power; from primitive fossil fuel to advanced anti-gravity power. Colonists were sent to two suitable planets, and a huge colony ship was launched to reach another galaxy. Mechanical and robotics systems were manufactured and perfected, and when even the day to day drudgery of cave work was automated, this gifted species turned its attention to biological explorations.

The decision proved deadly.

A laboratory accident released an experimental organism that quickly spread throughout the planet, ending the life of every being of this race on the planet Saurian. Within days, intelligent life on this planet ceased to exist.

Intelligence, however, did not. The computers carried on.

Lights still functioned, robots still worked tirelessly, and instructions left in the Computer High-end Advanced Robotic Linguistic Integrator system were still carried out. The instructions were scrupulously carried out, in fact, but with no rational judgment guiding them.

Thus it was that Directive #107-3142-99-7 concerning the exploration of oxygen-bearing planets, and Directive

#017-4910-03-1 detailing the taking of live samples, combined directly to affect the inhabitants of the third planet of a "G" type star called Earth.

After band class the next day, Jolene was sitting in the diner three tables from Dan and his friends when she decided it was time. She had purposely sat with Mary Chen. She knew Dan thought highly of Mary because Mary was the 1st chair (best) trumpet player in the band. Dan sat 2nd chair out of 24 trumpets and usually came very close to beating Mary during tryouts. Jolene explained to Mary what she wanted to do and asked for her help.

Mary was delighted to help!

Mary Chen liked and respected Dan very much. He had stepped in to support her in class when she was feeling sick one day, and he played her solo so well the director didn't even notice it wasn't Mary playing. Dan didn't argue when Mary said she was ready to play the solo the next day, and he never bothered her to do other solos unless she offered.

Still, Mary knew Dan wanted to beat her for the 1st chair trumpet position, and she decided that if Dan got involved with Jolene in the musical, he might not practice as much on his trumpet! It was clearly in her own best interest to help Jolene, 'Pin' Dan.

Mary went over to Dan's usual table and sat down unexpectedly.

"You know, Dan," she said sweetly, "I never thought I would need to take YOU by the hand and lead you where you need to go. Don't you ever look at the bulletin board?"

Surprised that Mary had come to the guys' table, Dan looked at her and replied defensively, "Well. . .sure, Mary. Every now and then I look at it, but I didn't see anything special there today." Dan looked at his friends who either shrugged their shoulders or shook their heads.

"But there is something special," Mary replied, "and it's been up a couple of days just waiting for you. Believe me, this is something you don't want to miss. C'mon." With that, she got up and went towards the bulletin board in the corner of the diner. Dan shrugged his shoulders, then got up and followed Mary.

"See? Right there." Mary pointed to the announcement concerning the musical Production WOLFSTOCK (© 1996 by Mary McMahon and Donald Woodward) that was to be staged. Dan glanced at the notice and read it quickly.

"Mary," he said patiently, crossing his arms, "the pit band for this only has two trumpet parts. I know you want one, and Adam already told me he really, really, really wanted to play in the pit band this year, and did I mind? I told him it was okay with me, and you two could cover the trumpet parts."

Jolene had been listening and pretended to be just walking by. She stopped and said, "Mary, you aren't showing him the right parts."

"Oh?" replied Mary. "What parts should he be looking at? Wait a minute—there's Bill. Gotta run Dan, Jolene!" and with that, she left the two of them alone.

Gotcha! thought Jolene in anticipation.

"These are the parts you need to look at, Dan. With your abilities, you need to contribute more than just playing trumpet in the pit." Jolene pointed to the cast parts on the notice, not the pit band parts.

"This is one of the finest musicals ever written, and the dancing and singing parts are outstanding. The problem is, the best six parts are written for couples. I want one of those parts, Dan, but the only way I can get one is if I have a strong partner who can sing and dance, like you." Jolene dropped her voice a little and looked directly up into Dan's eyes. "I know you sing very well Dan, and you are an excellent dancer. I want you to be my partner in this musical. Will you do that for me, Dan? Can we audition as a couple?"

While she was speaking, Jolene casually placed her foot on top of Dan's foot.

Dan stared back at Jolene, startled, flattered and flustered all at the same time, and not at all sure what was happening. Dan thought Jolene was the most beautiful woman he'd ever met, and he didn't want to mess up this opportunity to work with her.

"Jolene, gosh! Thanks for the kind words and invitation! I. . .I really don't know what to say!" he stalled for time to think. "You know I play on the green spaceball team, and the next season starts in just six weeks, and I'm afraid my dad expects me to play again. Spaceball takes a lot of time, you know, and I don't know if I can do that and perform in a musical at the same time."

"No problem, Dan," Jolene said and smiled, as she looked up at him. "Just ask your father if you can be my partner in the musical this season instead. There's always another season for spaceball," Jolene said scornfully, "but this musical is unique. We may never have a chance to do it again. Never!" She stepped down harder on his foot. "It's very important to me, Dan," she said as she leaned closer to him. "Very. . .important."

"Oh. . .uh. . .sure. . .well. . .uh. . ." Dan stammered as he tried to figure out how he should answer.

"Repeat after me, Dan," Jolene said forcefully. "'Jolene, I will ask my father if I can try out for a part in the musical.'"

"Sure, I can do that," Dan responded quickly.

"No! Repeat the words, Dan!" and with that, she stepped on his foot with all her weight. This position also brought her face very, very close to Dan's face, which flustered him to no end. He could smell her perfume, and her body was unusually close to his and warm.

"Jolene, my. . .my foot. . ." he stammered out of desperation to say something.

"Repeat it now, Dan!" she commanded, standing on his foot and staring into his eyes.

Dan gave in immediately. "Yes, Jolene, I will ask my dad about the musical."

"Pledge?"

"Pledge."

Jolene smiled and stepped back off his foot, but she didn't remove her foot from on top of his. "Thanks, Dan," she said sweetly. "You and I are really the best partners for this musical." Jolene glanced down at her foot resting on Dan's, and then stared back up into his eyes. "I'm counting on you to let me get the part I want." With those words, she smiled at him, stepped on his foot again which brought her face very close to his, looked into his eyes again and said, "Pressed." Jolene waited to see if Dan objected in any way, and when he didn't, she turned and walked away with a big smile on her face.

Dan limped back to his table with a very puzzled look on his face. He took a drink of soda pop and then muttered, "Girls!" under his breath.

"So. . .what was that little scene all about? Jeremy asked curiously. "I take it she wants something?" Dan's friends had watched what happened at the bulletin board.

"Oh. . .yeah. . .well. . .Jolene wants a partner so she can try out for the musical."

Adam asked, "And she wants you as her partner, I take it?"

"Yeah. I told Mary I was going to let you play trumpet in the pit this time, Adam, and Jolene must have overhead me. She told me I needed to try out for a cast part, and she almost broke my foot making a point of it." As he bent over to rub his foot, Dan didn't notice the smiles and glances his friends exchanged. They knew that standing on his foot meant Jolene had just 'Pressed him, and they also knew Dan didn't have a clue about what had just happened! Jolene was probably the one girl almost every boy in the school would like to date, let alone be 'Pressed' or 'Pinned' to. She had clearly chosen Dan, and he didn't have a clue!

Well, well, well, this should be interesting to watch develop, they thought with glee. *I wonder if Dan has any idea what he's in for? Jolene is one intense girl!*

'Pressed! Jolene thought excitedly to herself as she walked away from Dan, *and he only objected a little bit! That wasn't too bad. Now if I can just get my dad to talk to his dad, we'll set the stage for something better than 'Pressing! You know, the more I think about it, I really do want to 'Pin' Dan. I'll give him a day or two to think about it, then 'Pin' him. Oh, this is exciting! Now, what more can I do to help things along?* Jolene thought.

I know! Clothes! Mother has been after me to buy some new clothes for school, and I know just what Dan likes. By watching who he watches in the diner, I know he likes skirts and dresses better than slacks, but jeans are okay. He likes dress shoes and high heels better than sneakers or flip-flops.

The day Liana wore a white blouse with black leather bolero vest, black leather short skirt, and black spike heel boots, Dan actually got up and followed her around, pretending of course to just be taking his lunch tray back!

Now, I wonder how far I can go in buying some new outfits?

It was Mother's idea, after all, and I know I can get some outfits that will really appeal to Dan!

Dating rituals change from time to time like a pendulum that swings back and forth in time. For most of history boys asked girls out on dates, but girls could not ask boys. Over time that situation changed to boys and girls asking each other out equally. By the time Dan and Jolene were in high school, the pendulum had swung to girls asking boys out more than boys asking girls out. With girl's involvement in wrestling, the concept of '*Pinning*' changed from giving a small piece of jewelry (a pin, as a prelude to an engagement ring) to a girl, to a body pressed flat with both shoulder blades touching the floor. *('Pinned.')* "'Pressing" was a precursor to 'Pinning,' and done just as Jolene had done to Dan.

Chapter 2
CAMPING

Dan stretched slowly as he lay inside his transparent Enviro tent watching the stars in the sky, wondering if the rest of the campers in his group had found as good a place for their "tent" as he had. He hoped so, but part of this requirement was for each camper to find and set up his own site high in the mountains of Colorado. Despite being Senior Camper, he was not supposed to help the younger campers.

Things used to be much different, Dan thought as he remembered the old Boy Scout manuals he'd scanned from last century. For instance, scouts used to hike to their campsite carrying everything they needed on their back instead of driving their floaters in, and then set up an unpowered cloth "tent" that was subject to leaking rainwater and getting blown over by the wind. Talking to anyone was not possible unless they were within shouting distance.

Nowadays, campers could use their personal floater for hauling gear, sleep protected in the Enviro safe from rain, wind, and bears, and 'SAT or receive a 'SAT from home or anywhere else. The universal 'SAT (Portable Cellular Satellite Telecommunicator) was a personal "cell phone" everyone had so they could receive calls anytime and anywhere. The

SAT's were loosely based on the original cell phones but used satellite coverage instead of local cell towers, and functioned as a notebook, alarm clock, and personal diary.

The floater also helped eliminate the worst part of camping—smelly outdoor toilets! Clean flush toilets were usually within a few minutes float from almost anywhere, and that fact alone meant many more people were interested in camping.

Of course, the old-time Boy Scouts weren't expected to camp at an altitude above 9,000 feet in the middle of the winter, either! The Rockies were bitterly cold this time of year. Thank heavens for the Enviro!

[The discovery of the portable force field was not intended for private use, let alone camping. Military research was looking for a way to protect whole cities from bombs and missiles, and also troops in the field.

While a force field was easy to do once you knew how the power necessary to cover a small city was more than could be generated except with large nuclear power plants. Small, dome-shaped fields about 10 to 15 feet across—easy! Smaller fields to cover a floater and protect it from the weather—even easier. Large city-sized fields remained impossible, at least so far. Research into a more efficient power source and control system continued.

Looking for a way to advertise and capitalize on force field technology so they could continue their research, lab technicians set up small force fields in the most unlikely places to show how humans could be protected. The Arctic, the Deserts, the Rain Forests, all became comfortable with a portable force field controlling temperature, humidity, and air pressure. While the force field was breathable but not airtight (wind or moisture didn't come through, but regular air did,) the area inside could easily be heated or cooled to a set standard regardless of the weather.

Oddly enough, it was a janitor at the research lab who not only came up with the name, but also the most common use and commercial market for the device.

Jonathan Sydney Melloncamp had Downs Syndrome and an IQ about 30 points below normal. He always worked hard at cleaning the labs, however, and was liked by the scientists for both his work ethic and his childlike wonder at things. Jonathan overheard the director of the lab talking with several other scientists about what the force field could do, and how it could condition the environment to make it more comfortable.

After that meeting was over, Jonathan asked the director if he could borrow one of the En. . .Enviro. . .whatever the thing was called. . .so he could go camping with his son who had serious allergies and normally could not stay outdoors overnight.

The director smiled and started to tell him "No," but suddenly realized if Jonathan could learn how to use the force field controls, anyone could! After a moment's thought, the director told Jonathan he would see what he could do but that he needed to wait a day before deciding. The next day, a team set out to make the Enviro controls simple enough and safe enough for Jonathan to use. The controls only took about 45 minutes to design and about three hours to "breadboard" the first test controller. The director agreed to loan it to Jonathan.

The attention given to Jonathan's "Enviro" at the large camping event was overwhelming!

Other campers with allergies were very interested in it, but so were many campers with family members who refused to go camping due to the physical discomforts and inconvenience. Jonathan showed many people how the Enviro could be made translucent, opaque or a solid color. He showed how it heated or cooled the air inside, and even radiated light to help find it in the dark! He told everyone with pride it was made in "his" lab.

The following Monday morning, the director's secretary at the lab was quickly swamped with 'SAT's from people who wanted to know how to purchase or rent one of Jonathan's "Enviro's." The price people were willing to pay (compared to the actual cost of building each Enviro generator) was astonishing! The director immediately promoted Jonathan to chief of Enviro sales, got him a secretary and bookkeeper of his own, hired a replacement janitor, and the rest was history.

The Enviro became the quickest selling product and the biggest boon to camping since the sleeping bag.]

Another difference between the old Boy Scout Troops and modern-day campers was the achievement levels or ranks. The highest "rank" used to be Eagle Scout (carried over directly from Boy Scouts,) and you had to earn it by age 18. Soon after the merger with the girls' groups, a higher achievement level called Stellar was added, reflecting the changing attitudes from the Educational Revolution and Society, and the rank "2nd Class" was removed as offensive to minorities. In a very controversial decision, no age limit was set for Stellar to encourage continued participation in camping. Many purists disagreed with this change, but the number of 30, 40, and even 50-year-old Eagle Scouts who returned to camping and completed Stellar seemed to prove the point.

The basic premise of the old-fashioned scouting was still the same for campers—camping and survival skills were #1, and everything else took 2nd place.

Wait a minute! Dan thought suddenly. *Safety!*

He sat up quickly, unfolded his pocket computer and looked for the files on this exercise.

"Query—Safety," he said, and quickly scanned the text as it scrolled across the field. He found basic, general and generic rules, but nothing specific.

"Query—Duties; Sr. Camper Leader". As he waited, Dan realized he should have checked this before, but had forgotten. "Query—Safety."

And there it was. OOPS!

It shall be the duty of the Senior Camper Leader to check and approve all personal sites during Survival camping before the 1st sleep period.

No problem, he thought with relief. *It's almost dark, but I'll bet no one is asleep yet. I still have time to check everyone's site.*

Dan stood up quickly (stretching the Enviro a little as he did and changing it to radiate so he could find it easily in the snow.) He checked the settings on his bodysuit, pulled up his hood and stepped outside. It was 3 degrees below zero Fahrenheit with a wind-chill of 22 below zero. Visibility was excellent although the light was starting to fade, so Dan started his floater and drove over the edge of the mountain cliff.

OK, let's see what I can see, he thought. As he steered around the face of the cliff, Dan counted five sites visually. He floated to the first.

"SAT—Key Jeff Williams," he spoke clearly as he recognized the floater.

"Yo, Dan!" came the reply. "I figured you'd make rounds, so I checked my group already. Jonathan and Sammy have great sites, here. . .and here." As Jeff marked his map, it repeated on Dan's.

"Bobby really needs to move about twenty feet. Would you check him as a safety issue? He's right. . .here." The location appeared on the computer map.

"Sure thing, Jeff. As usual, you're ahead of the game already."

"Thanks, Dan. Have you thought about what Jolene asked you?"

Jolene. He'd thought about little else since she had cornered him, literally trapped him, in the school diner to make her pitch. His foot still ached where she stepped on him, twice.

"Affirm, I've thought about it a lot." Mostly how he could convince his dad he didn't want to play spaceball this season.

"Do it, Dan, don't just think about it. It is a rare opportunity to partner with Jolene on anything, let alone something as special as the musical."

"I hear you. Let me check Bobby. 'SAT me if you need me."

"Will do," he heard in response.

Bobby had set his Enviro up under a large tree that had fallen sideways. The tree looked like it could slip further at any time. *Great Stellars*, Dan thought as he looked at the site. *Doesn't he have any sense? Now how can I do this?*

"Yo, Bobby," he 'SATed.

"Hi, Dan. Isn't this a terrific location, or what?"

"Affirm, Bobby. That fallen tree will block out all the snow. That's why you're under there, right?"

"No," Bobby replied, sounding puzzled. "My Enviro will take care of any snow."

"The tree will hide you from bears, then?"

"No, Dan!" Bobby said scornfully! "Bears hibernate in the winter! You know that!"

"Well, I'm sure glad your Enviro will protect you if that tree slips and comes down," Dan suggested. "How much force have you got it set for?"

"The max, of course. I always set it for the max."

"And the max on your model Enviro is. . .?"

"A little over 800 pounds, I think," Bobby replied hesitantly.

"What would you guess that tree weighs, Bobby?" Dan asked.

"Let's not guess, Dan—let's find out exactly!" Bobby said, whipping out his pocket computer. "25 feet by, oh. . .let's say 2 feet in diameter times. . .density point 8,"

"It's frozen, Bobby. Better try point 9 at least."

"OK, point 9. . ." he said thoughtfully. Then he said, "Ouch!"

"How much, Bobby?"

"3000 pounds! Dan. . .is it OK if I move my Enviro?" Bobby asked quickly.

"Absolutely! You get to choose where to put it."

"Great! I think I'll put it right. . .over. . .here." And with that Bobby picked up his generator and moved away from the tree. The field surrounding the generator moved with him.

"Gotta flit, Bobby. 'SAT me. . .'"

". . .if you need me, I know, I know!" Bobby said.

Everyone else checked out OK, except Brandon who had set up in an avalanche shoot! He was also about 200 feet lower than the 9,000-foot requirement. Dan "questioned" him into moving, and then floated back to his own Enviro.

Teaching can be fun, he thought, surprisingly. Of course, His dad said that to him at least once a day every day. Clearly, his dad had ideas about him becoming a teacher.

His dad. Jolene. *There must be some way to resolve this situation. Dad likes spaceball so much, I can't believe he'd let me quit, and I can't do spaceball and the musical both. Maybe I just need to think about it a while,* he thought as he lay on his back to watch the stars. Very quickly he was asleep.

Chapter 3
THE GREAT CONFRONTATION

"*. . .So, you see, Mom, if you could just talk to Dad for me first, then maybe we could both convince him together," Dan suggested hopefully.

"No, Dan. I'm not going to intervene in this. This is between you and your father."

"Mom!" Dan said indignantly.

"You will ask your father about this," his mother replied firmly. "You know how important spaceball is to him! Go ask him now."

"But he's working now, Mom!" Dan protested.

"He's always working, Dan!" she replied. "Go!. . .Ask!. . . Him!. . .Right!. . .Now!"

Well, I tried, thought Dan glumly.

Dan went down to the basement, waited until his Dad looked up, so he didn't break his concentration, then made his pitch.

"Dad, I've been thinking about what I'm doing with my life, and how I'm spending my time. I've come to the conclusion that I need some new experiences, and I believe I'm ready for a change." *Good start,* Dan thought, *appeal to the more serious side.*

"That's good, Dan," his dad said absent-mindedly as he used the computer worklink. "I'm glad you are thinking about change." Dad's lab had a state-of-the-art hyper wave Server, and while Dr. Jackson physically went to work so he could supervise the research, he could really do everything else from home. Original research had to be done in person, and Dad's lab was doing key research for the government, only Dad never talked about what it was very much.

"Categorize how you spend your time now. List the changes you'd like to make, and we'll discuss if you are able to add something more, or if you must delete something from your schedule."

Categorize, List, Discuss, thought Dan. *Boy, Dad always takes the logical approach to problems! Luckily, I'm prepared this time. Maybe that will be enough to impress him. I sure hope so.* "I've already started the process Dad, and you can screen it or look at the printout here." Dan handed his dad a paper with the following chart printed.

Activity	*Weekly Time*
sleeping/dressing	9 hours/ 7 days
schoolwork	3 hours/ 5 days week
at school	4 hours/ 5 days week
trumpet practice	1 hour/ 6 days week
research	1 hour/ 2 days
camping or prep	1 hour/ 2 days
eating	1.5 hours/ 7 days
personal hygiene	1 hour/ 7 days
church services	2 hours/ week
spaceball practice	3 hours/ 6 days

Activity	**Weekly Time**
recreation	1 hour/ 7 days
target shooting	1 / 4 hour / 1 day

"Hmmm. Good approach, son," his dad said after he read it, then frowned. "However, I'd like to see a little more time for trumpet practice. You'll never beat. . .what's-her-name?"

"Mary, Dad."

". . .Mary on only one hour of trumpet practice a day?"

"Dad, Mary lives for her trumpet. She practices four hours every day, and trumpet is her whole life. In fact, I think she even sleeps with her trumpet! She doesn't do camping or spaceball or any of the other things that I do. I come within 1 or 2 points of beating her as it is, and nobody else is even close to either one of us. I can live with 2nd chair, as long as it's to someone as dedicated, hardworking and talented as Mary."

"Good point, son," Dad said thoughtfully. "I'll accept that reasoning. Now, what activity or class did you want to add?"

Crunch time thought Dan. *Here's where it hits the fan.* He took a deep breath.

"I've been asked to be in the musical at school, Dad." He waited for the explosion.

"The musical? You mean, play trumpet in the pit band again, right?"

"No, Dad. Jolene asked if I would be her partner on stage."

His dad looked up and stared at him for the first time, and said finally, "Jolene?"

"Jolene Fisher, Dad."

Dan waited.

"Jolene?" his dad said again as if the sound of her name

could make her appear.

"Her dad is Doctor Fisher. He works at your lab doing. . .something?"

"Oh! . . .Yes, yes. . .. Molecular Anti-Gravity Bindings," Dad said absently. "His team has made remarkable progress on. . ." Dad's voice tapered off. "Now, let me get this straight, Dan. You're asking me to let you act? . . .on stage? . . .in the school musical, is that right?"

"Yes, Dad."

"And it's because you think it will be a good, or at least a new experience, right?"

"Yes, sir."

"And you were personally invited to do this by Henry's daughter Jolene Fisher?"

"Yes, Dad."

"How much time will "acting" in the musical take?"

"Practices are about three to four hours a day, Dad, and will last for 10 to 12 weeks." *There, the kiss of death!*

Dad was quiet for a while, then leaned back and crossed his arms and looked at Dan.

"Why did Jolene ask you?"

Caught off guard by the question, Dan thought, *Good Lord! Is he really considering it?* "Uh, well. . .she knows I like to dance, Dad, and she knows I can sing because she hears me most Sundays at church services, and. . ." he couldn't say it.

"Yes?" Dad said slowly. "What else?"

Dan took a deep breath. "She thinks I'm OK. . .at least. . .for a guy."

"Hmmm." Dad studied my list quietly for a full minute and then turned back to his work.

"Approved. Notify the school spaceball coach tomorrow that you are taking this next season off. Post your rehearsal schedule on the fridge. Inform your mother when and where the performances will be. And," he said glancing back over the top of his old-fashioned glasses at me, "add ten more minutes a day to trumpet practice. I still think you can beat Mary." With that amazing pronouncement, he was lost again on the work link.

Unknown to Dan, Jolene had hounded her Dad to talk to Dan's father about the musical. Dr. Fisher finally gave in, discussed the matter with Dr. Jackson who in turn discussed it with his wife, Linda. All three adults felt acting in the musical would be much more valuable for both children than just playing spaceball again would be for Dan. Not surprisingly, they all secretly liked the idea of their child spending time with another young person they thought would be a "good" influence. Of course, none of the parents could say that out loud to their children!

Dan went back to the kitchen to see his mother.

"Well?" she asked, looking up from her book.

"Approved! I can't believe it, Mom. He didn't even argue with me when he knew I would have to skip spaceball for a season. He. . .told. . .me!"

His mom smiled. "We are all individuals with different likes and interests, Dan. Just because your father loves spaceball is no reason for him to insist you must play."

"Frigid, Mom. You and Dad are the greatest!"

"Thank you, dear. Now go do your schoolwork. And don't forget the extra time on trumpet."

"Yes, Mom," Dan said as he headed to his room, and it never even occurred to him to ask how his mom already knew about the extra ten minutes for trumpet practice.

After Dan had gone to his room, his mom got up and peeked around the corner and down at her husband in the basement. They silently exchanged smiles and nods of satisfaction. No words were needed.

Jolene appreciated the early copy of the script and songbook for the musical she got from Mr. Pierce. It gave her a chance to really get into the dancing. She thought the best way to keep Dan interested was to hit him with the dancing first. The script alone was hilarious. She knew Dan would like it, and the songs went way back to the 1950's and a time when a rock and roll singer named Elvis was known as "The King."

What I really need, Jolene decided, *is a hook. Something to fix his attention so that he doesn't think about spaceball or dropping out of the musical. I think I need to 'Pin' him. That's just the hook that will keep him tied to me.*

She looked at herself in the mirror and was pleased with what she saw. *But I've never gone steady,* she thought, *never 'Pinned' any boy, or even 'Pressed' one until Dan yesterday.*

Jolene asked her mother if she had time to help her pick out some new outfits. Her mother was so surprised and delighted that Jolene actually asked for her help that they both left within minutes for the best shopping mall around. True, it was much easier to buy things online, but buying clothes was always more fun when you could try them on in person.

Jolene was surprised and amazed her mother let her get four new outfits, including some shoes, boots, and accessories. She had hoped she might get three outfits but thought she would probably only get two. When her mother approved the third and fourth outfit, Jolene couldn't believe her luck!

Luck had nothing to do with it.

What Jolene didn't know was that her mother overheard Jolene talking to herself in the dressing room mirror. "Yes! I think Dan will really like this outfit, and I can't wait to show him!" Jolene's mother approved of Dan as her daughter's choice for a partner in the musical very much and decided she could help quietly by letting Jolene get the extra outfits. She also thought Dan would be a very suitable man for Jolene to date, but, of course, she didn't dare say that out loud.

Back home, Jolene tried on the different outfits with different shoes, boots, and accessories to see what looked best. By changing around, she decided she could really make seven new outfits out of the four she just bought.

Okay, now it's time to decide which one to wear when I 'Pin' Dan" she thought with satisfaction.

What do you really want to do, girl? Jolene thought to herself as she chose her outfit with extra care. *What would please you?* And after a long time gazing into the mirror in her room, she finally admitted to herself what she really wanted to do. It had nothing to do with the musical. That was just an excuse.

She really wanted to 'Pin' Dan and be his steady date!

Chapter 4
HIKING

"Okay, campers," Mr. Nolen started the meeting; "The ranger said the rattlesnakes are both active and plentiful this year. I guess the heat makes them frisky and aggressive." There were chuckles from the campers at this analysis.

"One other problem is the Gila monster. If it moves on four legs, looks like a lizard with bright orange and black stripes, leave it alone! The ranger said the score so far this year is Rattlesnakes and Gila monsters 2, People 0." He went on more seriously. "You all know what to do in an emergency. Any questions?" As usual, there were none.

"Except for Dan," Mr. Nolen said, "you all have a hiking partner. Watch out for your partner, follow the instructions in your CompGuide, and have a good time! Everyone ready?"

There were murmurs of agreement from all the campers.

"Okay, Dan. Lead us out. I'll bring up the rear."

This exercise was one Dan really liked. No floaters, no 'SAT's, no Enviro's, no pre-cooked meals, just a bodysuit and food you had to cook over a wood fire. If you could get a wood fire started, that is. This was as close to old-fashioned Boy Scouting as you could get!

As Senior Camper Leader, Dan led the line of hikers into the high desert, with Mr. Nolen serving as rear guard.

Eight miles thought Dan. *Four miles of up and down, but mostly up. I hope the new campers wore the right socks.* After the first 15 minutes Dan called for a break and boot check and, sure enough, some of the new campers had to adjust or change their socks.

Dan kept an easy pace to allow the new campers time to enjoy the surrounding area. This site in New Mexico had taken them two hours of travel by commercial floater, and few of the campers had experience with this type of climate. It certainly wasn't like the Midwest!

It took the group six hours to hike to the campsite, but what a view they had from there! The local Native American tribe granted permission for them to camp on tribal ground based on the camper's reverence for the land. It also didn't hurt anything the campers held the Indians in awe for their tracking, camping, survival and hunting skills. They appreciated the tribe providing teachers for them, and the tribe appreciated the fact the campers wanted to learn the right way to do things as well as learn the traditions of the tribe.

Most Native American tribes had prospered since the 20th century, and the EdRev had provided outlets for education never experienced before by some minorities. With education came employment. With employment came better housing, better family lives, and an upsurge of interest in their heritage. With this interest came what was needed most for many groups to prosper—pride!

The Native Americans had been leery the first time the campers showed up with girls along. When they realized the boys slept separately from the girls, they reluctantly accepted the girls, different though it was from their own culture.

It was soon obvious that the girls were even more eager to learn tribal customs and Indian lore than the boys. The girls' previous group hadn't allowed camping, and that was why it finally had to merge with the boys' group into the new group called Campers of America.

The change also caused the tribe to allow their own women to come and teach tribal cooking secrets, which everyone really appreciated. From the simple beginning of cooking lessons came instruction in sewing skills, tanning skills, and a host of other female related areas.

The three days of this campout flew past, and no one really wanted it to be over. The campers were impressed with the life skills the Indians had, and the Indians were impressed that the "long noses" (an old term for non-tribesmen) really wanted to learn correct customs instead of what they saw on 3V.

For instance, Sam, one of the younger campers, asked their Indian guide if it was true you could get water by digging a hole, suspending a black plastic bag over the hole, and collecting the condensation with a cup under the bag. He claimed he learned that trick on a special "survival" show on Tri-V.

"That will work, but it is a technique we learned from the white man," the Indian guide called "Running Bull," said with a straight face.

"Oh," the young boy replied with disappointment. "Why is that? Why did you have to learn it from us?" Sam asked.

"The only plastic my people have is what we buy at the white man's store. We don't make plastic." Although he said it with a straight face, the twinkle in his eye showed his amusement at the question.

"Then. . .how. . ."

"We get water in our deserts in several different ways. First, we can tap the bottom part of certain types of cactus. Second, we can dig at low points in the dry arroyo beds. Third, we can get water and help at several points on the top of the ridges. Fourth, we pass secret locations where water can be found from generation to generation."

The young camper considered these alternatives. Finally, he asked, "On the top of the ridges?"

"Sure. See that pile of rocks on top of that ridge?" The Indian guide pointed to a distant ridge.

"Uh. . .no. . .I can't really see a pile of rocks that far away because it all looks like rocks to me, Running Bull. How do you get water out of a pile of rocks?" Sam asked.

"At several sites around our territory, we have set up markers like the one my friend Sam, here, cannot see. There is water there."

Sam clearly had his doubts.

"Water runs downhill. How can you possibly get water from the top of a ridge?"

"Trust me," Running Bull said, "there is water there."

Thinking he was about to learn an Indian secret, Sam asked, "But. . .but how did the water get there?"

"Oh," the guide said with a perfectly straight face, "we went to the store and bought some packages of beef jerky and 10 one-gallon plastic water jugs for those silly enough to run out of water or food, and stashed them under the cairn of rocks."

At this point, the entire group burst into laughter at the look of indignation on Sam's face.

On the hike back, they finally spotted a rattlesnake, and Dan and Mr. Nolen made sure the younger campers got a good look without getting bit! For most of them, it was the first 'rattler they had ever seen in the wild. The campers were allowed to observe and see the rattler from all angles, but not get too close or tease it.

All told, it was an exciting, informative and delightful weekend for everyone. It was a tired but happy group of campers that slept most of the float home.

Of course, every single camper was asked the same question by their parents when they got home.

"Are you up to the norm on all your schoolwork?"

Robotic anti-gravity ships could speed up, then flip over halfway and slow down at speeds that made space flight feasible. Time was only another measurement to a robot or computer and questioning a directive not even possible. Taking live samples, which had been intended to mean plant samples, was done literally, and many animals were caught. Unfortunately, so were some intelligent animals.

Chapter 5
THE "EDREV" AT SCHOOL

The Great Education Revolution of the Early 21st Century (commonly known as "The EdRev") changed "school" into something that worked for many more people than before. It wasn't that education didn't work before the EdRev, it was just that the results were more dependent on where you lived than how smart you were, or how hard you worked. Success relied too much on local wealth ("The rich got smarter, the poor. . .etc.) and failed miserably in too many places because they couldn't afford the equipment, supplies, and staff to succeed. Some schools had "dropout" rates where more than two-thirds of all students who started high school as freshman failed to graduate or even stay in school until senior year.

The basic problem in education was simple. "School," even in the middle of the 21st century, was still based on and run like a late 19th century institution. It was more Industrial Revolution style than Information Age style. It fit neither the present day electronic style of learning, the advances in knowledge of how students learn, nor the temperament of the students being taught.

Society and technology had progressed tremendously, but "School" had not. School was still stuck more than 150 years in the past.

Under the "EdRev," schools stopped punishing students who should have been rewarded, and rewarding students who should have been punished. Before the EdRev, good students who finished assignments early and should have been allowed to enjoy time reading in the library or working on the computer or the like were "punished" with "extra" work so they "wouldn't sit idle wasting time." Poor students who were able to complete all their work but just didn't bother were "rewarded" by having assignments they missed eliminated from the grading period. Some were also misplaced into "Special Ed" classes. This was so the school could pass the federal mandates that started with "No Child Left Behind" and continued with several other well-meaning but unfunded and fundamentally flawed ideas, like "Common Core." While school talked about "quality," it was really based on "quantity" instead.

Examples of quantity over quality in education were abundant. Teaching to the last minute of the class, mandatory full-time attendance (i.e., babysitting), mandating subjects no longer valuable to society or necessary for history, insufficient funding to maximize learning through technology, and cramming too many students into a classroom. These were all considered more important than actual "learning."

The EdRev was a direct result of the first major shift in educational philosophy since that 19th century school.

Before the EdRev, CONTENT (the memorization of facts) was everything! All learning was based on memorization rather than understanding. The problem with memorization was human knowledge was doubling every five years, and too many schools were still teaching out of textbooks twenty years old! Many "facts" in these books were clearly outdated, obsolete and often downright wrong!

For example, how were students supposed to take seriously a textbook that stated, "...and someday in the future, man might actually travel to and land on the moon!" when every student could name at least five permanent moon bases already in existence! Many students also had e-mail "pen pals" that lived on the moon and corresponded with them in several of the sciences about the latest research done on the moon.

The World Wide Web and the Internet plus the home computer should have changed the philosophy about memorizing content, but "school" ignored them. Worse, "school" actively restricted student access to the internet to "teacher directed only" activities. Some things still needed to be memorized of course, like the multiplication tables, but educators finally realized what business, industry and even the military had learned years earlier.

It's not WHAT you know but HOW FAST you can find the answer!

An illustration of this point came during one AutoCAD class. Given an assignment to "design your very own 12 million-dollar mansion on three floors in three-dimensions," a student wanted to put four bowling lanes in his mansion basement. Since no one knew the dimensions of a bowling lane, the teacher declared an "Immediate Internet Competition" (just to make it legal for students to access the internet during class) to find the answer.

58 seconds later, a student announced to the class the correct dimensions of bowling lanes he found on the Internet. He rushed up and wrote the dimensions on the whiteboard.

Likewise, a similar question about the size and wingspan and dimensions of an F-22 Raptor Fighter Jet (44' 6") for a student "redesigning" one was answered via the Internet in about 30 seconds.

Again, in the 21st century, it's not WHAT you memorize, but HOW FAST you can find the answer. Neither of these examples contained "facts" valuable enough to memorize.

The breaking point came when home-schooled students using the Internet began beating the scores of students who went to traditional classes at school. Educators resisted for years splitting or comparing the results of the two groups, but a federal judge in Northern Illinois mandated the change after a group of parents filed a lawsuit demanding a comparison. The judge used the *Brown versus the Board of Education* case of 1954 in Topeka, Kansas (Separate but Equal) as a precedent.

The results of the comparison were stunning.

Home-based students in Northern Illinois using Internet-based programs for instruction (without the daily help of a live teacher) scored an average of 19% better than students of the same age enrolled in traditional schools.

A surge of anger swept the country as these results became known, and parents everywhere demanded the same type of comparison for their local schools. In the rural areas of the country and the big cities where schools were usually much poorer than the suburbs, the differences were even more astonishing. Internet-based instruction students ranged from 19% to an outrageous 45% better on standardized testing.

Outside of Illinois, the percentages in favor of Internet learning were even higher. School boards were besieged with demands to change to computer learning instead of traditional lecture and classroom style. Within one year the change had begun, and it was mostly completed (81%) within five years.

The Educational Revolution had finally come to pass. The lecture-style classroom was dead. Long live the classroom!

The EdRev had seven major components.

First, the "CORE" Curriculum Division. The four CORE subjects were math, language, science, and social sciences. Linear computer-aided instruction software was developed in all four areas from grade 3 through grade 16, and the age of a student no longer determined the speed of their forward progress. With the pocket and home wireless Internet computer, the theoretical ideal of "as fast as you want or as slow as you need" became a reality. Students could literally work at their own speed, and still be monitored by their teachers at school. Grade levels like "6th" or "11th" meant nothing except as a reference "norm" for when something had previously been taught. Progress reports were based on this timeline and grades like *.5 years above the norm* (.5+) or *.2 years below the norm* (,2-) replaced the meaningless grades like "A," "B," "C," "D" and "F" which had long been corrupted.

After the EdRev happened, everyone learned the same thing to an 85% mastery level. They just did it slower in some cases and much faster in others.

Problems that had plagued schools for years disappeared overnight. Tracking (General Ed, College Prep, or Vocational?) and both Special Ed (remedial or slower classes) and Accelerated classes (AP, Honors) were redundant under the EdRev. Since every student had an Individual Education Plan (I.E.P.), every student could learn at their own best speed.

Second, the "ENCORE" subjects, primarily music, art, theater, physical education, vocational and dance received better scheduling and more attention. Dr. Howard Gardner's ideas on multiple intelligences were recognized as the leading theory in learning as well as how important these subjects were in the development of the human brain. "Schools" before the EdRev pushed only three of Gardner's seven intelligences, ignored two, treated one like a religion and didn't understand the other. In fact, an analysis of all the classes and activities of a pre-"EdRev" school revealed Musical Theater, Swing Choir, Pom Poms and Cheerleading, many teams and Marching Band as being the only groups to use all seven of the intelligences! Ironically, most of these groups had been called "activities" before the EdRev and seldom received academic credit or even regular class time!

Third, school "buildings" now meant multiple gyms, multiple music rooms, and theater spaces, several art studios, a large auditorium, a large cafeteria (called the diner,) expanded science labs and lots of computer workstations with individual offices for teachers. The conversion of traditional lecture style classrooms into computer workstations meant buildings could accommodate up to three times as many students as before. (Some students preferred mornings, some afternoons and some evenings. A few even preferred weekends, which is what allowed far more students to be served at the same location.) This conversion of lecture rooms to computer labs saved billions of dollars every year and paid for all the EdRev changes plus a healthy reduction in property taxes for taxpayers.

Fourth, many junior and senior high schools were consolidated into larger, more efficient sites since students 10 or older could routinely float up to 10 miles from home to go to school. Due to the advent of the individual floater safe enough for 10-year-olds, "school buses" and associated costs were reduced almost to extinction. Also, less than one-third of the students were present in the building at any given time, particularly at the high school level. The school diner became the meeting place of choice for students and was open from 6 AM until 11 PM. Older students were scheduled to work one 8-hour shift about every month to use manual labor skills, and the diner was a safe gathering place. Students liked it because it had their kind of food. Parents liked it because it was supervised, however loosely.

Fifth, the concept of homeschooling combined with the home and wireless pocket Internet computer made mandatory school attendance redundant. Recognizing the "carrot" was far more effective than the "stick," schools starting rewarding students with days off school for high academic achievement. Five-day school was retained only for students who needed a very structured environment; the more a student achieved at home, the less time they had to spend at school. The concepts and problems of both AP (Advanced Placement) or Honors classes and Special Ed and remedial classes disappeared under the EdRev. Every student learned the same material, only at different speeds and rote memorization (except for multiplication tables and the like) became a thing of the past.

Sixth, teaching was recognized as an "art" rather than a science. The best teachers had always been "artists" in delivering material to the students and keeping student interest high. All the college classes in education could not make a person a "teacher" if they didn't have a talent for or the aptitude for teaching. Salaries were greatly increased and became high enough to attract and keep the best college graduates instead of those who couldn't do anything else. With basic instruction done via the computer at each student's best speed, teachers were free to engage in the one-to-one instruction known for over four thousand years as the most effective method. Gone were the lectures, the hall duties, bus duties, bathroom patrols, lunch counts, surveys to send home, tests to grade, forms to fill out, and countless other time-wasting frustrations that drove the best teachers out of education. Gone also were about a third of the teaching positions that had been filled by ineffective teachers teaching nothing but outdated fluff. Teaching became a vastly more respected profession.

Gone also was the concept of Monday through Friday daytime only school. Education became 24/7 with teachers, good teachers, doing night shifts and always available by phone or e-mail whenever a student needed help. Not surprisingly, the "best" teachers had always been available to students outside of regular school hours. In fact, one of the criteria for retaining teachers after the EdRev was how often they spent their "own" time helping students! A quick review showed many coaches, band directors, theater directors, and activity directors were already putting in up to 40 hours a week beyond their regular classroom time.

Seventh, with the shift in athletics from extramural to intramural, huge amounts of money that was spent before the EdRev on travel could now be dedicated to learning. Sportsmanship and fitness became the primary goal of athletics. The whole idea of "killing the other team" was stupid when "the other team" was made up of your best friends and classmates. The most admired students now included the star academics, artists, and musicians as well as the star athletes.

Jolene approached Terry with her idea. Terry played baritone saxophone in the band (as well as being in the same camping group as Dan,) and Terry liked Jolene a lot. For one thing, he thought she was the most beautiful girl in school. For another, Jolene had tutored him well enough to keep him from the mandatory 5-day per week school requirement, and he figured he owed her big time.

Besides, he liked both Dan and Jolene and thought Jolene 'Pinning' Dan was just great. He even had an idea about where and how Jolene could perform the ceremony and explained his idea to Jolene. Jolene was thrilled, and Terry promised her he would set the stage.

"Hey, Dan," Terry said just before band class, "have you heard the echo yet?"

"Echo? No, I haven't. What echo do you mean?" Dan asked as he got his trumpet out of the case.

"If you lay down right under one of the convex skylights over the wrestling mat area, you can hear voices from all the way down the hall."

"Really?"

"Yeah. I'll show you after band," he told Dan, then hurried off to let Jolene know the stage had been set, and where Dan was going to be.

Band practice was over, and Dan was resting on the wrestling mat area in one corner of the commons area waiting for the school diner to open. He was stretched out on his back with his eyes closed listening to the voices echo like Terry told him when he became aware something had blocked the light.

"Hi, Dan," Jolene said softly as she stood over him, ready to pounce. "No, don't get up."

Dan opened his eyes and started to sit up, only to be pressed back into the mat by Jolene's foot on his chest. Jolene had chosen her outfit with care and was wearing a short, black leather jacket with matching skirt, and black medium heel boots. (She decided to save her high heel boots 'til after she 'Pinned' him.) She had tiptoed over to him so as not to warn him with the sound of her footsteps.

"Ummpff." Dan's breath whooshed out as his back hit the mat. He had seen other girls do this foot-on-the-chest thing to other guys, but never paid much attention to it.

"Hi, Jolene. Hey, that's a great outfit," Dan said. "I don't remember you wearing that one before. Is it new?"

"Yes, Dan, it is new, and I have several other pieces that go with this outfit."

"Other pieces?" Dan asked, wondering why she was practically standing on him.

"I also have a longer skirt, all leather jeans, and spike heel boots that match," Jolene said. "But I didn't want to wear those boots today. Maybe later." she confided.

"Oh?" Dan replied, still trying to figure out what was going on.

"Now, Dan. Have you thought about what I asked?" Jolene asked, stepping down a little on Dan's chest.

"Yeah. My dad's a spaceball nut, you know," Jolene increased the weight on his chest, "and I didn't think I could do spaceball and the musical both," more weight, "so I checked with Dad to get his opinion," Jolene was almost standing on him! ". . . and he said yes I could be in the musical and sit out this spaceball season!" Dan croaked the last words out! Jolene smiled broadly and took the weight off his chest. She didn't remove her boot, though.

"That's great news, and I'm thrilled to hear it, Dan! My dad thinks your dad is one of the nicest and smartest people he's ever met." She dropped a packet on the floor by his books. "Read this script today, and I'll come over to your place at 7 tonight to go over the lines."

"Tonight?" Dan started to protest, "but. . ."

He didn't get to finish before Jolene stepped on his chest and stood there with both feet!

"Pinned," she said quietly as she stood on his chest, looking down into his eyes.

There were cheers from other girls passing by in the hallway.

"Way to go, Jolene!"

"Mark him good!"

"Use him like a rug, girl!"

"Tonight at 7!" Jolene said, still standing on him. For a second he thought she was going to step on his face with her boot, but then she stepped off the other side.

"Be ready, and don't disappoint me," she said as she briskly walked away.

"No problem," Dan said, as loudly as he could, "I'll be ready." *That is if I ever get my breath back! What is it with these girls and their games? I'll bet she left marks on my chest!*

Oh my gosh, he's mine! He's really mine!! Jolene thought excitedly as she hurried to tell her friends. *He just lay there when I stepped on him and 'Pinned' him, and he didn't contest it. Thank you, female equality! Thank you, Thank you, Thank you!*

Dan was congratulated many times during the rest of the day, sometimes by kids he didn't even know. At first, he wondered how they knew about his agreeing to try out for the musical so quickly, or why they even cared? His friend John Nelson finally set him straight.

"Man, oh man, Dan! Let me shake your hand for good luck! Melting the Ice Princess! How did you do that?"

"What are you talking about, John? Melting what Ice Princess?"

"What Ice Princess? Are you awake, pal? I'm talking about Jolene!"

"Oh. Jolene," Dan said, absent-mindedly rubbing his chest where she stepped on him.

"You really don't know, do you?" John said in surprise and suddenly stopped walking down the hall. "Dan," he explained patiently, "When Jolene stepped on you and stood there, she 'Pinned' you, like being pinned in wrestling? When you didn't tell her "no" or to "get off," you accepted the 'Pinning.' Didn't you know that?" he asked, pityingly.

"Ummm. . .she said "Pinned," but I thought she just wanted me as her partner for the musical. I really think that's all she means," Dan finished lamely.

"Dan, kids are not congratulating you about musical tryouts! It's all about Jolene. It's all about her choosing you and pinning you and has nothing to do with the musical."

"Jolene," Dan said.

John just smiled and shook his head. "You'll see, Dan. We'll see," he amended.

Chapter 6
DAN'S HOUSE

I read the script Jolene gave me of the most famous Australian musical ever written, WOLFSTOCK©, and never laughed so hard in my life! This was a great script; it was funny, provocative and the music was simply outstanding! If it hadn't been for Jolene asking me to partner with her and Adam asking to play trumpet, I would have loved to play in the pit band.

WOLFSTOCK is actually a musical production in two Acts set in the style of a 1950's Rock-n-Roll musical. The musical score contains eighteen original musical numbers including fifteen 1950's style songs and three dances. The pit band is for fourteen players including 1 mandatory violin (for the Gypsy music). Act 1 contains 10 songs and Act 2 has the other 8.

WOLFSTOCK is about an everyday, average, ordinary teenage boy who will turn into a werewolf on his 16th birthday because a werewolf bit his mother just before the boy was born. The boy, Jay, thinks turning into a werewolf is great, and hopes it will add excitement to his otherwise dull and boring life.

There are some great lines in the script, like when Jay is told:

"Don't you know what werewolves do? They chase girls in the woods at night." Jay replies with a grin, "I can handle that!"

"And they bite them in the neck."

"I can handle that, too!" he replies with a bigger grin.

Jolene came over just before 7 PM, and I introduced her to both my parents. She was wearing the same outfit but had worn her high heel boots instead. With those boots, Jolene was only about three inches shorter than I was and looked absolutely stunning. (I'm surprised my jaw didn't drop to the ground!) My parents formally gave her the 'Freedom of the Dome,' which startled me. I had heard about the privilege but had never heard it actually given to anyone. It meant Jolene was welcome to come over at any time for any reason. We went up to the dome's loft area and read lines, and then Jolene explained what else would be happening.

While she explained events to me, Jolene started taking off her boots, skirt, and blouse (to my surprise and discomfort!) revealing (to my relief) her dancing tights underneath.

She had a 'burn of the pit band music, and we worked on the dances she already knew. I was wary of touching her, but as soon as the music began and we started dancing, I forgot about everything except the moves and the steps. From Act 1, we worked on "Gonna Get Me a Motorbike," "Who Can She Be?" "The 1950's Overture,"and "On This Night Waltz."

We both finally collapsed on the couch, and I said, "That was great! I think that's the best I've ever danced." I looked over at Jolene and decided I had to ask. "You are so graceful, so smooth and so precise with your moves, Jolene. Why in the world did you choose me to be your partner? Now, don't get me wrong," I added quickly, "because I'm thrilled you asked me. I love it! It's just that. . .well. . .I can name several guys who I think dance much better than I do."

"Technically, Dan," she agreed. "They may dance better 'technically' than you, but they do it like a technician without feeling. You not only have a very good feel for how a dance flows and how the rhythm pulses, but you also seem to adjust your moves to fit the music perfectly." She smiled and looked right into my eyes. "I've never danced with anyone who. . ." she searched for a word. . ."flows with the music as well as you do."

"Probably because I play trumpet," I joked, to hide my surprise at her praise. I had no idea she thought I was that good.

"I know that! I sit in the flute section right in front of you, remember? I really think it's because you sing as well as play a band instrument. For instance, you seem to automatically adjust from the crazy up-tempo songs like "Get Me a Motorbike" to the more tender love songs, such as "Who is that Girl?" Of course, marching band helps a lot in dance. Did I remember to tell you, your character sings a solo in Act 2? Well, never mind. We can work on that another evening," and she got up to gather her books and started to put on her street clothes.

I hesitated, but then decided I had to know.

"Jolene? About this morning? In the diner? I was wondering. . ."

"You didn't know what I was doing, did you?" she interrupted quietly as she slipped into her skirt and started pulling on her boots.

"Well. . .no, not really," I admitted. "I don't pay much attention to things like that, and I thought. . .well. . .you were just stepping on me to make a point, or that it was just some passing female game. John Nelson clued me in to what you meant by it. At least, what he thinks you meant by it."

"So. . .you understand now what I meant?" she asked with no expression in her voice or on her face.

"That you 'Pinned' me?" She nodded.

"And that means you claim me to be yours?" She nodded again.

"And it puts me off limits for other girls? They can't ask me out? Is that really what you meant, Jolene?"

"Yes, that's exactly what I meant, Dan, but if you didn't know that, it doesn't count," she said sadly.

"It does count, Jolene!" I replied strongly. "You knew what you were doing, even if I didn't. If I had known, I wouldn't have done anything differently. No matter how you look at it, it counts, Jolene, it counts!"

Jolene just looked at me but didn't say anything.

"Please, Jolene, I bet every other guy you 'Pinned' has been thrilled. Don't let me be the first to mess up your record. Please?"

Jolene thought in amazement, *He doesn't have a clue!*

She said slowly, "You. . .are the only guy I have ever 'Pinned,' Dan, and you messed it up because you didn't know what I was doing."

I hesitated only a second, then placed my body in front of her feet. "I know what it means now, Jolene." Too late, I remembered what boots she was wearing.

She immediately put her boot on my chest before I could change my mind, but then she hesitated.

"I've got on heels tonight, Dan," Jolene warned softly. "This morning I was wearing flats. You're going to feel the difference. Are you sure?"

For once I did the right thing, kept my mouth shut, and

just smiled up at her. Besides, she probably wouldn't. . ."

Jolene didn't wait any longer for me to answer. She immediately stepped on my chest and stood there with both boots. "I claim you," she said quietly but formally. "Pinned." She continued to stand on me, and I realized she was waiting.

"Pinned." I croaked back to her. She immediately shifted her weight to those heels, and said, "You almost messed up my first 'Pinning,' Daniel!" she scolded, and with that, she stepped off me and walked out the door.

She was right. Heels hurt a lot more than flats, but it was a happy hurt.

Yes, Yes, Yes! thought Jolene as she floated home. *I prepare a perfect setup, and the guy is too dense to know what was going on. My God, I loved stepping on him with my boots, watching his face turn red. He's mine, all mine! I think I'll 'Pin' him every day, just to emphasize he's mine, but also because I love stepping on him. I love the thought of someone as big and strong and good looking as Dan being a rug for me to stand on.*

I can still feel his arms around me as we danced. It's a mystery to me why no other girl ever 'Pinned' him before, but he probably scares them away. I know Liana would love to 'Pin' him, but she's too late. His eagerness to please me tonight, his stretching out at my feet even when I had on heels, shows he wants to do the right thing. He really had no clue I never 'Pinned' anyone before, but just assumed I had.

I have a treasure in Dan, and I plan to keep him a long, long time! This musical is just the beginning of the rest of our lives!

Chapter 7
THE MUSICAL

Dan was surprised at how much organization went into a musical theater production, and how much of a commitment it would take to get a position in the cast. He was also amazed at the number of students who wanted to audition for a part.

The director, Mr. Pierce, let the students know up front everyone would be expected to be at every, repeat, every practice.

"Two unexcused absences and we replace you. There are about 150 students signed up to try out for a part, and we only need 14 in the cast plus 20 in the chorus. Anytime we have cast members missing, other people must read the lines, and everyone loses. Actors so familiar with their part that they don't look or sound like they are acting give the best performances! Everyone will be assigned an understudy, and your understudy will take part on your second unexcused absence."

Mr. Pierce outlined the schedule for practices.

"You need to know the schedule before you even begin. This is a major commitment on your part. Be sure you can handle it before you try out!"

Week one would be devoted to singing (or listening to) all the songs and music and auditions. Cast members would use 'burns' of the music since the pit band would not be ready yet. The pit band would start once per week practices since they could learn their parts quicker than the cast and chorus and the musical was just one of their many performances. Tryouts would occur at the end of week one when everyone has had a chance to hear the music and read about the different parts.

Week two would be devoted to readings of ACT I, with the cast members and chorus split. The cast could read lines while the chorus could learn the dance routines.

Week three was the same, except the cast would concentrate on ACT II readings.

Weeks four and five would be devoted to "blocking," a term used to show the cast and chorus where to move on stage. The chorus would also begin teaching the cast the dances they had learned.

During these first five weeks, the stage crew would be designing the sets and building them on stage.

Week six, the pit band would practice every day by themselves while the cast and chorus did "run-throughs" to work out bugs and give the lighting crew some idea of where to aim the lights.

Weeks seven, eight and nine would be full working rehearsals with pit, cast, chorus, and lighting. These practices could be stopped at any point to fix problems, change the music or blocking, or adjust lights. Week nine the cast and chorus would wear costumes but not make-up.

Week ten was "Tech Week." The cast would add body mikes to all speaking actors, and the sound crew would try to preset the volume for each individual actor. The lighting would also be adjusted, and any last-minute changes could be made.

Week eleven would be complete run-throughs on Monday, Tuesday, and full-dress rehearsals on Wednesday and

Thursday. Opening night was Friday night, with performances on Saturday night and Sunday afternoon.

Week twelve would be performances on Tuesday, Thursday, and Friday nights and Saturday afternoon, with teardown following the Saturday matinee. All in all, the troupe would perform the show in its entirety seven times, plus some short "teaser" scenes as the local junior high and elementary schools.

Compared to the sports teams Dan had been on, he realized this event was a major and well-organized undertaking.

Jolene and I went through all the procedures we needed to do to audition during week one, and we were one of nine couples who auditioned together for the three couple's parts. We each had to read by ourselves, work under the lights on stage, and read some lines cold (without practice.) Mr. Pierce had unusual ideas about sound. He wanted us to project as if we didn't have any microphones, and he sat way in the back of the auditorium to judge how we sounded. If he couldn't hear you without a microphone, you didn't get a part.

The cast was posted on Friday afternoon, and you can imagine our feelings when Jolene and I were one of the three couples selected! Jolene gave me a huge hug, and it seemed to last forever. She had tears in her eyes, and she thanked me several times for being her partner.

It was the first time she had ever hugged me like that, and I have to admit I liked it. I liked it a lot! Jolene was cast as Janice, the head of the female group. Her character is bossy and sometimes insensitive, but still very likable. (I thought it was perfect typecasting, but of course, I didn't dare say that out loud!) One of Janice's main contributions is that she tries to fix up Jay (the main character) with Shirl, a female group member who starts out wimpy and over-shadowed by the other girls, but who develops interestingly as the show goes along.

I was cast as Marty. My character is supposed to be girl-crazy (a role I felt I could handle quite well, thank you), cocky, self-assured and rarely flustered. Marty had some great lines, but he also played the straight man for Janice, Deb, Shirl, Rick, and Jay.

One of the early exchanges goes something like this:

RICK: So. . .what are you getting for your birthday?
JAY: A record player.
MARTY: Sounds good to me. Get it? SOUNDS good to. . .
JAY: (tiredly) We got it, Marty. We got it.
MARTY: Hey! Let's go talk to the chicks.
           (*They take their drinks and go over the girl's table.*)
MARTY: Hey, it's your lucky day today, girls!
JANICE: (sarcastically) Why? Are you leaving right away, or what?

I'll have to admit; my favorite characters were Madam Berzurka and Loupy Garou.

Loupy was the werewolf who bit Jay's Mom just before Jay was born, and Holland (the student playing Loupy and a born clown!) used a thick French accent to enhance the character. (Loupy Garou means "werewolf" in French, hence the name of the character.) Holland always wore a black tuxedo since he was also the owner, director, and ringmaster of his own traveling circus. It was at the circus that he bit Jay's mother before Jay was born.

Holland was so good with his accent and so effective as a werewolf that Mr. Pierce made a big concession. Holland couldn't carry a tune in a bucket, and his part had a big solo to sing. Mr. Pierce let him say some of the lines in rhythm like old-fashioned rap instead of singing them all. Holland was so good at this rap style that most people in the audience didn't even realize he wasn't singing everything.

I think that's one of the reasons why Mr. Pierce is so effective as a teacher and a really great director. It's because he knows when to break the rules and allow something different.

Brooke, a stunningly beautiful girl with waist-length jet-black hair, played Madam Berzurka. Madam Berzurka was a gypsy, and Brooke played the part to the hilt, using a thick gypsy accent that really highlighted her lines. One of the funniest touches in this musical was every time anyone in the cast said the name "Madam Berzurka," the pit band played a five-second burst of music. It happened so many times in one scene that the actor playing Jay's father actually leaned over the pit band to complain ". . .who from now on we'll call something else!" Normally, actors ignore the pit band, but this "complaint" to the music conductor was written in the script.

When either Loupy or Madam Berzurka were on stage, it was hard for the rest of us not to laugh and break out of character. They were both extraordinary actors, and clearly the stars of the show!

Musical practices turned out to be more fun than I ever imagined. The experienced cast (done this many times, thank you; know what I'm doing; of course I'm good!) accepted me first on Jolene's say so, and then on my own singing and dancing. It's hard to describe how good that made me feel. It's also hard to describe my feelings about dancing so close to Jolene. She and I seemed to move like one person, and the more we danced, the better it got.

I could get used to this, I thought at one point. *I could really get used to this.*

During week three Mr. Pierce asked me quietly after practice, "Dan, when was the last time during spaceball practice you got your arms around a girl like Jolene?"

"Never!" I replied, looking puzzled, and he smiled and walked away.

Oh! I thought, suddenly realizing what he meant. *Good point. Very good point! At this rate, I may never go back to spaceball.*

Chapter 8
FIELD TRIP

"Dan, I need a big favor," Jolene asked as we walked to our floaters after lunch.

"Name it, oh high-pitched-voice, and it shall be yours." The flute section sounded terrible in band today since several girls were trying out professional open hole flutes and couldn't close the holes well enough to sound good.

"Thank you, oh higher-louder-faster guru!" she laughed. Trumpet players, except for Mary, were always pushing the tempo (faster,) playing up the octave (higher,) and generally trying to outblow the rest of the band (louder). Mr. Kissinger really chewed on both sections today during band practice.

"I'm overdue for a field trip out west, and my dad won't let me go alone. He knows how good a marksman I am with my PerLaz, but he says hitting paper and hitting an animate object in a crisis are two different things."

"Your dad's absolutely right, Jolene. But never fear; Deadeye Dan is here. I hate to brag, but outdoor survival stuff is one of the things I do best."

"I know that! You've told me about it often enough!" she said sarcastically.

"So, what is your stated premise, and where do we need to go?" I asked, pleased with myself.

"I've been assigned the "Early Development of Erosion leading to Extreme Erosion over Time," and the only logical place within reach is. . ."

"Echo Canyon!" I said grimly at the same time she said it.

"How did you know that?" she replied with a puzzled expression.

I hesitated long enough she repeated her question more forcefully and indignantly.

"Because," I confessed slowly, "my group of campers, about 30 national guardsmen, some state police officers, some county sheriff's deputies, and 20 civilian volunteers searched Echo Canyon for three missing campers who reported strange happenings and flying saucers just before they disappeared." I looked her in the eye. "100 people searched that canyon for two days, Jolene. It was not a pleasant experience." I confessed quietly.

"Oh!" she exclaimed and then frowned. "But they found them in the end, right?"

"No, we didn't," I answered slowly, "and I knew one of the campers. Jerry Thornton was as careful a camper as I am."

She thought about that awhile.

"I suppose," she sighed, "it might be safer to just take a failure on this assignment, then?"

"And lose your chance at Top Scholar?" I said indignantly! "No way! Let me ask some of the campers in my group, and maybe we can get a large enough group to make it safe."

"Thanks, Dan, I'd appreciate it," Jolene answered with a frown.

I spent quite a bit of time on the 'Sat that evening, and at least as much time the next morning. I couldn't convince anyone to go with us and I tried every trick in the book. I even spoke to some of the parents but to no avail.

During the afternoon, I had to confess my failure to Jolene. It wasn't easy.

"No deal, Jolene," I told her. "Every single parent said no when asked for permission to let their kid go to Echo Canyon. Every one of them!" I still had trouble believing that.

"So. . .what do I do now?" she asked.

I thought about it. "Let's go downstairs and talk to my dad."

"Echo Canyon?" my dad asked in surprise as he looked up at us. "That's the place by our western lab where those kids were lost, isn't it Dan?"

"Yes, Dad. I've asked the other campers, and none of their parents will allow them to go there. I thought that maybe a larger group would be safer, as well as knowing about the problem would keep everyone on their toes."

"Of all the places you could go, why in the world do you want to go to Echo Canyon?" Dad questioned. "You know it may not be safe there." Clearly, he was worried about it as well.

"That's my fault, Mr. Jackson," Jolene admitted to my dad. "My assignment is the Early Development of Erosion leading to Extreme Erosion over time. Echo Canyon is the only place within reach where you can observe that." She paused, and then went on. "Maybe I should just. . .take the failure and skip this assignment?" she asked half-heartedly.

"No, that's not the best way to deal with a problem like this." He looked at us both thoughtfully, and then came to a decision. "Let me spend 30 minutes to see what I can find out, then come back down here. Dan, have you shown Jolene your collections yet?"

Startled, I replied, "No sir. They are all in my room Dad, and. . .well. . .you and Mom said. . ."

"Approved. Jolene has the Freedom of our Dome. Go show her, Dan," and he was lost in the web, searching for database items on Echo Canyon.

I was so amazed I took Jolene's hand without thinking about it and led her to my room in the basement of the main dome. Jolene was so amazed I had taken her hand, she followed me meekly and quietly.

"What is this business about I have the Freedom of the Dome?" she asked me, as we sat in my room. She had chosen to sit on my bed, which made me uncomfortable for some reason, and which, as usual, was not made. "Just exactly what does it mean?" she asked.

"It stems from an old Naval custom where the captain of a ship could grant honored passengers or other officers in transit unlimited permission to be on the bridge, meaning control room, of his ship. In this case, I guess it means it's okay for you to come to my room."

"Why are you so uncomfortable that I'm in your room, Dan?" Jolene teased.

"My parents were very specific that I was never to have girls in my room without their approval," I answered righteously.

"How many girls have come to visit you that you couldn't bring to your room?" she asked innocently but with a twinkle in her eye.

"Oh. . .well. . .I think I can give you a good estimate of how many girls have come to visit me. Let me think about it. I believe it was, or is. . .close to. . ."

"None?" she asked into the silence. My own silence was her answer. "I thought so. Your room is really a mess, you do know that, don't you?" she asked gently.

I never thought about it much before. "Yeah. I guess you're right." I looked around my room and was suddenly embarrassed in front of Jolene by the clutter and disarray.

"Okay, Dan," she said to change the subject, "Show me your collections."

Jolene was really offended by some of my collections, particularly the ones involving animal scat. At one point in time, she appeared to be so angry, I thought she would leave. Instead, she pointed to the ground, and once again I placed myself at her feet.

Luckily, she had on soft boots, or our collaboration might have ended right then and there, along with my life! I'm not sure the idea of mercy has any meaning to girls, at least not in this situation. I promised to clean up my act and get rid of the more offensive collections. Boy, did she tell me to get rid of some!

After several probes reported interference by live creatures before ceasing to transmit (and probably exist), steps were taken to protect the sample takers. A small beam projector was developed that temporarily interfered with organic life functions. The projector would be used to prevent the live creatures from disturbing the sample takers.

As soon as Dan and Jolene were gone, Dennis 'Sated Jolene's dad.

"Henry, we have a problem. Your daughter caught the assignment to Echo Canyon, and she wants my son to go with her. Can you still fit in your gear?"

"My tactical gear, you mean? Haven't had it on since 'The Troubles.' How is it that our kids caught that assignment, Dennis?" Dr. Fisher wondered.

"Because our kids are smart, and they fit the profile, that's why. The question is, Henry, are we going to let them go?" There was silence from the other end for a while.

Henry finally answered slowly, "I guess we have to, Dennis. We helped set it up, and we approved it when we didn't know who would be selected. You know our children are headstrong enough to go no matter what we tell them. Our only option is to monitor from the lab and come running if things go bad. Could we reach them in time if, well. . .that problem appears again?"

"General Lacey has been after me to stay current. He will positively jump at the chance to put me in his debt again! Go check your gear Henry, and I'll call you back."

After a short conversation with General Lacey which proved to be very fruitful, Dennis Jackson called Henry Fisher to give him the details.

"Henry? Approved, and you won't believe how much help we'll have. Lacey has been itching to get another shot at. . .well, you know. Did your gear still fit?"

"Yeah, but it's a little tighter than I remember, Dennis," Henry confessed. "It was hidden between my snowmobile suit and my University of Iowa football jacket. It must have shrunk from all that time in the back of my closet," he joked.

"Right. You really should try that stuff on more often, Henry. I'll brief the kids in a few minutes, and it's a go for next Monday. I'll pick you up."

My dad called us back into his work area, and we sat side by side on the bench he usually had covered with books and printouts. He looked worried as he looked at the two of us, then he began speaking very slowly and seriously.

"Dan, Jolene, this is a dangerous thing you've been asked to do. I'm convinced you would both sneak out there anyway no matter what your father or I said. I talked it over with your father, Jolene, and we both agreed to let you go. However, we are going to insist on a few safety measures. You also need to wait until Monday before you go."

"Thanks, Dad,"

"Thanks, Mr. Jackson," Jolene said at the same time. "We have a marching band competition on Saturday anyway," she explained.

"You're both welcome. Jolene," Dad said, looking at her directly for the first time, "I need to spend some time with Daniel. Would you mind if I steal him away from you, now?"

"Not at all, Mr. Jackson. Dan is a pretty special guy." And with that, she stood up and gave me a big hug and a quick kiss on my cheek in front of my dad and said her goodbyes. I was a little shocked she was so sweet and kind since she had just yelled, scolded and all but stomped me to death a few minutes ago!

Girls! I don't think I'll ever figure them out.

Chapter 9
PREPARATION

"**S**on, we really need to talk about this trip of yours to Echo Canyon," Dad said as soon as Jolene was gone.

"Yes, Dad?"

"You mean the world to me, and I will never forgive myself if something happens to you or to Jolene. Your mother would never forgive me either. I am going to do everything I can to make you both safe, do you understand that?"

"Yes, Dad."

"I am also going to tell you some things you shouldn't know, things you can't ask questions about, and things you may never talk about to anyone. Can you understand that as well?"

I sat quietly, debating if this was the time to tell my father what I already knew. As he waited for me to answer, I realized this was probably the best time to tell him. After all, I'd kept it a secret for almost a year.

"You mean. . .about the alien spaceship, Dad?" I asked quietly.

The look on my dad's face told me I caught him completely off guard with my question! He was so surprised by my response, that when he tried to speak, he couldn't. He quickly recovered his composure, then said grimly,

"You'd better tell me what you think you know, how you know it, what proof you have, and who you've discussed it with. This is serious, son. Think it through, and wait until I tell you, then start." Dad reached over and started the 'burner rolling, to make a record of our conversation. "Oh, run up and shut the basement door, please."

I quickly ran up the stairs and shut the door.

I gathered my thoughts, came back down and waited for him to nod, then started.

"Last things first. I have not said one word to anyone, including the other campers who were there. Sometimes you adults forget kids hear things you don't think we hear, or you don't think we understand!" I said somewhat scornfully.

"I was there, Dad. I was actually in Echo Canyon for the search.

My group found the burn marks on the side of the slope, and the man-sized silhouette burned against the cliff. The captain told us it was lightning, but lightning doesn't strike from that angle or leave a body-size shadow like that. We also found campfire remains and were told it was an old campfire. Dad, that campfire was still warm, and when I stirred it up, I found foil-covered potatoes and meat and carrots prepared just like I taught Jerry Thornton! The food was still moist and warm and edible. That campfire was only a few hours old, Dad, not an old one like we were told. I know it was made by campers or people who used to be campers."

"We were told the thunder that day was from a storm on the other side of the mountains. It wasn't thunder, Dad. It was an Orbital Laser Cannon firing in a multiple bracket intercept pattern. They use the actual sounds in the Space Fighters game at the video arcade, so I know what it sounds like."

"A camper in John Nelson's group actually discovered what appeared to be a landing site. He showed John, John showed me, and I showed it to a corporal who couldn't see it even when he was standing on it. The corporal did call his sergeant who took one look and immediately herded my group away from the site and back to the mess tent for a meal and rest. The lieutenant then cordoned off what I believed was an actual landing site."

"After we ate, I went over by the radio van and lay down behind a hedge to take a nap. At least, that's what the captain thought when they found me "sleeping" there hours later. They questioned me about what I might have overheard but finally accepted my story about sleeping."

"I heard it, Dad. I heard all of it!"

"I heard the radio traffic about the spaceship and the failure of the intercept pattern to take out the bogey. And the soldiers thought I was sleeping and wouldn't have understood anything even if I did hear it!"

"I know about the alien ship Dad, and that's why I'm scared," I said quietly. "I might really be in over my head on this one, and I know it," I concluded.

Dad was silent for almost a full minute, then cleared his throat and said, "General? . . ."

"Incredible!" came an unexpected reply from the audio speaker. "Daniel, it astounds me you deduced the truth and pleases me you kept it to yourself. Dennis, you should be proud of your son."

"I am, General, but if you remember the assignment we set up, sir, you will appreciate that I am more than a little nervous that Dr. Fisher's daughter and my son were selected."

"You know the parameters that were set up because you set them up, Colonel," the voice said firmly. "I would have to say these two young people fit the profile to a T. Smart, resourceful, dedicated, talented and lucky." The voice paused and went on more slowly. "I would also bet they are both stubborn, willful and difficult to discourage. You have no chance of keeping them from this assignment, Dennis. I hope you understand that?"

My dad didn't answer. Instead, he looked at me, cleared his throat and asked, "Daniel, if I told you directly you could not go to Echo Canyon, would you disobey me and go anyway?"

I stared at my dad for several seconds and then replied slowly.

"Dad . . . it's not up to me to decide. Or you either. Jolene has the assignment, and I know darn well she will go regardless of whether I help her or not, or anything else." *Lord, how can I say this? How can I say what I have to say?*

"What you are asking me," I continued slowly, "is if I will abandon Jolene to whatever danger is there because you tell me not to go there to protect her. I understand you have fears for my safety, Dad, but. . .sir. . ."

"Just a minute, Daniel, don't say any more!" the speaker's voice interrupted commandingly. "Colonel Jackson, you have painted Daniel into a corner, and he is desperately trying to find the right way to say what you know he must say. I strongly suggest, Colonel, you re-consider the question." The voice paused several seconds and went on more gently. "Dennis, you know what he did on that dairy farm for a total stranger, and you know he would never abandon someone he likes as well as I think he likes this young lady. Well. . .Dennis?"

My dad was staring at me while the voice was talking, then smiled briefly and shook his head and took a deep breath.

"Dan. . .I withdraw my question. The general is right, and I was wrong to ask. Remember this incident as an example of how hard it is to always do the right thing as a parent," he added ruefully, "when you grow up and have children of your own."

"Okay," the voice said briskly, "Now that we have that out of the way, let's get to something more pleasant. Dennis, I want Dan to have every reason to come back safely from Echo Canyon. Given his previous actions, his accurate deductions plus his silence about the whole matter, I believe I can offer him something worthwhile."

"Attention to orders!" the voice said formally. (Startled, my dad stood up quickly, and a second or so later, so did I.) "On behalf of the Space Force High Command, I hereby award Daniel Jak Jackson a merit appointment to the Space Academy, as soon as he can pass the entrance exams." The voice then added conversationally, "How does that sound, Dan?"

"The Space Academy?" I blurted. I could hardly breathe, let alone talk. "The Space Academy?"

"That's right, Daniel. Your country needs all the qualified people it can get in leadership positions. You have already proved you know how to put others before yourself. That lesson is one too many adults never learn."

I couldn't believe my ears! the voice continued.

"Explain anything you feel he needs to know, Dennis. I trust him. Clear space, Dan, Colonel."

"Clear space, sir." Astounded, I could only look over at my dad who was still standing at attention. "Dad . . . was that for real?" I still couldn't believe it.

"Yes, son," my dad said, relaxing finally. "General Lacey is very much for real."

My eyes got big.

"That was General Lacey? I mean . . . the real General Lacey? The one who saved the world during the War?" my voice seemed to keep getting higher and higher.

"That's him. By the way, insiders don't call it 'The War.' We call it 'The Troubles.'" My dad looked at me ruefully and shook his head. "I had really hoped you would to go to the University of Illinois and be in the Marching Illini band like I was, but I suppose Colorado Springs does look more attractive."

I still couldn't believe it! The Space Academy in Colorado Springs was the number one choice of almost every boy and girl I knew, and yet they only accepted the top 1000 candidates a year from the whole world!

"Okay, Daniel," Dad said in a tone of voice that brought me back to Earth. "Let's get back to business and focus on what we need to do next. Besides, the last time I looked," he added dryly "they only accept LIVE cadets at the Academy. Let's see if I can teach you enough to stay alive long enough to get to the Academy!"

Chapter 10
TARGET PRACTICE

The straw that broke the back of the ultra-liberal gun-control movement was the massacre at Little Bayou in southern Louisiana. Until that time, the anti-gunners had pushed tighter and tighter restrictions on any use of a gun by anyone for any reason.

At Little Bayou, a colony of "Basics" ('we must return to nature and use only basic devices') similar to the Amish who didn't allow firearms were brutalized and some murdered over a two-day period by a gang of early release ex-cons looking for a place of their own to hide.

Angry neighbors were stunned when told the local, county and state police forces were prohibited from engaging the gang under the latest gun control measure, the No-Gunfight Law for police officers. Carried to its ultimate absurdity, gun control had slowly stripped even the police of the right to use a firearm. Use of a gun was considered a criminal act, so under the absurd No-Gunfight Law for police, only criminals could use guns. This they did—consistently and brutally with no fear of retribution by the police.

Outraged, the angry citizens took action by themselves.

A brother of one of the victims worked at a local lab that was experimenting with a handheld defensive laser system that was non-lethal. This laser system did not qualify as a firearm since it didn't fire a projectile or use a propellant. Several early prototypes were "borrowed" by this relative, and he "loaned" them to neighbors and friends who then "went to have a talk" with the gang of killers.

Somehow, none of the gang of killers was ever seen again.

Speculation was they had foolishly tried to swim across the swamp to escape "talking" to the relatives and friends of their victims and had themselves fallen prey to alligators and other predators. As it was, no one ever talked about what happened that day at Little Bayou, and the truth remains shrouded in mystery. Opinion polls taken in the days following the events, however, showed 90% of the citizens of this country approved the actions taken by the relatives and friends. Soon after the incident, the United States Supreme Court ruled, ". . .these laser devices do not fall under the category of guns, and so could not be regulated by any existing gun control law." Everyone wanted a laser of their own, and the local lab got rich selling the plans.

In any event, the publicity given to the "PerLaz" (short for Personal Laser) as it was dubbed in the press lead to immediate success in the marketplace for those who licensed the plans. The companies with tooling in place and employees sitting idle were the almost defunct gun companies, who made a "killing" manufacturing and selling the PerLaz. After the PerLaz became a common item, the homicide rate plummeted to its lowest level in years. Statistics taken two years later showed the homicide rate fell by 87% within 18 months of the introduction of the PerLaz. People no longer had to be passive victims, but finally had a device with which they could (legally) fight back.

Several years later, belatedly recognizing the fact that an armed citizen was indeed a safer citizen, Personal Laser

Training was required of every person before they could receive a license to drive a floater. The PerLaz (temporarily disabling at 4 feet, painful at 10, ineffective beyond 25) was an idea whose time had come, and society became much politer. It also became much safer.

"Dan, if what we suspect is true, your PerLaz is useless. You need something better to take, and you need to learn to use it right away."

"But Dad," I protested, "I'm a dead shot with my PerLaz!"

"So were the Orbital Laser Cannon crews. We recorded what appears to be five direct hits that were either deflected or blocked. Either way, they had no effect on the bogey. You may be a dead shot, but I don't want you shot dead, or worse!" Dad said grimly.

I knew a state of the art Orbital Laser Cannon puts out umpteen gig-a-watts of power, and if that had no effect. . .

"Dad. . .isn't that information classified?"

"Very highly classified, so don't repeat it," he agreed. "The current thinking is that a kinetic energy weapon may penetrate or disrupt whatever field they use, so it's time you learn how to shoot this."

'This' was Dad's Glock 17 Semi-Automatic 9mm pistol. "I carried this on the street as a police officer before you were born, and it saved my life at least twice. It's accurate, hard-hitting with the +P+ ammunition, and it has magazines with capacities that were manufactured for police use only."

Dad showed me the most effective stance and hand positions, and I prepared to fire.

"Remember, it kicks much harder than your PerLaz, Dan."

The sights were very much the same, so I lined them and squeezed the. . .BOOM!. . .BOOM!. . .BOOM!. . .Trigger.

What the heck? I was surprised at how hard it bucked in my hand.

Dad smiled. "You've been taught to squeeze, squeeze, and squeeze on the PerLaz so as not to overheat it. On a semi-auto pistol, that gets you three separate shots. Let's see how you did." And with that, he hauled in the target.

One hole was just below the X ring, a second in the 7 rings directly above the X, and the third off the target but still on the paper in a vertical line above the X and near the top.

"+P+ kicks hard, son. In rapid fire, the shots tend to rise. You have to hold it down more."

With the target back in place, I prepared to fire again.

BOOM! . . .BOOM! . . .BOOM! It felt better this time, and I signaled for Dad to bring in the target.

One hit below the X ring, one on the X, and one just above the X. A coffee cup could have covered all three holes. *Not bad for 25 feet with my second three shots.* I thought.

"The best grip for a Glock is to push forward with your trigger hand and pull back with your other hand on the front of the trigger guard. That locks the Glock into position better than anything other than a hand rest," Dad said.

Dad continued to drill me on combat reloading, clearing "stovepipe" jams, and I must have fired 200 rounds before he was satisfied I had the basic idea.

"Dad, is it legal for me to carry this? I mean, what about the gun laws?"

"Yes, Dan, as long as you carry it in a holster in plain sight, it is legal. After several disasters involving armed bandits, the Supreme Court overturned all local and state laws on gun issues and returned to the original intent of the Second Amendment of the Constitution. They ruled the intent was for citizens to be allowed to protect themselves and their families through the use of firearms. Minors do need written parental permission, however, and I'll give you a letter you must keep in your holster at all times."

"So much for the basics." Dad continued. "It's time for some advanced work."

"I need to leave for school pretty soon Dad, or I'll be late for band."

"Not today, Dan. I informed the school you would not be coming in today and cited the Personal Safety Clause which gives parents the right to substitute other training or treatment." He smiled grimly. "In your case, it will be both training and treatment."

Dad floated us to the County Simulator, which really shocked me. "I thought you were against the use of the 'Sim' as a training device Dad!" He had told me that often enough.

"I am against it," he agreed. "I am totally opposed to the Simulator when it comes to learning math or history or something of that nature. The Simulator was designed for combat, police tactics, and gross motor skills, like shooting. I can't teach you what you need to know in just one day, Dan, and this may become a life or death issue, not a test you get a grade on!" With that amazing explanation, he handed me a Restricted Enhancement Capsule (which I swallowed before he could change his mind) and we began.

Dad kept me practicing for several hours while the REC was still active, with frequent breaks to correct the fine points. He had never discussed his police work with me before, and I was fascinated with his knowledge of tactics and personal survival tips.

He shared such things as "Always go wide around a corner. If someone is waiting to ambush you, his job is harder because of the distance, and your job is easier because you can see him quicker," and, "Always watch their hands. Forget all that stuff about watching their eyes or their stomach muscles. If they are going to try to hurt you, it will be with their hands or something they are holding in their hands." He also told me a police officer must show compassion. "My job was to protect people, son. Always err on the side of protecting the innocent."

Dad and I grew much closer by the end of that day, and I looked at him and what he was telling me in a different light than I ever had before. My dad was a warrior, something I had not realized before today.

Chapter 11
COMPETITION MARCHING

"OK, BAND," Mr. Kissinger said through the Public-Address System. "This will be a complete run-through of the show for Saturday's competition. The stopwatch and burn disk will be rolling, all the props are in place, and we're doing everything except uniforms. Give it your best shot, and don't hold back this time!" He added formally, "Drum major, you have the band!"

"BAND! . . .'Ten-HUT!" the drum major shouted, and we all snapped to attention and froze into complete stillness. Every percussionist played one loud note just as we hit Attention.

"TAKE-THE-FIELD (pause) READY (pause) MOVE!" Drum major Liana commanded her words in time with her clapping the beat. The band marked time for four beats, then began forward movement onto the football field to go to our beginning positions. One drummer tapped on the rim of their drum, "Tap, pause, tap, pause, tap tap tap, pause. We all marched in time to the drum beat.

We got into position, turned to the back of the field, did our 1-minute warm-up, turned back to the front and halted.

"Are the judges ready?" boomed the voice on the P.A. The judges, who were actually alumni of the band who came back to help with this practice, waved their clipboards in the air to signal they were ready.

"The judges are ready. Drum major, is your band ready?" asked the P.A. voice.

Liana walked slowly to the front third mark, halted, then snapped a fancy 4-part salute.

"The band is ready. Ridgeway Marching Rebels, you may take the field for competition."

Liana walked to the podium and clapped the beat to give us the tempo. The percussion started playing the first 4 beats, and the rest of the band began playing. Our first song (called the 'Off the Line') was music from an old rock group, the Monkees. It was "I'm Not Your Steppin' Stone" and had a very strong introduction. It was an excellent arrangement, and the drill started with the band in four tight 1-step (shoulder to shoulder) triangle clusters that quickly expanded into huge 8-step (5 yards apart) triangles. The flags and rifles were in-between the triangles on two 45-degree diagonals, crossing at the 50-yard line and the front third mark (called the "hash" mark.) When the main melody started, the entire band marched towards to front of the field.

At the second phase, the outside two triangles marked time while the inner triangles and percussion continued forward. The guard (flag & rifles) turned 90 degrees and headed towards the end zones, opening the way for the inner triangles and percussion.

On the third main melody phrase, the four triangles merged into two huge blocks, one on either side of the 50, then the blocks started to contract with the players on the outside sliding sideways towards the 50.

The percussion had a 32-count transition while the winds continued to close to 4-step intervals, then quickly moved the last 8 counts into one large company front shoulder to shoulder from both 30's to the 50.

We pushed the company front straight to the sidelines with our horns to the box (brass bells pointed up at the press box) and blew as strongly as we could. The sound of 140 wind players plus 28 percussionists was incredible, and the parents and friends in the stands went nuts!

The company front marked time 8 steps before the sideline, then arched out in a final 16-count back push. The arc was to make it harder for the judges to hit us on alignment.

The whole first song with an intricate drill that took 8 hours to design, 2 hours to chart on the computer, two days practice to learn and perfect was over in just 2 minutes, 10 seconds. The performance felt good, and we continued after an 8-second pause.

The second song was "Mexican Hat Dance." It was a neat little traditional song, and Jolene had a soli with 3 other piccolo players. The tubas played the first part of the melody while they marched down the 50 towards the crowd. Hidden behind the tubas, the piccolos followed in their footsteps until the last four counts when the tubas opened ranks. The piccolos seemed to appear from nowhere, and the crowd always roared their approval at being tricked!

The third song, our American Flag presentation was definitely our hardest number. Taken from the musical "1776," we presented the American Flag to the tune of "Momma, Look Sharp." Not only was the tempo very slow for marching (about 76 beats per minute,) the song was in triple meter. It was a real tearjerker, and the judges always gave us good marks for difficulty. Mary and I had a trumpet duet with muted drums in the background, and once we won a trophy for best solo/soli in Class.

Our closer was a modern hit tune "Martian Sands," and the drill was a free-form design with constant movement but no obvious formations until the last 16 counts. It was OK, but I didn't care for either the music or drill very much. Some people thought it was our best song, however, so I guess it just proves different people have different tastes.

We completed the practice show, trooped the stands (passed in review) then waited for Mr. Kissinger to come down from the press box and talk to us. I went over to where Jolene was standing with the other piccolo players.

"Hi Jolene, ladies. I loved your pop-out surprise. Whose idea was it for the tubas to kneel as you passed through?"

"Thanks, Dan," Kimmee said. "It was Jolene's idea, of course. She's the only girl strong enough to get six big guys to kneel before us little girls!" she said sarcastically.

Jolene frowned for a second, and then said, "Actually, it took no convincing at all. I mentioned it to Jim, told him it would look like we were coming out of their bells, and he couldn't wait to tape it so we could see what it looks like." While she was talking, Jolene went closer to Dan and leaned against his shoulder. "Besides, most guys know where they belong anyway," she said, resting her foot on Dan's.

"OKAY BAND, LISTEN UP!" shouted Mr. Kissinger. We quickly got quiet.

"That was a very good performance! Very good! I think that rather than just run the show again or work in sectionals or on M&M (marching and maneuvering,) it's time for you to see yourselves before tomorrow's competition. Everyone to the auditorium, and we'll use the big projector. It will be "Monday at the Movies" on Friday this week."

We all cheered at the thought of no more marching for today, and at seeing ourselves on the projector screen.

The auditorium had an ultra-high-power quartz iodine projector capable of producing a bright picture on the 30-foot by 20-foot drop-down screen on stage. I knew from past experience that about 20 rows from the front gave the best perspective, so I grabbed Jolene's hand and hustled her into the center of that row. The sound system used 'Voice of the Theater' speakers, ancient but still among the most powerful and clean sounding available.

The lights dimmed, the show started, and we watched in rapt attention the practice performance we just did. We cheered just like the audience, and I was really impressed at how things always seemed to flow from one move to another. How in the world did the color guard change flag colors so quickly? And when and how did the rifles put streamers on their rifles? I was looking for where the piccolos came from, and how they got behind the tubas, and I still didn't see it!

"You were right," I whispered. "It looks like you came out of the Tuba bells."

Jolene smiled and whispered back, "I know."

We cheered at the end, and Mr. Kissinger reminded us about what time the buses were leaving and all the necessary details for tomorrow.

"You look and sound very good," he told us, "but we're going up against both Rockland and the Dundee Scots tomorrow. It needs to be a perfect show for us to have any chance of beating either one of those bands. You've done well today, so I'm going to cut you free early. Go home, get some rest, and I'll see you tomorrow."

"BAND: Ten-HUT!" Liana shouted. We all came to attention and froze into position.

I'm in a block of ice and can't move a muscle! I thought to keep myself from moving.

After about three or four seconds of 140 of us frozen into position and not moving a muscle, Mr. Kissinger shouted, "Dismissed!"

Jolene was meeting her mom, so we couldn't go home together. I said my goodbyes and hurried to my floater, trying to get home early enough to "help" my mom pick out what we would eat for supper. Unfortunately, two other floaters were in my way. I still had a chance, but then I saw Liana and three other self-appointed guardians approaching, and I knew I was in for another grilling.

"Dan!" shouted one of the three, "Wait a minute! We need to talk to you."

"Hello, ladies. Nice to see you. . .again." I stressed the word 'again' on purpose, hoping they would take the hint. No such luck.

"It's come to our attention that the person who 'Pressed you may be going too far in what she expects you to do for her, or what she expects you to tolerate. Is Jolene going too far? Is she hurting you, or making you do things you don't want to do?"

I stared at them for a few seconds, trying to control my anger.

"No," I said slowly. "Jolene has not asked me to do or done anything to me that I object to." They looked glum at my words. "Wait a minute!" I added quickly, and their expressions brightened in anticipation. "She did make me eat my vegetables when I ate at her house, but that's all."

They looked eager, then disappointed, but couldn't really say much more. They did tell me (again) I could break the 'Pinning' if I wanted to, and (again) I declined.

They left, I left, and by the time I got home, supper was already on the table.

When we got to the University Stadium the next day, we discovered the practice field was set up too close to the stadium, and we couldn't practice playing our show because it would interfere with the bands actually performing in the stadium. Typical. No matter how well planned an event is, something always must go wrong.

"No problem," Mr. Kissinger told us. "We'll do a sing-through instead." A sing-through is when we march our drill and sing our parts instead of playing. It's usually fun, and we ham it up a lot. The percussion played on the rims of their drums, not the heads, so we could still hear the rhythm and beat.

The sing-through felt good, and Mr. Kissinger sent us to the buses to change into uniform.

Normally, changing into uniform on the buses is no problem. Two buses are for the guys, and two buses are for the girls. Lately, however, some of the girls (led by Jolene and Liana, I must admit) have decided to change on whatever bus they rode on. Since Jolene and I rode together, she was changing into uniform in the aisle right next to me. I manfully tried to ignore the fact she would see me in my underwear, and scrupulously avoided looking at her in her undergarments as well. I felt quite superior until I realized Liana had changed earlier and had watched me undress the entire time!

"Liana, Please!" I sputtered. She just smiled at me, but at least she did turn away.

Our band lined up, waited our turn, and then played the best performance we had ever done! It was an electric feeling, and we could just feel the current go through our bodies! Afterward, we went to the concession stand and got some hot dogs and sodas, and then sat in the back stands to watch the other bands.

The Dundee Scots, complete with kilts and bagpipes, were good, but I was pretty sure we were better. Rockland, on the other hand, gave an incredible show that filled me with awe. I didn't think it was possible for anyone to be that good, or for anyone to beat them.

All the bands lined up for the grand finale, and we were slotted in between Dundee and Rockland. The announcer read all the scores and places of the small band class, then the medium band class. We were in the large band class.

"And now for the results in the large band class." the P.A. boomed.

The announcer read the scores of the 7th through 5th place bands.

"In Fourth Place, with a score of 86.7. . .the DeKalb Barbs!" The DeKalb band came to attention, their drum major saluted the judges (and Liana Saluted them,) came forward to get their trophy and then put their band back to Parade Rest.

"In Third Place, with a score of 88.1. . .the Dundee Scots!" *Yes! Yes!* I thought. *We beat them!* The drum majors did their ritual, and Liana saluted them.

"Ladies and gentlemen," the announcer commented, "the difference between second place and first place tonight. . .is one-tenth of one point." *We were that close?* I thought, *that close to beating Rockland? We must have done great to come that close!*

"In second place, with a score of 89.9. . ." the announcer paused for everyone to get quiet; "the Rockland Marching Rockets!"

I was stunned. I couldn't believe it!

The Rockland drum majors came forward, and Liana called us to attention, then saluted them. She put us back to parade rest.

"And in First Place, with a score of 90.0. . .the Ridgeway Marching Rebels! Let's hear it for all the bands, Ladies and gentlemen!"

Liana called us to attention and then she marched forward to accept the 1st place trophy.

She came back to our ranks and held it up, and we cheered!

Of course, it wasn't over yet.

The highest scoring band, in this case, us, is allowed to perform their show one more time. This post-performance meant a lot since it was all the other bands that would be watching us from the front stands and track.

If we did great the first time, we were spectacular the second! Having your competitors cheer and applaud your show was even better than the regular audience because the other band students all knew and understood how hard we had worked. At the mixer after the show, we got a chance to talk with kids from the other bands. The students from Rockland were very gracious, even though we broke their 5-year winning streak. Our drummers talked to their drummers, our color guard swapped trick moves with their color guard, and one of the most beautiful women I had ever seen asked if I wanted to study trumpet with her father? She hinted she'd really like to do some trumpet duets. . .and other duets. . .with me. I was about to exchange phone numbers and addresses with this goddess when I saw Jolene glaring at me from about 15 feet away. I could feel the heat of her anger even that far away! I thanked the goddess trumpet player very much but told her I had to decline. Talk about a close call!

I made amends with Jolene on the bus ride home, and she came over that evening for pizza and pop. We talked about the show, and how incredible it felt to win, then exchange ideas with the other band members.

As usual, I had gotten a lot of questions during the mixer about our trumpet Soli during "Momma Look Sharp!" Several other brass players asked how we managed to blend together so well, and how could we possibly keep in step since the music was in triple meter instead of duple. I gave them the secret of slightly veering to the left when we started on our left foot, and then to the right the next measure. They were amazed at how simple and effective that was, and I had to demonstrate it for them. Two female trumpet players wanted to practice it with me, and I made sure Jolene didn't see me practicing with them since they were both leaning on my body as we moved! It was a lot of fun to mix with the other band members. A LOT of fun.

Marching band competitions have it all over athletic games in that regard!

Chapter 12
ECHO CANYON

"Oh, Dan! You may think it's spooky because of your bad memories, but I think this is one of the most beautiful places I've ever been!" Jolene exclaimed as we descended into Echo Canyon. The canyon was a typical box canyon with a large stream that cascaded over the closed end. It was this stream creating the canyon by cutting a respectable path through the center. The canyon was about 3 miles long and almost a half-mile wide at the open end, but only about 200 feet deep and wide at the closed end. Large trees lined the whole rim of the canyon, making it seem deeper than it really was. I started us at the closed "box" end. We picked that end because the waterfall showed the latest erosion that could be seen.

The four-place floater Dad had rented for us was much nimbler than I would have believed, and I had no difficulty setting it down precisely where I wanted.

The floater was only one of a number of amazing items on which our dads insisted. For example, our belts.

"Put these belts on and walk slowly down to that tree," my dad told us. Jolene looked at me, and I shrugged, so we did as we were asked. About halfway there, I felt a vibration in the belt that became increasingly weaker as we continued.

Jolene stopped before I did (probably because she had better sense,) and we turned and hurried back to the floater. The closer we came to the floater, the more the vibration.

"OK, Dad," I said. "What is that all about?"

Dad smiled and said, "First, you can always find the floater by how the belt feels, even if you can't see it. Second, this very special but ordinary looking family floater is really a covert combat vehicle I borrowed, and the Enviro field on it extends outwards 5 yards. Your belts will stop vibrating just after you leave the actual Enviro field. Third, if you carefully lift the red decoration on the buckle, you will find the emergency control to activate the shield. This shield will deflect all but the heaviest laser from a main battle tank, but it only lasts 10 seconds before it drops back to normal."

"Fourth, while you are in the floater, the shield will deflect much stronger lasers and last longer since the shielded area is smaller."

Inside the floater, a sign was posted reading:
The rule of thumb is:

1. Stay within 15 yards of the floater at all times
2. Run, don't walk and get in the floater if threatened.
3. Activate the shield and float like XXXX away. (Someone had scratched one word off.)

"Activating the shield will set off alarms in several locations, and help will be on the way in seconds. Don't wait too long to turn it on."

"Yes, Dad."

"He who runs away lives to go to the . . ." he paused and glanced at Jolene, then continued, ". . .to special places later in life. Do you understand?"

"Yes, Dad." *Boy did I understand!*

As amazing as the floater and belt were, Dad's instructions to Jolene were nothing short of astounding.

"Jolene, you are an extremely capable young lady, and I appreciate your intelligence and strengths . . . but Dan must be in complete control for this trip. There can't be one second of arguing, deciding if you want to do what he says or not, or delays for any reason. Dan's sole job is to safeguard you while you do your report." Jolene looked more serious than I had ever seen her.

"Dan has already had his first life and death crisis, and someone is alive today because of his quick thinking and swift action. You are trusting him with your life, and you need to do exactly as he says, when he says it. Will you do that?"

"Yes Dad," she answered, but I don't think she realized what she said. My dad noticed, of course, but his glance at me silenced my laugh before it got out.

"Very well, clear space, Jolene," and he gave her a hug. "Clear space, son," and I got a hug as well," then he whispered to me, "Take your time getting there. Give us time to get into place." I grabbed Jolene and hurried her to the floater before she could see the moisture in my father's eyes.

Just before we floated, I saw my father standing at attention, and he gave us a parade ground salute. Startled, I returned it, but I don't think Jolene noticed.

The best way to gather the required samples, particularly of larger mobile creatures, was to set up secretly and wait for a single or small group to come in range, then use the beam projector to collect the sample. Or samples. The samples could then be loaded on the ship that remained safe outside the atmosphere until summoned.

We were both wearing full bodysuits, so the crisp air was delightful rather than numbing. Jolene 'burned as she walked, and I stayed on point no more than 10 feet from her. Her 'burning was very thorough, and I heard her with part of my mind while I watched for unusual signs. I noticed a tiger spider dangling his antenna, a large bug approach, and. . .

POUNCE! The bug was history.

"Bait!" I cried out loud, with a sudden understanding of our position!

"What?" Jolene asked, startled at my exclamation.

"Sorry, Jolene. I. . .I was watching a spider catch a bug." And with that, she turned and resumed her 'burning.

We are bait, I thought again. *But you must have some way of stopping the spider, or the bait becomes toast! So where are the catchers?* I raised my eyes and started searching the canyon walls.

"By the way, what was that life and death decision you made? Your dad seemed very proud of it." Jolene asked.

I stepped over a log and made sure nothing was on the other side. "I saw a farmer trapped under his tractor and got him out safely from underneath." I was constantly scanning the area around us, looking for something, anything, out of place. I was also looking for any sign of someone ready to help us if we ran into trouble.

There was nothing to indicate anyone or anything, was within miles of our location.

"Surely there's more to it than just that?" she persisted.

"Well, I had to go underwater and under the tractor to get to him, and the tractor was still slipping." She just looked at me. "I had to help! I was the only one around, and he would have drowned if I didn't get him out. We are our brother's keeper, just like they tell us in church services. Besides, the tractor didn't completely fall over until several seconds after we were out."

"You knew him?" she asked.

"No, but he was hurt and in danger, and I couldn't run away and leave him to die."

Dan was scanning the area so hard he failed to see the way Jolene looked at him.

Up by Dad's western lab, Jolene's father said, "They are getting close, Dennis."

"I know, Henry," Dennis Jackson replied. "Just keep watching."

None of the samples collected from this planet had survived to be taken back to the home planet. Over a period of years, the robots had learned: 1. Not to go faster than 2 G's (twice the gravity of this planet); 2. How to duplicate the mixture of atmospheric gases; and 3. To provide grain crops to be used as food. They had yet to learn the difference between salt and fresh water, and that the atmosphere gases must be renewed. The new hyperdrive, however, meant a sample could be returned at 2 G's in only 10 revolutions of this planet instead of the 1210.5 revolutions (4.1 years) of old. It was a good possibility the next samples would still be alive when they arrive.

"The erosion has gone unusually fast along this section," Jolene 'burned as she walked, "and one unusual indication is a cave that should not normally be found. . ." she continued.

Cave? I thought. *There wasn't a cave here!* I moved to get between her and the cave.

"General! We've got the unknown radio signal! We've got the unknown signal again! All stations stand by!" And the warning went out.

Jolene continued burning, "The cave almost appears to be artificial, and I can see. . .Dan, is there something in there?" We both heard a strange humming, and then two small boxes moved. . .no floated! . . .out of the cave towards us. They were about a foot to a foot and a half big and floated above the ground about 6 inches. They also moved pretty darn fast!

"GO! GO! GO!" I shouted! It was our emergency signal to retreat to the floater. To her credit Jolene didn't hesitate, she immediately turned on her heel and sprinted back. I was running backward, keeping an eye on the. . .robots? Jolene was climbing in, and I was halfway there when I saw a rod raise up out of a robot and then swing down to point at us. I don't remember drawing Dad's pistol, but suddenly it was in my hand.

I didn't wait. BOOM! . . .BOOM! . . .BOOM! And I saw pieces of the robot fly in all directions. It stopped moving towards us, but the second one started to raise a rod and BOOM! . . .BOOM! . . .BOOM! I fired again. It kept coming. How could I have missed?

Dad's words came back to me. "In combat, rookies always shoot high, son, and you're definitely a rookie. Keep your aim low and keep firing until the target stops moving."

I aimed lower, and BOOM! . . .BOOM! Fired again. The robot tipped over on its side, spinning around.

"Hurry," Jolene screamed! And I turned and ran for the floater. She pointed to one side, brought up her PerLaz and fired, and I saw two more robots approaching with rods already drawn. I fired as I ran. BOOM! . . .BOOM! . . .BOOM! and one of them stopped moving. I switched my aiming point to the other robot and fired again. BOOM! . . .and it was like I ran headlong into a brick wall! My world went red and hazy.

I could feel myself falling in slow motion, but all I could do was twist to hit on my shoulder. It was like being stuck in a nightmare where everything moves fast but you.

The fourth robot came closer, then stopped, turned away from me and aimed the rod at the floater.

The red haze was gone as soon as the rod moved away from me, but I couldn't get on target before I saw Jolene stiffen in her seat, then slide sideways to the floor of the floater.

Furious at myself for not protecting Jolene, I used my fury to make my arms move into shooting position. I had the sight picture; did I have the strength? BOOM! . . .BOOM! . . . BOOM! And the 4th robot exploded into pieces.

I had to get in the floater, but my legs wouldn't move! It felt like I was moving in mud!

Jolene didn't know about a special feature Dad told me about in that floater. I knew I could never make it inside quickly enough to escape the other robots I could hear, and I knew she had been hit and maybe couldn't move at all, so I pushed the remote RECALL button. The floater Enviro buttoned up, and the floater lifted and headed like a rocket to the preprogrammed spot at Dad's Lab. Jolene was safe, but I was angry. *Is this what happened to Jerry Thornton? This time,* I smiled grimly to myself, *at least, one person will escape to tell the story.*

I ejected the magazine, inserted another, and was back in business, or so I thought. The numbness was starting to wear off, and I could feel my strength coming back.

One of Dad's tips came back to me.

"When you're hit, you're dead; so stay dead! If you can see your attacker, stay down and wait to fight back until he comes in range and you can't miss."

Good advice, I thought as I lay there in the sand, waiting.

There was a deep humming I felt in my chest rather than just hearing it, and I felt the wind move overhead. Cautiously, I peeked through the bush, and there, no more than 50 feet away from me, was a flying saucer!

I couldn't believe my eyes!

The saucer was a disk shape like two dinner plates, one upside down on the other. It was about 20 to 25 feet in diameter, silver in color and had three legs to support itself as it rested on the ground. I could see it didn't sink very much into the sand, so I guessed it was not very heavy. It didn't seem to use rockets or anything like that, and I didn't hear engines or engine sounds except for the humming. Then, the humming stopped.

The silence made it seem very eerie and menacing.

Suddenly, one side of the ship started to move. A panel that was hinged at the bottom started to unfold and reach to the ground.

I was afraid I knew what was going to happen next!

Chapter 13
CAPTURED

"No, No, No!" Jolene screamed, as the floater lifted off and accelerated away. *I can't run away,* she thought as the numbness wore off her arms, *I can't leave Dan! Where is this thing going?* She hit the control program and saw in flashing red letters "EMERGENCY RECALL."

I will NOT run away! she thought angrily, but a flashing orange button that read "EMERGENCY RELOAD?" caught her eye.

Yes! she thought and savagely banged the orange button with her fist. *Maybe I can fight back and help Dan.*

As she turned her head to look back, she saw a disc-shaped object zoom towards the cave at incredible speed. *Oh my God! She thought, is that what happened to Dan's friends? Is that what's going to happen to Dan? Not if I can help it!* she thought, her anger growing.

Deep inside the floater (which really was a combat craft in disguise) a string of 20mm projectiles fed into the breach of a cannon. Immediately, a large red light appeared on the monitor. "A R M E D," and then "Emergency Recall Canceled." She felt the floater slow, and the yoke come to life.

Grimly, she whipped the floater around, applied maximum power and headed in a wide circle back to where Dan was trapped.

"General! The floater canceled the recall and is heading back to the site! The indicators say it's now armed, sir!"

"Armed?" General Lacy and several others blurted together?

"Yes sir. General, If I remember right, there's a hidden reserve of 20mm cannon shells in that type of craft, and it activates automatically when the recall is canceled."

"Saints preserve us!" A lieutenant said quietly.

"Sir, we have the disk, we have the disk!" the technician shouted excitedly, and he pushed the Scramble alarm.

I stayed still and watched as a panel swung down from the side of the disk. *I'll be frosted!* I thought. *The UFO nuts were right all along! They DO exist!* Two little box robots came down together, then two more, then two more. They stayed in pairs but moved in different directions so I couldn't get a clear shot at all of them.

I wonder about that opening in the saucer, and what's inside? I don't have enough ammo for this, but maybe I can take out their central control.

I aimed at the opening into the disk. BOOM! . . . BOOM! . . . BOOM! . . . BOOM! . . . BOOM! . . . BOOM! . . . BOOM! . . . BOOM! . . . BOOM! . . . BOOM! I fired 10 shots into the interior of the disc, then jumped up and ran away as fast as I could force my legs to move.

I went about 10 yards, then zigged behind a bush, reversing my direction.

Dan didn't see the sand erupt behind him. He made about another 8 yards and zagged back. He looked back, tripped on a root, and went down just as a stronger blast from the disk itself went over him. The fringe of the blast hit his leg and was enough to make him scream, and as he tried to get up, he realized his leg wouldn't support his weight.

Jolene is safe! Jolene is safe no matter how much I'm hurt! No matter what happens, Jolene is safe! I thought with satisfaction.

I dragged myself into the shelter of a bush and started looking for the robots. *There they are!* BOOM! . . . BOOM! . . . BOOM! . . . *switch aiming points*, BOOM! . . . BOOM! . . . BOOM! . . . *Two more robots down. One shot left.*

No! I remembered Dad shouting, *don't wait to reload if you know you're low.* Reload until the last magazine clip. *Right, Dad,* and I pushed the eject button, then reloaded my last magazine. *Two shot groups, I have to use two shot groups instead of three!*

There was a noise behind me and, and as I turned there were two robots coming towards me only 20 feet away with their rods already pointing in my direction.

Oh God! I really wanted to go to the Academy, and I never told Jolene how beautiful she was!

I quickly raised into position and fired. BOOM! . . . BOOM! . . . switched my aim, . . . then, . . .

No red haze like Dan experienced before. This time it was immediate blackness, and Dan was sinking to the bottom of a deep, dark pool.

The personal locator showed Jolene where Dan was, and as she slowed to pick him up, she saw him turn and fire, then go down like a frozen statue.

"NO!" she screamed, and she watched the robots advance towards Dan. Jolene lined up the floater, put the cross-sights on the robots and pressed the firing button.

Six 20mm shells tore through the decorative cover on the floater and blew the two robots into bits and pieces that flew everywhere. She hadn't realized the power of those shells, or she might not have fired so close to Dan.

As she landed, Jolene saw the disk start to rise, then settle back down. It tried again then settled again. Suddenly, armored infantrymen appeared from all directions. It had taken them about one minute and 45 seconds to cover the almost two miles from their hiding places. They quickly converged on the disk, and their rifles took care of the other little robots once and for all.

The Battle of Echo Canyon was over.

The A.I.s had captured the saucer, secured the area and set up a perimeter in case any other robots appeared. The battle had lasted only one minute and 42 seconds, with one human casualty.

Chapter 14
MED-VAC

When Jolene got to Dan, he was unconscious and curled up on his side. She checked to see that he was breathing, then that he wasn't bleeding too severely from the pieces of the robots she destroyed that hit him, then if he was burned anywhere. He appeared to have only minor cuts and bleeding except, of course, he was unconscious and stiff—very stiff. That was when her tears began. He had a good pulse, but it was very slow and getting slower. It was much too slow for normal, and unbelievable for someone who had just done physically what he had done.

Before she could do anything else, six AI's in full augmented infantry combat gear converged on their location and formed a perimeter around them while the medic put a device against Dan's chest. "Are you OK, Ma'am?" he asked, checking her visually for injuries at the same time his instruments were checking Dan. After a few seconds, he turned and checked the readout on Dan.

"Yes, I'm fine. What's wrong with him?" Jolene asked the medic.

"His pulse is very weak," he replied. "He needs MedVac, and right now!" the corpsman said as he glanced at Dan's pistol. "Cripes! He's holding that too tight, and the Glock doesn't have a regular safety!"

Dan's tight grip with his finger on the trigger meant the Model 17 held in Dan's hand could fire at the slightest movement.

"His dad taught him how to shoot it, and told him to bring it today," Jolene told the medic. "He shot those . . . things . . . that were trying to get us."

"I know. We saw it all, Ma'am. I'll just make this safe," and he reached over and released the magazine and ejected the cartridge in the chamber. "Keep this," the medic said, handing Jolene the magazine. "It's expensive, and if he lives, I know he'll want it back."

It wasn't until the medic's bland statement of doubt as he handed her the magazine that Jolene felt fear grip her heart again.

"Johnson! Rogers!" the medic shouted. "HotVac! Take them both!"

70 seconds later, the MedVac with Dan, Jolene and two AI's aboard was airborne and en route to the Regional Critical Care Hospital 110 miles away. Over the years the military learned that time to treatment was critical, and the MedVac went to maximum military boost with complete disregard for local speed, noise and altitude laws.

Both fathers in full tactical gear arrived as the MedVac was boosting, and hurried to find out what happened, and how their children were. It had taken only three minutes for them to arrive from the lab. When told of the MedVac destination, they immediately left for the hospital.

Dan thought it was like swimming in a dark sea, with strange sounds but no light. He could feel movement but couldn't understand what any of the sounds were. *I'll think about it a while*, he thought, then fell asleep, again.

The MedVac flared dangerously fast, and the two armored infantrymen picked up Dan and Jolene, jumped out and sprinted for the ER before the MedVac actually touched down. The hospital staff had been alerted they were receiving two patients, but this hospital had never received patients from armored infantry before and didn't realize how quickly AI's in full boosted combat gear could move. The AI's ran past the orderly pushing a gurney out to the MedVac, almost knocked both swinging doors off the hinges, and lay both patients on the table before the doctors knew they were in the ER.

"She's OK, Doc, but this one needs help with his breathing fast!"

And so, the second battle began.

Dan could feel motion on his skin. Not just his skin, his hand. *Something was holding and rubbing his hand. That's it*, he thought satisfied that he figured it out. There was something in his mouth too, but it didn't taste like food, and it didn't really hurt however uncomfortable it was, so he ignored it. And then he slept again.

As he slept, the Biological REgulatory And Temporary HElp unit (BREATHE for short) was monitoring his functions, and slowly restoring them to normal. The multiple hits he had taken from the paralysis rays had started his body on a downward cycle that, unaided, would have terminated his life forces.

It was an unusual occurrence. The ship was damaged but not destroyed. Samples were inside the ship, but the ship could not take-off to transport the samples back to the home planet. Also unusual was the fact communications via the new hyperlink were still intact between the ship and the central computer, and the ship dutifully reported all the occurrences as they happened. The fact the sample-taking ship had now become a sample itself escaped both ship and planetary central computer.

"Jolene, you have to eat and sleep sometime," Dr. Jackson said gently, as he tried to get her to leave Dan's bedside. "You know, they will take good care of him, honest, even if you aren't around to make sure they do," he joked.

Jolene just looked at him and shook her head no.

Dr. Jackson said ruefully, "They still haven't told us what they found yet, and your Father and I would really like to know what happened. You are literally the only person who was there and. . ." his voice broke a little, ". . .can still talk about what happened. Please, Jolene!" he pleaded, "I need to know what happened to my son!"

The raw emotion in his voice reached Jolene, and she glanced over at her dad, then went to Mr. Jackson and put her arms around him. What started as a consoling hug for him deteriorated into a fierce clinging embrace for her when Jolene finally gave in to her grief.

"He saved me!" she sobbed. "He risked his life to save mine! He got me out of there, and deliberately stayed behind to cover for me!" With those words, a flood of tears was released.

Through the darkness, Dan recognized a sound. *Jolene?* he thought. *Jolene crying? But she was safe, wasn't she?* He had to know. Dan started to fight his way to the surface of the black lake.

"Jrrrgh?" Dan croaked in a voice barely working, his eyes opening for the first time, but not really seeing anything. "Jo. . ." he moved his hand.

Instantly Jolene rushed back to his side, grabbed his hand and said, "I'm here Dan! I'm here! We're both safe! We're safe!"

Safe, thought Dan, and he closed his eyes and let go to sink back into the dark lake.

"Excellent!" said the doctor who had entered the room because she heard Jolene sobbing and observed what happened. "He responded to your voice, Jolene, and the anguish in your voice. I think he really cares for you deeply," she added quietly. "I believe it's only a matter of time now before he recovers," she said and then checked Dan's pulse.

"Back to normal. It appears the paralysis is wearing off. I think he will wake up soon, and probably be very hungry." To Dan's father, she said, "Tomorrow morning we'll disconnect the BREATHE and see how he does on his own."

Cares for me deeply? Jolene thought. *Is that what the doctor just said? Cares for me deeply? Oh, Dan, you don't care for me half as much as I care for you! My God! What am I thinking?* She went back over to Mr. Jackson and resumed her hug, only without the tears this time.

"Thank you for bringing my son back," he told her emotionally.

"No, thank you, Mr. Jackson, for having a son who put my life ahead of his own," she replied. They both smiled briefly at each other. "He's the one who got us out of there," she said, looking back at Dan. "He's the one."

The ship reported mechanical devices controlled by the samples were picking it up and placing it on a portable surface. This report caused a warning marker to pop up in the central computer, and it considered the nature of the samples in question. It compared the file on intelligent life with the description of the samples. The file showed intelligent life as having four legs, a tail, scales, and fangs. The description did not match the samples. Still, the samples were clearly tool users, and the central computer assigned a probability of 40% they had a higher level of intelligence.

Cares for me deeply! Jolene could hear the doctor's words echoing again and again in her head. *Cares for me deeply. He was ready to sacrifice himself to save me, and I have never even told him how I feel about him! He knew when he pressed that button the floater was his best chance of escaping, and he knew he faced the same fate as those other campers, yet he cared enough about me to send me out of danger, maybe at the cost of his own life.*

I used him, 'Pressed him,' 'Pinned him,' bullied him into the musical, walked on him like a rug, but I never ever told him that it was all because. . .because. . .say the words Jolene! . . . because I love him!

It was the first time she had admitted her love for Dan even to herself. Up until now, it had been just a game, just a series of pleasurable events in a pretend world.

Is it possible to know when you meet the right person even if we are both so young? Is Dan the man I am destined to spend my life with? How old do you have to be before you can admit to loving someone who isn't in your family? These thoughts and questions went around and around and around in Jolene's mind.

Responding to the anguish in Jolene's voice was, in fact, the turning point in Dan's recovery. Dan woke up later to find Jolene asleep in a chair next to his hospital bed, still holding his hand. *My God, she's beautiful, even when she's asleep,* he thought. *"Why didn't I tell her that before?"* He squeezed her hand gently, and she woke immediately to find him looking at her intently.

"You're safe, Dan," she said quickly. "Safe."

Dan took a slow deep breath and sighed. "Safe. How did I. . ." the words sounded strange as if he was just learning to speak.

"The Cavalry came over the hill to rescue us just in time, like in any good movie," Jolene joked with a weak smile.

"The cavalry? I don't understand."

"Just after you got. . .shot. . .some army guys in funny uniforms that made them run very fast came and rescued us, threw us in a MedVac, and flew us to this hospital."

"AI's? AI's rescued me?"

Dan had to think about that a few seconds and try to see what he remembered.

"Wait a minute," he protested. "You said, 'rescued us?' But you were safe!" he protested again. "I sent the floater away so you would be safe."

"Sent me away so I couldn't help you, you mean!" Jolene said fiercely. "You're going to pay for that, Daniel Jackson!" Jolene leaned over Dan and kissed him gently on top of his head. "And pay for it," Jolene said more reasonably as she kissed his forehead, "And. . .pay. . ." and she kissed him fully on the lips.

The nurse who walked in on this little scene quietly turned and walked right back out of the room. She decided Dan's temperature and pulse would definitely not be accurate right now anyway.

"Oh, Dan!" Jolene wailed after a while, and her tears began.

Chapter 15
THE AFTERMATH

"Tomorrow, Dan. Not today, but tomorrow," the doctor said with a smile and nodded her head to Dr. Jackson. As the doctor turned to leave she added, "And don't try to sneak out on me, Dan, or I'll send the AI's to bring you back!"

"Tomorrow will be too late," Dan said unhappily to his dad after the doctor left. "I want that part in the musical, Dad. I can't believe how much I enjoyed it, and I know they will replace me. They've got to."

"It can't be helped, Dan. However, I think you still have a chance. A legitimate injury might influence them to consider letting you keep the part," Dr. Jackson said.

Of course, Dr. Jackson already knew they still wanted Dan to play his part and Jolene hers. Mr. Pierce himself (who was a reserve Lieutenant) had called and told Dennis the new lights for the stage had been delayed, and they would need to postpone the musical performances by two weeks. He said if he did that, Dan and Jolene could keep their parts. *Still, it wouldn't hurt the boy to realize the consequences of getting hurt,* his dad thought. *It might prevent him from doing something really stupid in the future.*

"I see no reason to keep you here any longer, Dan," the doctor said the next day. "I'll sign your release papers, and you can go home this afternoon."

"Why not right now?" Dan asked impatiently.

"Because you have visitors coming who want to verify you are in good health, Dan. They will be here soon, and after they talk with you, and you eat all your lunch, including all the vegetables," she added sternly, "THEN you may go home."

A short time later, Dan's parents came into the room with Jolene and both her parents. Two men in military uniforms followed them.

"Hi Jolene," Dan said eagerly. "Hi Mom, Dad. Hi Dr. and Mrs. Fisher." Jolene immediately went over to his bedside, took his hand and said quietly, "Hi Dan." All four parents immediately noticed the possessive way the two teenagers looked at each other, but none of them said anything about it.

Dr. Jackson said, "Dan, Jolene, Mrs. Fisher, let me introduce you to these gentlemen. This is General Collins, the commandant of the Space Academy, and this. . .is General Lacey." Jolene and her mom were startled when they realized who the two men in uniform were. Henry, of course, already knew who they were.

"Dan, Jolene, I thought you might like to know what really happened out there, and how important your part was," General Lacey started out.

"We were bait," Dan said with a frown. Jolene looked up sharply at Dan's tone of voice. "You were using us to attract those. . .things."

"Yes, Dan," General Lacey admitted slowly, "you were bait. But you weren't unprotected or unobserved bait. We had one full company of AI's hiding out there, waiting for you for an entire day before you arrived."

"You see, we had been getting electronic readings for some time and knew an unknown ship visited Echo Canyon frequently. We sent AI's and infantrymen out, and nothing happened. We sent out what looked like civilian parties, horseback parties, and groups of hikers, campers, RV's, you name it—we tried it. Nothing happened until that small group of kids went."

"If we had known those campers were going into Echo Canyon, we would have stopped them," he added grimly.

"A post-analysis CompAn (computer analysis) suggested sending more children, only better prepared and armed. We chose your school and left it up to the SchoolComp to select a student based on a large number of requirements for the assignment. At that point, we were going to substitute adult look-alikes if the students were not suitable or not willing."

"You and Jolene were the best possible combination we could have hoped for, and your parents agreed, however reluctantly, that you could both handle it."

"Jolene, what you don't know is that Dan deduced the existence of the alien ship during the search for the missing campers and has kept quiet about it for more than a year."

"Incidentally, Dan, you impressed the armored infantrymen no end with your shooting, your accuracy, and your tactics. The sergeant of the squad told us that after you graduate from the Academy, he'd be proud to serve under you."

"The Academy?" Jolene asked quickly. "Graduate from what Academy?"

"The Space Academy. We awarded Dan a merit appointment based on his observations about the events he discovered, the accurate deductions he made, and the silence he kept about the whole affair." He added proudly, "He didn't tell anyone about that ship!"

"What?" Jolene glanced at Dan in disbelief, then back at the general. "Are you telling me. . .he had an appointment to the Space Academy. . .BEFORE we went to Echo Canyon?" Jolene exclaimed.

"That's correct," General Lacey said proudly, not recognizing the danger signs.

"And he KNEW he actually had an appointment?" she asked intensely.

"That's correct."

Uh Oh, Dan thought. *I wish you hadn't said that!*

Jolene slowly turned back to Dan. "And you still pressed that button to make me run away while you stayed behind?" she demanded.

"Now Jolene, I only wanted to. . ." Dan protested only to be overwhelmed by Jolene's anger.

"OF ALL THE IDIOTIC, STUPID HAIR-BRAINED STUNTS YOU COULD HAVE PULLED!!" Jolene shouted at Dan. "Risking your life or risking an injury that would keep you out of the Space Academy, on my HOMEWORK ASSIGNMENT?" Jolene's voice kept getting higher and louder, and if her eyes had been lasers, Dan would have been toast. She leaned over and shouted directly in Dan's face. "If you EVER do something STUPID like that AGAIN. . .."

"Jolene, please!" her mother interrupted, grabbing her daughters' shoulders to restrain and pull her back. "You and Dan can discuss this later, dear, in private?" she said, reminding Jolene that others were still in the room. Still seething with anger, Jolene relented, but she never took her eyes off Dan.

General Lacey cleared his throat. "Yes, thank you. Let me continue, please. Here is what we found."

"Dan disabled seven portable. . .robots. . .with his pistol and damaged the disk by firing through the only breach in its shield, the open door. We calculate you had no more than 10 seconds to recognize the opportunity and take advantage of it, Dan. No one else was close enough to do anything, and the damage you caused prevented the ship from escaping."

"Dan," he continued slowly, "your world captured an actual flying saucer because of your quick actions. I can't thank you enough, nor would there be money enough to pay you for what you have done. If there is ever any way you think we can repay you, it's yours."

The biggest blank check in history, and I immediately thought of something that they could do; something that might even take me off the hook with Jolene.

"Thank you, General Lacey. May I remind you, sir, there were two of us in Echo Canyon that day? I've been told a certain young lady with no training whatsoever took out several of the robots herself. Isn't that correct, sir?"

"Yes, that's correct. . ." the general said slowly, paused and then went on. ". . .and so, you want us to grant Jolene an appointment to the Space Academy as a favor to you, right?" General Lacey asked with a smile on his face.

I heard Jolene, and her parents gasp.

"I'm sorry, Dan," General Lacey said, "but I can't accept that as a favor for you. General Collins, if you please?"

General Collins smiled, pulled out some papers and said, "Attention to Official Orders: On behalf of the Space Force High Command, I hereby award Jolene Sue Fisher a merit appointment to the Space Academy, as soon as she passes the entrance exams."

Jolene was too stunned to speak, but her parents stammered out their thanks. Our parents shook hands with the generals and each other.

"You still have a favor coming Dan, but this isn't it. We beat you to this one." General Lacey said smugly.

"I hope to still be commandant when you two come to the Academy," General Collins said. "I'm sure you both realize you'll get no favors while attending as cadets?" Dan and Jolene both nodded.

"Good. I knew you were both intelligent. Now I know you have street smarts as well. By the way, I did bring these for you both. They help to advertise the Academy." General Collins gave both Dan and Jolene a highly prized Space Academy leather sleeve jacket.

General Lacey said, "There is one other item we must take care of. I told you the AI's were impressed with your combat skills, didn't I, Dan? They have their own system of awards, and they insisted you were eligible for one of them. General Collins, if you would please?"

"Attention to Orders. On behalf of the North American Military Forces, the

2nd Division of Armored Infantry hereby awards Daniel Jack Jackson the Combat Infantryman's Badge to be worn on his future uniforms. In combat against a technically and numerically superior foe, Daniel did the following:

First, he recognized the situation as a trap and sounded the alarm, alerting his principal.

Second, he covered his principal's withdrawal.

Third, he destroyed three armed enemy devices with small arms fire.

Fourth, after being wounded, he destroyed a fourth armed device.

Fifth, disregarding his own safety, he sent his principal out of harm's way.

Sixth, in the 10 seconds available, he disabled an advanced enemy air vehicle.

Seventh, after being wounded a second time, he destroyed three more armed enemy devices before being wounded a third time and rendered unconscious. Will enter the service from Illinois."

"Dan, you are not 'Just a Kid' as far as those AI's are concerned! Your actions epitomize the best qualities of an infantryman. The CIB is the highest and most coveted award those armored ground pounders have. Congratulations!"

Chapter 16
LIFE RESUMES

Dan had gone to talk to Mr. Pierce to see if he and Jolene could still perform in the musical. He was prepared to plead his case, if necessary, and outline the special circumstances that caused him to miss practices. He was even ready to explain in detail what actually happened in Echo Canyon, at least to Mr. Pierce.

"Do you still want to be in the show, Dan?" the director asked seriously.

"Yes, Mr. Pierce, I do. I know I've missed too many practices, but. . .well. . .it wasn't really my fault. Could I still have my part, and Jolene too?"

"If these were ordinary circumstances, Dan, I would have to say no. Missing as much practice as you did would be too much, even for a severe injury. In this case, however, we had to postpone the opening date because the new lighting for the auditorium didn't arrive on time. And. . .your understudy is nervous about doing your role. He came to talk to me about it and told me if there was any way you could still do it instead of him, it was okay. You got lucky, Dan." Mr. Pierce stopped talking and just looked at Dan. "You still have your part. As does Jolene."

"Yes!" Dan exclaimed happily. "Thank you, Mr. Pierce!"

"You're welcome, Dan. Oh, by the way, my best friend had his squad on the ridge at some place called Echo Canyon the other day. His job was to cover the MedVac if needed, and, since my reserve commission is tied to his squad, he filled me in on everything that happened." Mr. Pierce paused a few seconds, looked Dan in the eye and cleared his throat. "Everything."

Dan just stared at Mr. Pierce. Pierce had been an armored infantryman?

"Thanks to you, he wasn't needed. Even if you can't tell the rest of the students what happened, I know all about it. Everything. Frankly. . .I'm pleased that a warrior such as yourself has a lighter, more delicate side that wants to do theater." Mr. Pierce sighed. "You have no idea how difficult it is for me to get that message across to some of my more obnoxious students."

Jolene was more afraid of talking with Dan alone as she knew she must than she had been that day in Echo Canyon. She knew their relationship had changed, and she was afraid her angry words at the hospital may have upset Dan enough that he might not want to be 'Pinned' anymore.

He saved your life, she thought, *and you reward him by yelling and embarrassing him in front of those generals! How stupid can you be, Jolene? Can you be brave enough to accept his dumping you without crying? He is told he can have anything he wants, and the first thing he asks for is the Space Academy for you! Even after you yelled at him! My God, girl! You don't deserve to be in the same room with this guy!*

Dan was equally afraid he had offended Jolene enough by not telling her about the Academy or the alien spaceship that she would believe he didn't trust her.

How can I let her know it wasn't that I didn't trust her, it was that I didn't tell anyone, even my mom, and dad? What if she wants to break off our pinning?

It wasn't for several days that Dan and Jolene finally had time to sit and talk about what had happened. They resumed musical practices, but without the small talk and banter that had been so enjoyable before. It was almost like they were strangers to each other. They were up in the loft of Dan's dome with soft drinks and snacks after practicing, and neither one wanted to be the first to talk about what happened.

Dan finally broke the silence. It was his house, after all, and he was the host.

"I want to thank you for coming back to save me, Jolene. It was a very brave thing to do. I just wish I had been. . .able to see you take out those robots."

Jolene just stared straight ahead.

"I mean, I was told you armed the floater, disabled the Recall signal and came back in time to help save me." Jolene continued to stare. "I'm not even sure how you did that or knew enough to do it, but I really want to say thanks."

Again, silence.

"It was a really brave thing you did, Jolene." Dan tried once more a minute later. "I'm glad you won your own appointment to the Space Academy."

Nothing. Dan waited, then tried again.

"I feel bad about what happened since I at least had something I could fight back with, while my dad thought a PerLaz would be useless."

The continuing silence was deafening.

"I can understand," he went on haltingly, "if you. . .don't want to be 'Pinned' to me anymore, Jolene. I mean. . .it's OK if you want to. . .get a better partner or something for the musical."

Good Lord, he thought to himself, *I'm rambling all over the place.*

Dan took his eyes off Jolene and said in a small voice, "Please don't hate me, Jolene, for what happened. I did the best I could. I tried my hardest to protect you," he said as he looked at the floor miserably while Jolene continued to stare at him.

He really doesn't have a clue, Jolene thought in amazement. *Not the faintest idea as to how I feel towards him or what I think about what happened. He thinks I want to unpin him, instead of me being afraid he would unpin me! You'd better go real slow, girl, and reach him on his emotional level right now. Don't blow this one, Jolene! Be careful!*

Jolene slowly slid over to where Dan was sitting and gently put her fingers under his chin to raise his head up so he would look into her eyes.

"Look at me, please," she said quietly, and when he did, she continued.

"Dan," she said softly, staring into his eyes and smiling, "You're an IDIOT!" she thundered.

"Thanks, Jolene!" he replied with evident relief. *At least she was talking!*

"Now, let me tell you what I think." Jolene paused and gathered her thoughts. "If you hadn't called out, I would have walked right up to those. . .things. . .to see what they were, and I would have been caught without warning. When you yelled at me, you literally saved my life. You stayed between those things and me, drew their fire so I could get in the floater, got hurt protecting me, and then destroyed the one who shot me so I could get away."

"You gave up any hope of rescue when you sent the floater away, and you knew that when you pressed that button. You knew that" she repeated in awe.

She moved even closer to him. "You were willing to die," she said slowly, "or worse, so I could live. The rest of my life is a gift from you. I still can't believe I'm going to the Space Academy! Without you, I might have gone into space all right, but only as a specimen to die somewhere alone."

"Hate you, Dan? Not on your life! 'Unpin' you? Not a chance!" Jolene leaned over and hugged Dan with all her strength. Dan responded, and they both sat on the furniture for a period that seemed to go on for a long time.

Finally, Jolene loosened her grip on Dan, sat up and said, "However, Dan. . ." and with those words, she gestured to her feet.

As Dan happily lay before her, he forgot she was wearing dress shoes with high, hard heels. She stepped on his chest 'Pinning' him again then moved her other foot towards his face.

"However," she yelled down at him again, "if you EVER do something as STUPID and risk your life that way again, I'll grind your face to jelly under my shoes! Do you understand me? I'll grind you until you're nothing but a grease stain on the bottom of my heels! Do you copy that, mister?"

It was impossible to hear what Dan's reply was, but he surely got Jolene's message.

Chapter 17
JOLENE EXPLODES

After Dan and Jolene patched things up between them, they realized they couldn't talk about what had happened in Echo Canyon. No one told them they couldn't, but they both knew that extraordinary events such as they had experienced needed to remain hidden until older and wiser heads could decide how much and what to tell the world.

Dan and Jolene thought patching things up, going home and going back to school would be a return to a normal life. However, they were sadly mistaken. Most of the students at their school knew something had happened, but all they knew was that Dan was injured and in the hospital for several days after going to Echo Canyon with Jolene.

Many of the girls thought Dan had tried to play around with Jolene and got decked and stomped for his behavior. They became very frosty when Dan was around, and Dan manfully ignored the snide comments during lunch, in the hallways and in-between classes. He overlooked the slights and the snubs he received and tried to ignore the girls who acted hatefully to him. His friends were also curious, but they knew he would tell them when he felt like it, so they waited.

Dan endured this situation far better than Jolene did.

Not being able to say what really happened was eating at Jolene's very soul. Listening to other girls' abuse Dan in conversation and guess all wrong about what happened made Jolene regret the promise of silence to which she and Dan had agreed. Worse still was the fact she had become a female hero to the other girls!

"Jolene, the 'Wonder Woman' who stomped her boyfriend and put him in the hospital!!!" is how she had been introduced to several younger girls by some of the more obnoxious upper-class girls at school. She became more and more moody as the comments behind Dan's back increased.

The situation came to a head one day in the diner when Jolene and Dan were having lunch. As usual, they were the only ones sitting at the table. Sally Olsen walked past their table and said, "You didn't stomp him hard enough, Jolene. Use your boots on his pretty face next time."

As quick as Dan usually was, he reacted far too slowly to prevent what happened next.

Jolene bolted out of her seat, grabbed Sally by the front of her blouse with both hands and jerked her off the floor, then screamed into her face loudly enough to silence the entire diner.

"You stupid moron! You idiot! You got the whole thing wrong! Dan got hurt protecting me! I didn't stomp him! He saved my life! HE! . . .SAVED! . . .MY! . . .LIFE!!" she screamed. "He rescued me from those things! He put his body between me and those! . . .those!" and that's when Dan finally intervened and interrupted. "Jolene, you can't say it!" he whispered urgently. "We can't talk about it!"

Jolene glared at a terrified Sally before letting her go, then threw her arms around Dan's neck and sobbed, "I can't stand it anymore, Dan. I can't let them think I. . ." and then, she kissed him, hard. . .and continued to kiss him for a long time. She wrapped herself around Dan to the point he couldn't escape, even if he had wanted to.

It was very obvious to everyone in the diner who was kissing and holding on to whom.

After a few seconds of stunned silence, the diner erupted in typical teenage applause, congratulations, and catcalls, and Jolene pulled back a little, looked into Dan's eyes, then turned and fled sobbing to the girl's restroom.

Dan just stood there, stunned for a moment by what had happened. He reached up to touch his lips where Jolene had kissed him, then started slowly in the direction Jolene had fled. Dan stopped outside the girls' restroom, unable to enter, and leaned his forearms and forehead against the cool concrete wall.

Two of Jolene's friends went into the restroom after her, giving Dan very strange looks on their way in.

Mary Chen had been sitting at the next table and heard everything that was said. She came up to Dan and asked quietly, "Are you OK, Dan? Are you OK?" When he shook his head but didn't answer, she tried again. "Is it true? Did you really do something to save her?" Dan still didn't answer, so Mary asked him again. "Did you really save her?"

"She was safe, Mary," Dan said quietly and slowly. "I sent her to safety, but she was too stubborn to stay saved. She came back to rescue me."

At that point, Mr. Pierce, followed by some other teachers who had also heard the commotion, arrived from the nearby teachers' lunchroom. He assessed what had happened and took charge.

"Mary, John, would you both please go with Dan to the nurses' office?" Mr. Pierce asked quietly. "Mrs. Crandall,

Barbara. . .Jolene is in the restroom. She needs to come to the nurses' office too. Would you bring her the back way please?"

Mr. Williams, the principal, felt the emergency medical sequence buzz on his pager and immediately headed to the nurses' office. One look at the whiteness in Jolene's face convinced him they needed to stay right there in the nurses' office.

Mr. Pierce and some of the students who came with them told Mr. Williams what they saw and heard. Mr. Williams was frankly puzzled. Jolene, in particular, had never been prone to outbursts of this type, but one student grabbing another student was almost unheard of.

He also knew these were two of his best students and neither one had ever been in trouble before. Well, there was the incident with Dan and the snake, but some other student let it loose, and Dan caught it and was just returning it to the lab when he passed Mrs. Thornberry in the hall, and she screamed and fainted! That wasn't really Dan's fault.

"I'm sorry, Mr. Williams," Dan explained quietly as they sat in the nurses' office. "We apologize for the disturbance. In our defense, we have both been teased badly about my hospital stay since we haven't been able to say what really happened. I think Sally's remarks to Jolene today were the last straw."

Given the obvious closeness of the two students, Mr. Williams knew he had to ask the next question, as distasteful as it was. He cleared his throat and asked, "Jolene, if you and Dan have done something that will lead to a medical condition for you, later on, we can get you help?"

The question sailed right over Dan's head, but Jolene knew immediately what Mr. Williams was asking. She glanced at Dan, realized he had no idea what Mr. Williams was talking about, and said calmly, "Not even close, Mr. Williams."

Jolene smiled for the first time since the incident in the diner. "Of all the things that have happened, that one is a long time away," she added wistfully, glancing at Dan again. "A long time, if ever."

"Good, I'm very relieved to hear that. Very relieved," and Mr. Williams relaxed a little. "Thank you, Jolene. I need to think about this situation, but I hope you realize I need to call your parents. Yours too, Dan."

"I understand that Mr. Williams," Dan agreed. "In fact, would you call my dad right now, please? I don't think either Jolene or I want to float home alone, and maybe he can come pick us up."

"That is a good suggestion, Dan. Let me . . ." he was interrupted by the intercom.

"Mr. Williams, you have a . . . a very unusual call on line 4. He insisted I tell you Code Alpha Red?"

Annoyed at the interruption but surprised and recognizing the Code phrase, Mr. Williams muttered his apologies to Dan and Jolene as he took the call.

"Yes?"

"Mr. Williams, I believe you hold a reserve commission as a captain in the infantry, is that correct?"

"Yes, it I," he said, puzzled.

"Are you talking with Dan Jackson and Jolene Fisher, or can they hear your side of this conversation?"

"Yes, to both questions. Who is this, please?"

"Don't say my name out loud, or let them know who you are talking to on the 'Sat. This is General Lacey from the Space Command Center. For this phone call, you can call me Abe."

". . .Uh. . .sure. . .good to hear from you. . .Abe. How do you know about Alpha Red?" he asked suspiciously, trying not to use the general's name or the usual honorific that goes with it. *General Lacey!* he thought in awe!

"I was a butter-bar lieutenant once myself, Captain, a fact you ground-pounders seem to forget," he said in amusement. "Captain, those two students in front of you went through a traumatic experience in Echo Canyon and have not been able to talk about it to anyone. The details of what happened are classified so high that I'm not even supposed to read it as I am writing it."

Mr. Williams chuckled at that line. It was a matter of faith among infantrymen that the brass didn't read their own orders, let alone think about them. General Lacey convinced him of his identity with that one phrase as well as the code "Alpha-Red" meaning "Clean up your act quick. The brass is coming."

"I can tell you this, as an indication of how important what those two young people have done. First, they have both been awarded merit appointments to the Space Academy."

"What?" Mr. Williams exclaimed, genuinely startled. He knew no student in the history of Ridgeway High School had ever been chosen for the Space Academy.

"You heard me. Dan had his before the. . .incident and Jolene was awarded hers after the incident. Second, the AI's who were supposed to protect them arrived three seconds after it was over and were so impressed with Dan's combat shooting and tactical success they insisted on awarding him the CIB. In fact, they told me if I didn't let them award him, their next drop would be on my headquarters!"

Mr. Williams couldn't believe it! The CIB! This young man sitting in front of him had earned the badge he would most like to have himself. Involuntarily, he glanced over at Dan who was still holding Jolene's hand.

"Uh. . .Abe? Can you elaborate at all?"

"Hmmm. Keep this to yourself, Captain. In one minute and 42 seconds, Dan destroyed seven armed. . .enemies, was wounded twice, disabled an advanced. . .well. . .something this world has wanted to see up close for more than a hundred and fifty years was wounded a third time and rendered unconscious before he quit. In the meantime, he sent Jolene to safety at his own expense. Jolene, however, refused to stay saved and returned to rescue Dan after he was down, hurt and unconscious. How does that grab ya?"

"Good lord, that does put a new light on the situation!"

"Doesn't it! May I offer some suggestions, Mr. Williams?"

"Of course. In fact. . .at this point," he sighed, "I would appreciate it very much."

"Okay, first, unless you absolutely have to, take no detrimental action against those two. When I can give you a full briefing, you will be amazed they are even back in school let alone trying to act normal."

"Second, do you have any type of assembly or awards ceremony coming up?"

"Yes, we do. We have our bi-weekly assembly this Friday at 2 PM."

"OK, good! It's time I took some pressure off those kids. Third, please put on your website announcements there will be a special guest speaker to make a major presentation, but don't identify me as the speaker. Invite all the parents as well as students to attend. I think it's time those two get some recognition for what they did. I plan on making their Academy appointments public at that assembly."

"Excellent idea. In the meantime, I'll," he hesitated, "take care of things here," Mr. Williams said carefully. "What about the media? Should I make a point of calling them?"

General Lacey thought about this briefly and then said, "Yes. Do that. I'll see you Friday, Mr. Williams, and thank you." With that, he disconnected.

Mr. Williams turned back to Dan and Jolene. "Sorry for the delay. I'll 'SAT your dad now, Dan."

Mr. Williams called Dr. Jackson who said he would be on his way immediately. The principal and nurse engaged Dan and Jolene with small talk until Dan's Dad arrived. Dr. Jackson thanked Mr. Williams for the 'SAT, and walked the two students out to his floater. On the float home, he told Jolene that her dad had asked if she could stay at Dan's home until he could come and get her.

"I was concerned your situation might pose a problem at school," Dr. Jackson said, "but I felt we had to wait and see. I do have one suggestion, but I need to get approval. He looked at both of them and said, "You both realize there are things you can't talk about?"

"Like General Lacey still calling you Colonel?" Dan asked his dad promptly.

"And those special uniforms you and my father were wearing?" Jolene added.

"And the special communication you seem to have with the general?" Dan said.

"And where you got that special 'rental floater' that conveniently had a cannon?" Jolene continued sweetly.

"And. . ."

"All right, all right!" Dr. Jackson interrupted. "Yes, yes, all that and more," he said ruefully. "I can see we weren't able to keep much from you two." While they were talking, they walked into his work area, and Dr. Jackson opened a special panel by his desk, pushed a button and spoke into the air. "Is he in today, and may I speak with him? This is Dennis Jackson."

On a speaker hidden somewhere, a woman's voice replied. "He's here, Colonel Jackson. Just a minute." Dr. Jackson looked at Jolene and Dan and just shook his head.

"What's up, Dennis? Is this about Dan and Jolene?" the voice of General Lacey replied.

"Yes, it is, General. The notoriety is getting to them, and I think it is time for us to head it off. Are you still willing?"

"More than willing, Colonel. Dan, Jolene, I presume you are both there?"

"Yes sir, we're both here," Dan replied for them both.

"I've got to talk to your dad about some things that you shouldn't know about yet. Would you leave us for a while? Thanks."

Jolene stood up, took Dan's hand, and they both went to get snacks and something to drink. Dr. Jackson waited until they were out of hearing, and then told General Lacey he could continue.

"I've already set it up, Dennis. I talked to Mr. Williams at the school before you picked them up and explained the situation. He agreed to include me on next Friday's assembly. I'll announce what happened and make the Academy presentations then. I think that should relieve some of the pressure the kids are feeling."

"Good idea, sir. Now how about an analysis of the disk? Do we know anything yet?"

"Boy oh boy, have we got a lot to learn about gravity! They hope to repair the damage Dan did within a month, and if they can repair it, we will have a working model. Once we get the saucer working, we can reverse engineer most of the rest of the power plant and actually fly the thing ourselves as well as build other saucers. That should go a long, long way towards our understanding how and why the drive system works. Anything else?"

"Not now, General. Thanks for your help."

"My pleasure. Clear space, Colonel."

"Clear space, General."

After Dan and Jolene left the school, Principal Williams thought about what had happened and as he did, he found himself staring at his wedding picture. He and his wife were both in uniform. *The CIB*, he thought, *the Combat Infantryman's Badge. It sure sounds like he deserves it. Dan has already accomplished more than I did while in uniform. I'm proud of those kids, and there is no way that I'm going to put a blemish on their record. We'll wait until after the assembly. Maybe "Abe" can tell me more.*

Chapter 18
DISCLOSURE

In the meantime, events were taking place that would upset the careful plans General Lacey and Mr. Williams had prepared. Indeed, they would upset the very fabric of the political world itself.

Somehow, members of the news media had discovered a sketchy story of what had happened in Echo Canyon. While the events of the combat situation were not known, the fact the military had in their possession a working, if slightly damaged, Unidentified Flying Object made hearts pound and race across the broad spectrum of news people. Reporters were dispatched to find out what they could about where and how this event had occurred.

All other things being equal, they would probably have found nothing and written the story off as another hoax. Too many times the media had gotten burned with a story that looked and sounded plausible, only to have it wilt under the intense light of close inspection.

Except for a curious combination of events that would stretch the credibility of the most suspicious, that would have been the fate of this event.

However. . .

Jesse Marion Rothschild III had patience enough to please a saint if it hadn't been for the fact he often played the devil's role in exposing things people wanted to be kept secret. Born with a platinum spoon in his mouth (his parents and family owned outright several large corporations, and held a controlling interest in many others,) this only child of a rich family would never need to work a single day in his life. He grew up a solitary child, as is often the case, yet developed a passionate interest in photography about the age of eight. His rooms were soon filled with cameras and photographs, and he quickly discovered the advantage of telescopes and telephoto lenses for long-range photography.

The best digital cameras still had many flaws, and JR (as he liked to be called) learned enough about the electronics of cameras in his late teens to whet his appetite for more knowledge. Given the best tutors money could buy, JR was able to make significant strides in improving digital camera technology. (His family had a habit of finding the leading experts in any field, offering them double the salary they were presently making for a minimum of at least two years plus an unlimited budget and free hand for research. They also offered shared credit with JR for any inventions and 20% of the profits as well as the possibility of lifetime employment if events went well. It is not surprising JR's "tutors" made more advancements than anywhere else on the planet.)

JR started specializing in long and ultra-long-range photography, and he and his tutors came up with numerous improvements in the digital camera. The first was to quadruple the resolution of the lens itself by using specially ground sand in its manufacture. The second was to triple the density of the already ultra-high-resolution storage disk used to retain the images. The third was an ultra-high resolution digital color laser printer that printed an image so fine it could be magnified 100 times before it became too grainy to understand. (An ordinary map magnifying glass enlarges only 8 times.) The fourth invention was a smaller version of the stabilized camera platform developed for motion picture camera photographers so they could walk (or run) and still shoot perfectly steady images.

Animals became JR's primary subjects, and he was able to get (and sell) incredibly detailed pictures of rare animals from all over the world. Before he specialized in animals, however, he did a brief stint as a photographer seeking movie stars and other celebrities. JR seemed to have an uncanny knack for finding where these people would be, arriving before they got there and then taking their picture unobserved.

It was the threat of a lawsuit from one celebrity for shots published with that celebrity in the arms of a woman, not his wife that caused JR's family to suggest he work on something less dramatic!

Consequently, it was during the pursuit of the rare blue mountain goat in the western United States that JR succeeded in taking his most famous and prized photographs.

JR quickly discovered that fast moving aircraft were very difficult items to photograph, and therefore perfect practice subjects between his safaris. While setting up for his blue mountain goat search, he realized the Air Force base a few miles distant gave him the opportunity to practice following a fast-moving object.

As luck would have it, no aircraft were flying after he set up, so he looked for something else on which to practice. As he scanned the airbase and surrounding area from a nearby hill, a flatbed truck coming through the back gate of the base caught his eye. The truck had a large object covered in canvas on the flatbed, and JR decided to shoot a sequence of 400 images to detail its passage through the gate.

He started the sequence just as the truck made a right angle turn into the gate. As the truck came through, it turned too sharply. The canvas snagged on the gatepost and came off the object as the truck continued forward.

Hmmm, thought JR. *That almost looks like a flying saucer. I wonder if they are shooting a movie somewhere?* At that moment, one edge of the saucer raised up as if it were going to take off then came back down again. Once more this happened. Armored infantrymen JR hadn't noticed before swarmed over the saucer, some disappearing inside. Others trained what looked like anti-tank rockets on it. A few seconds later, the AI's came back out carrying something, and everyone seemed to relax.

Following its instructions, the ship again tried to lift off and return home periodically. Immediately one of the samples entered and turned off the power supply to the drive. Turned off but did not destroy the power supply. Again, the central computer consulted its files on intelligence and using the actions of the samples instead of their appearance, decided the probability the samples were intelligent was 65%.

Beep! The camera signaled the sequence was over, and JR thought idly, *I wonder how sharp that sequence was? Oh well, I'll have Dr. Toth look it over,* and he popped the disk out of the camera and put it in his pocket. He inserted another disk and trained the camera on the hills above the base where the goat had been reported. *Now the important work begins,* he thought, not realizing the disk he just put in his pocket was almost worth his family's entire fortune.

Dr. Toth took one look at the sequence, called the other tutors to scope it with him, and they went en masse to talk to JR.

The photos were published the next day along with banner headlines reading

AI's CAPTURE UFO
Disk Tries to Escape

The cat was out of the bag.

"This is General Lacey, sir," he said into the 'Sat.

"Thank you, General. Wait one for the president, please," and the general waited with sweaty palms.

"General Lacey?" asked President Ericsson. "I read your report about Echo Canyon. Did those two kids really do what you said they did?"

"Yes, Mr. President."

"Are they the ones responsible for the news leak?"

"No, Mr. President. We found out what happened and how it leaked. Colonel James Robert interviewed Mr. Jesse Marion Rothschild III. Mr. Rothschild was out taking pictures of some blue mountain goat and was looking for something moving to shoot as a reference and just happened to get the disk on the truck entering the base on film. It seems he didn't even know what he had photographed. He carried the disk with the photos around in his coat jacket pocket for two days before he gave it to some workers in his lab to screen. They were the ones who realized what it was, and they persuaded Mr. Rothschild to let them publish it. It was just bad luck, Mr. President."

"Humph. I take it we can't just deny this occurred then?"

"No, Mr. President. The photos he took were with a state of the art photography system, and much too detailed to pass off a hoax. In fact, he took a sequence of 400 pictures spaced one-half second apart. Colonel Robert viewed the entire sequence and said it looks like a jerky movie that lasts a little longer than three minutes. You can clearly see the disk attempting to take off, and the weapons covering the disk, the AI's going inside, and coming back out again."

"OK, denying it is out, but we need to salvage something out of this politically. Have you given any thought to doing something nice for those two kids?"

"Yes sir. I awarded both of them an appointment to the Space Academy if they can pass the entrance tests. They are both in the top 10% of their class, and would make wonderful additions to the service."

"Excellent! It's also very good for PR. Have you made the appointments public yet?"

"No, Mr. President, but I have an idea that will give us even better publicity if you have a moment to listen. . .?"

The ship had been designed by sentient beings that included several instruction manuals for the operators to use. The robots built the ship to the exact plan as designed, including space for a pilot and visible controls for the ship computer system. When the samples began probing the interior of the ship, one of them deduced the controls that caused the ship to produce the manuals. The intensity of the samples examining the manuals was relayed back to the central computer who raised the probability of intelligence to 80%.

Chapter 19
AWARDS ASSEMBLY

Word has somehow leaked out that the guest speaker was a Very Important Person who was coming to make a major presentation. No one knew who it was, but there were many more parents as well as students than usual in the auditorium for the Friday assembly.

Dan and Jolene's parents had both been told that General Lacey would speak and had been asked not to let the kids know what was going to happen. The parents agreed since they suspected Dan and Jolene would find someplace to hide instead of showing up.

The school's auditorium could hold about 750 people, and most of the seats were filled. What was unusual was the number of cameras and 3V agencies present. Mr. Williams started the assembly and gave out the normal awards that were usually done. Then, he continued by making an introduction.

"At this point in time, I would like to introduce one of our two guest presenters today. Ladies and gentlemen, students, may I present General Abraham Lacey of the United States Space Force." After a moment of surprised silence, the audience rose to its feet, and thunderous applause filled the air. General Lacey was perhaps the best known and best liked military figure in the country, and certainly, the most appreciated since his actions during 'The Troubles' prevented a major war from starting. He came out from backstage.

Lacey waited until the applause quieted down, then said "Thank you, Ladies and gentlemen. Thank you very much! I seldom do presentations like this anymore because the noise hurts my ears." There were chuckles and laughter from the audience as he rubbed one ear.

"I came here to make a special presentation to two Ridgeway High School students, but recent announcements in the media have prompted me to expand on what I intended to say." He paused for several seconds and then continued slowly and distinctly.

"At this time, and speaking officially for the Government of the United States, I can confirm that the United States Military Services have captured and possess a workable flying saucer of unknown origin." The noise and babble from the crowd started and crescendoed to where it was almost two minutes before the general could continue. Flashcubes started going off, and the media present came to full alert.

"I would like to claim credit for this monumental event on behalf of the Armed Forces of this country, but in all honesty. . .I can't. This extraordinary event occurred because of the bravery, the quick thinking, and the willingness of two young people to put their own lives at risk in fulfilling what they thought was a schoolwork assignment." The audience had become totally silent, intent on hearing every word.

Dan and Jolene squirmed in their seats and glanced sharply at their parents.

"This event did not take place without a fight, ladies, and gentlemen. These two young people entered into Echo Canyon knowing other young people had disappeared from there, and that there was a dangerous unknown element in the area." Whispers of 'Echo Canyon' could be heard up and down the auditorium.

"They sprang a trap," he said grimly. "They sprang a trap set by unknown beings whose goal was to kidnap humans from this planet and transport them someplace else." Angry voices sounded from the audience, and again it was several minutes again before General Lacey could continue.

"Fortunately for the human race, the young man involved was far better equipped than normal, and prepared to go to any length to protect the young lady with him." Dan and Jolene started sinking down in their seats.

"The Battle of Echo Canyon as we now call it lasted just one minute and 42 seconds. During that one minute and 42 seconds, the following events occurred.

"First, out of an artificial cave, two, what I'll call robots, floated towards the pair of young people. The young man recognized the trap and shouted a warning. The young lady immediately raced back to the safety of their floater. The young man stayed between his lady friend and the robots, and when the robots pointed a weapon at him, he destroyed both with his father's police pistol. Luckily, his father had taken the time to teach him how and when to use it," General Lacey added dryly.

"That is robot 1 and robot 2." Outside of an occasional gasp, you could have cut the silence in the auditorium with a knife.

"Second, as the young man retreated to the floater, two more robots appeared. He destroyed one and hit the other once, before being shot himself with its paralysis ray. He then fell to the ground, unable to move."

"That is robot 3."

"The young lady fired her PerLaz from the floater, diverting the robot's attention from the young man, and was herself shot with the paralysis ray. In the meantime, the young man, now free from the ray due to her efforts, recovered enough to destroy the robot that had shot them both."

"That is robot 4."

"Unable to move well enough to get into the floater, and not knowing how badly the young lady was hurt, this young man did one of the bravest things I have ever known. He remotely instructed the floater to button up, lift off, and head for safety. . .without him."

"Think about that action, Ladies, and Gentlemen," General Lacey said flatly.

"With complete disregard for his own safety, this young man was prepared to sacrifice himself so that his female companion might escape and live." The silence in the auditorium was absolute.

"Excuse me, just a moment please," the general said, as he took a deep breath and a sip of water before continuing.

"As the paralysis diminished, the young man observed a flying saucer land about 50 feet from his position, lower a ramp, and at least six more robots leave the saucer. At this point, he had to realize his position was hopeless, yet he took the one action by which he might save himself. From 50 feet away, he fired ten shots into the opening in the saucer above the ramp, the only area unprotected by a shield on the saucer."

"It was those ten shots into the interior of the saucer that allowed the armored infantry to capture it seconds later. His shots prevented the saucer from leaving this planet."

"As the young man tried to escape again, he was hit a second time, this time in the leg, and pinned down. He fought back and destroyed two more robots."

"That's robot 5 and robot 6."

"Being unable to move, he was flanked by other robots and attacked from the rear. He fired again and destroyed one more robot and damaged another. . .that's robot 7 and robot 8. . . before being shot a third time. . .after which he fell to the ground. . .completely paralyzed and unconsciousness." General Lacey waited a full 20 seconds before continuing.

"In the meantime, the young lady in the floater recovered, disabled the emergency recall which had automatically armed that particular floater, and headed back to the site. She arrived back in time to see the young man go down for the last time and, using a floater and cannon she was unfamiliar with, destroyed the two robots trying to kidnap him. With complete disregard for her own safety, she landed and reached the young man ready to give medical attention." General Lacey paused again to wait for the noise to diminish.

Dan looked over at Jolene with amazement. He whispered, "You never told me you did that!"

Jolene whispered back, "It was nothing compared to what you did, but there was no way I was going to let them kidnap you! Absolutely! No! Way!"

General Lacey had continued. "Three seconds later, the armored infantry arrived, took charge and med-vac'd both young people to a hospital. It had taken only one minute and 45 seconds for the AI's to arrive at the fight, and they destroyed the other robots in hiding, plus captured the saucer." He paused again, and looked out over the audience, then continued very slowly. "One minute and 45 seconds was 3 seconds too long. Had these young people not fought back so well, probably neither one of them would still be on this planet today." General Lacey paused about 20 seconds before continuing.

"Friends, the reason I am telling you this is because the young man and the young lady of whom I speak are students at this school . . . and both are sitting in this auditorium right now." General Lacey had said that very quietly, but there was nothing quiet about the reaction from the audience. Lacey waited a long time for the sounds to diminish then continued.

"It had been my intention to make a presentation to reward these courageous students, but my boss told me I didn't go far enough. He also said he wanted to do it himself."

"Ladies and gentlemen, students, may I present the President of the United States, Steven B. Ericsson!"

As President Ericsson came from behind the curtains and limped across the stage, the audience again rose to its feet to welcome the most distinguished visitor the school had ever had. When the applause finally died down, the president spoke.

"Thank you, General Lacey, Mr. Williams, ladies and gentlemen, students. Please, everyone, be seated." President Ericsson looked out over the audience.

"I was told your school band could play 'Hail to the Chief' if I wanted, but I knew they would be missing one trumpet player and one flute player who would otherwise be busy." There were polite chuckles from the crowd, but no one except Dan and Jolene's friends suspected whom the president was talking about. "Besides," the president went on, "I didn't want to warn the two students involved and have them skip this ceremony today!"

"I believe it's time we recognize these outstanding young people in person and invite them to come to the stage. At this time, would you please give a very warm welcome to Mr. Daniel Jak Jackson and Miss Jolene Sue Fisher? Both of you, please come down to the stage." The audience immediately rose to its feet, and as everyone including the president applauded he added, "They might escape robots and flying saucers, but they can't escape their president."

Jolene and Dan glared accusingly at their parents and then walked slowly to the stage with thunderous applause following them the whole time. They both came up and shook hands with the president, General Lacey and Mr. Williams. The president continued.

"General Lacey, if you would please," and the president handed him the microphone.

"Attention to Orders!" General Lacey said formally. "On behalf of the Space Force High Command, I hereby award Daniel Jak Jackson and Jolene Sue Fisher merit appointments to the Space Academy, as soon as they can pass the entrance exams." The audience liked that very much, and their applause was loud and long. The media had rushed to the front, taking pictures of everyone on stage.

"It was General Lacey's idea to grant both students a merit appointment to the Space Academy," the president said, taking back the microphone. "I concur with his judgment, but I don't think he went far enough. This country can do better than just pay for college for these two! We can also spare them the hazing necessary to prove future officers how to show poise in awkward situations. They have already done that." The president turned back to them.

"Daniel, Jolene, please raise your right hands." When they did, the president continued.

"Do you solemnly swear to defend and uphold the Constitution of the United States of America, to defend it against all enemies, foreign and domestic, and obey all lawful orders given to you by a superior officer? If so, answer, 'I do.'"

Jolene and Dan glanced at each other, then said, "I do."

"By the power vested in me as president of the United States, and for meritorious service above and beyond all expectations, I hereby commission you both into the Officer

Corps of the Military Service of the United States of America, and confirm your appointments to the Space Academy." As the president spoke, General Lacey pinned the "Butter Bar" (Gold Bar) of a 2nd lieutenant on each of their collars. "It looks better on a uniform," he shouted so he could be heard over the cheering and applause. Dan and Jolene's parents were then invited to the stage and met and shook hands with the president. The media was going nuts with pictures and videos of the ceremony. Only the Secret Service agents present managed to keep the media from mobbing the stage.

"There is one other award to be made," General Lacey said, quieting the audience "and I believe all the veterans in the audience will agree it is well deserved. The armored infantrymen who captured the disk were so impressed with Dan's combat skills, they insisted he be awarded the Combat Infantryman's Badge. What do you think, Vets? Does he deserve it?" The response was immediate and thunderous.

The congratulations and questions went on and on, and it seemed like there was no end in sight. The media wanted to concentrate on the flying saucer events, while the president and general wanted them to focus on Dan and Jolene. Every time the reporters asked General Lacey or the president a question about the saucer, it was deferred and redirected back to Dan and Jolene. When the reporters finally concentrated on Dan and Jolene, the general and the president drifted to the back of the stage area, and then slipped out the back door.

"Clever, Abe," the president said as they went down the backstage stair steps and headed towards Montrose Avenue. "I take it you've done this before?"

"Of course, Mr. President. How else does one live long enough to be a general?" and the two men smiled at each other.

When the media realized both dignitaries had slipped away, they left in pursuit of the bigger game. Dan, Jolene, their parents and the group that was left retired to the relative safety of the school diner.

In the diner, Dan and Jolene were bombarded with questions about their adventure that continued until late in the evening. Someone thoughtfully ordered a meal for them, and as they ate it, they were finally able to explain to everyone what actually happened in Echo Canyon.

Although they would never remember what they ate, Dan and Jolene regarded that meal as one of the best they had ever eaten.

As a side note, many of the girls that thought Jolene had put Dan into the hospital came up and apologized for their actions. Unfortunately, they apologized to Dan instead of Jolene and fawned all over him. When Dan sensed Jolene was about to explode in anger, he grabbed her hand and took them both out of reach of the crowd.

With the space drive and the paralysis ray safely disconnected, the scientific community was quietly going nuts examining the saucer. Revelation after revelation was made concerning the design and manufacturing technique of the saucer and its contents. After observing the ship's camera for a while and judging it to be actively working, the scientists wondered if communications could be initiated. They set up a television monitor in plain view of the camera. A basic video on the development of man on Earth was projected and then repeated twice.

The ship relayed this unexpected signal to the central computer, which recognized the implicit message of communication and raised its probability of intelligence in the samples to 100%. Since intelligent lifeforms were never to be taken as mere "samples," the central computer directed the ship to desist from escaping and cooperate fully with the new lifeform.

At this point, another over-riding directive in the central computer came into play. The original inhabitants of the central computer's planet had placed the search for other intelligent life forms second behind only its own search for biological perfection. Having found intelligent life, every effort was to be made in communicating with them.

Since the lifeforms were examining but not damaging the ship, the ship was instructed to slowly open all service ports and interior areas and observe what happened.

It was only an outrageous coincidence this opening occurred at the same time as the following conversation between humans inspecting the ship.

"Doc, I can't figure out how or if this panel comes off. Do you have any suggestions?" The technician was frustrated and ready to start prying panels loose. If Dr. Fisher hadn't been present, he would have done just that.

"I don't need those panels off yet, Bill, but try the magic phrase if you like." Dr. Fisher was examining the way the disk was put together: did they use nails, rivets, screws or some other means of joining pieces. If they used screws, were the threads left-handed or right-handed. He wasn't really paying much attention to what Bill was doing.

"What magic phrase? You mean, 'please'?"

"No, but that's a good one. What I meant was, 'Open the pod bay doors, HAL.'"

"What? Oh. Doc, that's a line from that old movie about space, isn't it? The computers name in the spaceship was HAL, right?"

"Yes, it is, Bill. You've got an excellent memory," Dr. Fisher replied, pleased and surprised that Bill recognized it. "It can't hurt anything, and it just might work."

"OK, Doc. If you say so." Bill cleared his throat. "Open the. . ."

"Towards the camera, Bill. Say it to the camera." Dr. Fisher interrupted, then pointed to the camera.

Bill smiled ruefully at Dr. Fisher but turned towards the camera.

"Open the pod bay doors please, HAL," Bill said firmly into the camera. He opened his hands at the same time to show graphically what he wanted. Bill felt a little foolish, but he liked working with Dr. Fisher and felt humoring him would. . .

"Bill. . .!" Dr. Fisher whispered quietly but intensely.

Bill turned his head quickly, to see almost every panel in the ship opening. "Oh. . .my. . . stars!"

"Bill, face the camera again and say, 'thank you' very clearly."

"What?"

"Say, 'thank you' Bill, to the camera. Quickly."

"Oh, yeah." He turned back to the camera. "Thank you."

"Now what, Doc?" Bill asked as he turned away from the camera. "I can't believe that really worked."

"Hmmm. It was probably a coincidence, Bill, but I think we have accomplished our mission here. It's time for the language and communication experts to come talk to HAL."

After this session, everyone else started calling the disk "HAL."

The ship completed a direct video link to the central computer, and the central computer had monitored the camera images in live time. Tool users', intelligent, not destructive, trying to communicate - this was clearly what the Creators had wanted to find. Accordingly, the signal that intelligent life had been found and confirmed went out to the designated Creators.

Unfortunately, all sentient life on the planet Saurian had passed away 35 years earlier, so there was no one to receive the signal. That left it up to the central computer to decide what the Creators would have wanted. It started a massive search of all files recorded in its memory since the computer was first powered up and came across ancient files about colonies on other planets.

Perhaps some of the Creators had survived, somewhere else. If so, they needed to be notified of this monumental achievement.

Perhaps. . .

Chapter 20
FIRST CONTACT

Daniel Jak Jackson was propped up on the couch doing homework on his laptop computer when his 'SAT rang. He reached for it, only to discover it was just beyond his grasp. Dan shifted his position and reached again. This time he only succeeded in knocking it onto the floor even further away. It kept ringing.

Visibly annoyed, Dan put his laptop on the coffee table where it promptly closed and turned itself off, got up, grabbed the 'SAT and spoke into it.

"Yes?" he said loudly. He knew this type of greeting irritated his mother, but he thought it was different and distinctive, and so continued to use it anyway. Besides, his greeting matched his mood right now.

"Wow! What side of the bed did you get up on today?" his caller asked pointedly.

"Oh. . .hi Jolene," Dan said much more politely and softly.

"I just wanted to make sure you knew about the change in the practice schedule for the musical, Dan," she reminded him. "You do realize we need to be at school in thirty minutes?"

Dan had completely forgotten about the schedule change.

"Sure, Jolene, I remember," he fibbed. "I still have plenty of time. . ." too late Dan remembered his floater was in for a battery change and mandatory safety inspection, ". . .to get to practice."

"Right! I'll just sit here and watch you run the five miles to school, okay? Or would you prefer I give you a lift on my floater, which just happens to be outside your house? Hmmmm?"

Dan knew when to throw in the towel.

"Okay. Thanks, Jolene! Once again you saved my budding career as an actor. I'll be out just as soon as I put away my homework."

"You're welcome, Dan," Jolene replied and then went on in much softer tones. "Although when it comes to saving people, I'm the one who still owes you big time."

Dan tossed his homework on the couch, put on his coat and raced out the front door to where Jolene was waiting in her floater.

"Thanks, Jolene," he said as he squeezed in behind her. "After all that has happened, I don't want to miss a practice for no good reason. I'm just thrilled Mr. Pierce let us keep our parts."

"I think it was a combination of the new auditorium lights not arriving on time, your understudy having very cold feet, and Mr. Pierce liking a hero in his cast that made the difference." As she spoke, Jolene gunned the floater, lifted off and set course to Ridgeway High School. She dialed in "Quick Trip," and then watched as the computers routed them the most direct way. "Plus, you're just plain lucky. Your part also called for someone with blonde hair and blue eyes that could sing and dance better than just average."

Dan was embarrassed.

"One more week," he said to change the subject, "and then we start spending all our time at school."

"I know that! How are you coming on your solo? Better than last time, I hope." Jolene expertly passed a transport floater, bounced up two levels to a faster routing, then turned inside a string of slower floaters and descended back to her assigned level.

"Oh, I'll be better today, that is unless I leave my stomach on one of these upper levels!" Dan joked.

"Are you criticizing my piloting Daniel?" she asked indignantly while passing underneath another slow transport.

"Oh, perish the thought," Dan replied.

"Because I never could figure out why you drive so slow."

"I want to get there alive," he muttered under his breath.

"What did you say, Daniel Jak Jackson?"

"I said, 'That's just the way I drive,'" Dan improvised.

"That's not what I heard you say," Jolene replied indignantly as she dodged around another transport and then turned into the school parking lot. There was a spot close to the door and, as usual, Jolene let the radar braking system bring the floater to an abrupt halt. Also, as usual, they were both thrown against their restraining harnesses.

Dan and Jolene jumped off the floater and ran for the door. They made it into the auditorium just as Mr. Pierce was calling the cast to order for the pre-rehearsal meeting.

"Thanks for picking me up," Dan whispered to Jolene as they sat in the theater seats "You're welcome, Dan. Anytime," Jolene replied. She then put her foot on top of his. *That's to remind him he is 'Pinned' to me*, Jolene thought to herself, *and also because I like having him under my foot!*

". . .remind you we will be doing complete run-throughs for the rest of this week, and full costume with make-up next week." Mr. Pierce looked at the cast over the top of his old-fashioned glasses. "I don't want any excuses about jobs or homework. Every one of you has been given a two-week hold on your academic progress timeline. That's because we expect you to be here on time and on target every practice, and not floating around chasing saucers and the like." That last line was spoken in the general direction of Dan and Jolene. The other cast members just smiled or chuckled. They knew full well how proud Mr. Pierce was of Dan and Jolene, and he showed that pride often by the way he teased them and made sarcastic comments about flying saucers.

"We begin Act 1 in 45 minutes. Costumes but no make-up, cast. Let's get moving, people!"

"Jolene, can you float me home after practice?" Dan asked as they got out of their seats.

"I can do that, Dan. Really, I'd never leave you stranded!" she teased.

"Frigid, Jolene," and they split to go to their dressing rooms to get ready while the pit band began warming up.

Fifty minutes later, the opening scene started. The stage was a spooky replica of a dark forest at midnight with fog (artificial of course) drifting everywhere and only blue lights to simulate darkness on the scene. Madam Berzurka, in full gypsy costume, began her solo about a "dark and spooky" night while chorus members in all black outfits flittered in and out of the trees pretending to be phantoms. The spotlight gradually narrowed and brightened while fading from blue to white and focusing on Madam Berzurka as she continued her solo. The pit band struggled to play softly enough so the audience would be able to hear the vocalist, but loudly enough so "Madam Berzurka" would be able to stay on key.

While Dan and Jolene were intent on their parts in the musical, other groups were equally intent on their own tasks.

Sometime earlier, the scientists studying the flying saucer nicknamed "HAL" had discovered its communications system was either instantaneous or was going to a "Mothership" close to Earth. "The Life Story of Man" DVD was played to the spacecraft's camera in an attempt to communicate with the aliens. Everyone was amazed that the response, though unintelligible, had come back within 10 seconds.

The scientists then removed the communication system from HAL and installed it at Chanute Space Force Base Lab. This allowed the Space Force to concentrate on the flying aspects of the aircraft, while the scientific community worked on the communications problem.

They tried the most basic type of communication first, a numerical sequence.

A blinking light was used to send "1 (1 blink,) 2 (2 blinks,) 3 (3 blinks,) 4 (4 blinks,) to the camera. The scientists had just started discussing how long it would take to get a response when the alien system replied.

Five beeps, six beeps, seven beeps, eight beeps. The alien system didn't have a light, so it used sound instead.

"It's working! It's working! It's working!" shouted one of the technicians in awe.

"Hold on, John. It could just be an automatic response. Try sending 9 and 10," Dr. Foster told the technician.

The blinking light was used again to send "9" and "10."

This time it took 27 seconds for the response, 11 beeps and 12 beeps.

"Why so long this time?" John asked. "Why 10 seconds the first time and 27 seconds the second? I don't understand."

"How long did we take to send the signal for 9 and 10? Anybody put a stopwatch on it?" Dr. Foster asked.

"Uh. . .no. It was about half a minute, Doc, but I didn't get it exactly. We weren't really expecting a response that quick, you know," he added sheepishly.

"Okay, maybe they matched both our sequence and our timing. Let's send the numbers 2, 4 and 6. If they send 8, 10, and 12, we respond immediately with 14 and 16. Make sure we time the response exactly, John."

"You got it, Doc. Here we go."

The technician sent 2, 4, and 6, then started one stopwatch. Over a minute later the response came back 8, 10, 12. Immediately 14 and 16 were sent, and 10 seconds later 18 and 20 came back.

"Wow, Doc! 10 seconds again. I can't believe how quickly they figured it out and replied."

"Hmmm. I wonder if the 10-second time span is due to how far away they are, or how long it takes them to figure it out?

"Boss, if we could hook up that English language program through this video camera, we could see how quickly they catch on. If they could learn English, we could talk intelligently with the first alien race that mankind had ever met!" Everyone involved with the communications system was eager to communicate, and they hurried to set up the program.

Dr. Foster and his staff, however, had no idea they were communicating with a planetary supercomputer rather than a live alien species. This misconception would have an enormous impact on the effectiveness, or lack of, their communications.

"Excellent idea, John. We were going to try that, but not for a month or two. Anybody have any objections?"

Dr. Foster waited a few seconds. "Hearing none, let's set up the language program now and see if it will work."

The staff set about the task of playing the English Language Program to broadcast for the communication system. One of the variables was the speed of the program. Since there was no way to monitor if it was being understood, they started with the speed set at normal. To say the least, it was a very intense moment when the DVD program was started.

In the back of the auditorium where Dan and Jolene were rehearsing, two uniformed visitors had entered unobserved and were sitting in the back, watching and talking quietly to each other.

"Which ones are they, Captain? Do you know them by sight?" the lieutenant whispered.

"No, but the general gave me these photos. This is Dan. . .and this is Jolene. Do you see them on stage?"

The lieutenant looked closely at the performers on stage.

"Yes. Yes, I do. That's Jolene in the pink skirt and white top, and her blonde, blue-eyed partner in the dance must be Dan." The lieutenant looked at the captain.

"They move pretty well, Captain. I understand they both play instruments in the band as well. Maybe we could get them on the drill team? I know they do competition marching at this high school. Maybe the Academy Drum and Bugle Corps could use them."

Annoyed, the captain whispered back, "That's the problem, Lieutenant. As soon as they pass the entrance exams, they are directly commissioned as second lieutenants. They won't be cadets; they probably can't participate in cadet activities, yet they won't know what every cadet needs to know! That's why the general stuck us with the problem of what to do with them!"

"Direct commission? What the heck, Captain? How did that happen?"

"They got those commissions DP, Lieutenant; by direction of the President. These are the two kids that shot up the flying saucer the AI's captured in Echo Canyon. The president himself commissioned them both, and General Lacey pinned their butter-bars (Gold Second Lieutenants Insignia) on. As usual, the brass makes a mess and expects us to fix it!"

"Oh," was the only reply the lieutenant made. They both continued to watch as the play unfolded, each trying to think of a fix for this "mess."

On the planet Saurian some light years from Earth, a file search initiated by the central planetary computer finally came to an end. The super computer was the only intelligence left on the planet after the "Creators" all died when a biological experiment turned toxic. The instructions after finding intelligent life on other planets carried a forceful command to immediately notify certain Creators.

The problem was, those Creators were all non-functioning. (Meaning Dead.)

Logically, the computer needed to notify the Creators. If it was unable to notify the Creators designated in its instructions, it needed to notify other Creators. To find any other Creators, the computer launched a massive file search designed to turn up any possibility some Creators were still alive.

After an entire day searching (after all, it was searching centuries worth of files for a whole planet), the massive search turned up three possibilities. Four colony ships had been sent out to two different planets, and one research vessel was launched as a self-sustaining colony. The problem was, there had been no contact with any of the three colonies in the last 35 years. Robotic ships had been sent by the planetary computer to make contact, but the ships ceased to communicate after entering a huge magnetic cloud. Perhaps an intelligent lifeform could penetrate the magnetic cloud where robotic ships had failed and find if any of the Creators were alive in the three colonies.

The logical conclusion reached by the planetary computer was:

1. learn to communicate with these intelligent lifeforms as soon as possible;
2. ask them for help finding the Creators by piloting spacecraft;
3. find the surviving Creators; and
4. notify the Creators intelligent lifeforms have been found.

The consequences of this conclusion by the planetary computer on Saurian were to have a profound effect on the lives of Dan and Jolene.

Chapter 21
HEADACHES

It had taken a month for the best technicians in the Armed Services to repair the flying saucer enough for it to fly again. They nicknamed it "HAL" after a computer in a spaceship from an early space movie. The instruction manuals were in a non-earthly language and unusable, but the pictures and diagrams were excellent. The controls on the saucer were too big for comfort, so they were replaced with controls more suited to humans. The principles of how this particular anti-gravity drive worked had more or less been puzzled out by trial and error, and a life-support package designed for high altitude aircraft was installed in the spaceship. This would provide re-cycled air and water as well as basic survival food if nothing else were available. (Flyers and sailors disliked the taste of this survival food and dubbed it GEE-GO, short for Garbage In, Garbage Out.) The most experienced test pilots had taken off and landed successfully, and commented the controls were easy enough for a teenager to use.

There was, however, one fundamental problem.

All the test pilots experienced headaches of varying intensity, and it was soon discovered the older the pilot, the worse the headaches. Various remedies were tried starting with simple aspirin, but the longer the test flying time and the older the pilot, the worse the symptoms.

After one test flight, the oldest (and most experienced) test pilot had to be removed on a stretcher from the spacecraft named HAL. Luckily this had been one of the first flights with both a pilot and co-pilot, and the younger co-pilot took over and brought the spacecraft back to base safely.

"Nothing, General!" Captain Johnson protested to General Lacey as they watched the lead test pilot being loaded onto a MedVac for transport to the infirmary. "Colonel Diaz did absolutely nothing out of the ordinary, or outside the parameters of the flight test. He shook his head a couple of times and complained his headache was getting worse. After he executed the fourth 180-degree turn, he muttered for me to take over, put both his hands on his head, and said, "I can't stand this buzzing any longer!" then slumped sideways in the seat."

"I immediately took over, aborted the test flight, radioed for medical backup and brought the spacecraft back to base."

"You didn't have any problems flying it or landing? Nothing interfered with you?" the general asked.

"No sir. That's got to be the easiest ship I've ever flown. I have no idea how well it will work in space without an atmosphere, but it's a dream ship here on this planet."

"Well done, Captain. You did exactly the right thing."

"Thank you, sir." Captain Johnson replied, saluting. The captain obviously thought his interview was over, but then General Lacey continued.

"Why don't we walk over to Base OPS, (Base Operations Office) Captain? I have a few more questions to ask you." They both started walking towards the building.

"OK. First, did you get a headache at all during the flight?"

"It was more like a dull ache than a headache, sir, but it only started while I was landing HAL. It didn't interfere with my flying at all." Captain Johnson shook his head a couple of times as they continued to walk. "As a matter of fact, it's completely gone now, sir."

"Good," the general replied. "Yours was short-lived, but we need to find out why the headaches occur, and what we can do to eliminate them. Pilots like Colonel Diaz as well as our only working flying saucer are too valuable to risk. If you hadn't been aboard today, Captain, we might have lost both a good test pilot and the flying saucer! Obviously, HAL flies very well so our priority must be changed from flying it to protecting the pilots." They walked in silence for a little while as they both tried to come up with a solution to the problem.

"Tell me, what were your flight assignments before you came aboard the Flight Testing Program here, Captain?"

"Sir, I flew in the Thunderbirds. Before that, I was Squadron Leader for the 122nd Tactical Interceptor Wing flying F-22E Raptors out of Alaska, sir. I'm scheduled to go back as commander of another squadron when my rotation as test pilot is over."

"The Thunderbirds! I'm impressed, Captain." General Lacey thought for a minute, then asked, "By any chance, did you ever hear about. . ."

"Yes sir. I not only heard about it but I was flying the Air Show in Asia when that dictator sent eight of his best MIG fighters to shoot us down. He wanted to embarrass the United States in front of all those people by shooting down our unarmed planes." The captain chuckled. "He didn't know the Raptor carries its missiles inside its belly until needed, sir. One of his own people gave us a warning the day before the show, so we were loaded with missiles and ready to play."

"We got ninety seconds' worth of warning from the AWACS plane, broke into three two-ship groups and sent one group to protect the AWACS. That left four of us against eight of them. They fired first, we used counter-measures, evaded and they missed, then we returned fire and splashed seven of the eight."

"And if memory serves me correctly, the pilot who pursued and splashed the eighth MIG exceeded speeds of Mach. . .?"

"Uh, about Mach 3.9, General. Almost 2400 miles per hour in a dive."

"That's well above the rated top speed for a Raptor, wasn't it Captain?"

"Yes sir, but, sir, it was an actual combat situation, sir, not an artificial test. I proved . . . I mean. . .we proved the Raptor was a lot more capable than we were told, sir, and we didn't let that MIG get away!" the captain said with pride.

They stopped just outside the OPS Building. "Think about this, Captain," General Lacey said quietly. "You know how HAL can move, start and stop, and change direction instantly. If HAL was armed and flown by an experienced combat pilot, could your Raptor flight splash it?"

Captain Johnson's silence was all the general needed to hear.

At the White House in Washington D.C., the president's meeting was not going well at all.

"Gentlemen, gentlemen! We need some action on this immediately! The public is aware we have a flying saucer, and every cotton-picking politician in the country wants it flown through their district! I've got 25 letters from engineering schools like Stanford, The University of Illinois, Purdue and M.I.T. that all want their students in on the enhanced anti-gravity drive. I've got 40 telegrams from UFO nuts that claim they can control the aliens if we just pay these nuts enough money! We've got to do something more than just what we are doing now!" President Ericsson said forcefully.

"Mr. President, Did I hear the saucer communication system still works? If it does, then obviously, we must try to communicate with the aliens. Have we tried that yet?" asked Marvin Westerling. Dr. Westerling was the secretary of state.

The chief of staff disagreed with the priority.

"Mr. President, we really need to get the military function sorted out before we do anything else. We can't possibly let the knowledge about that saucer out of our hands until we know it's harmless, or at least what it is capable of." This was from the chief of staff of the Armed Forces Committee.

"Okay," the president agreed after a few seconds thought. "Yeah, that makes sense." He turned to one of his aides.

"Helen, get me General Lacey on the 'SAT." He explained to the members of the committee, "Lacey has had time to look at it and should be able to give us some kind of estimate on its capabilities."

The committee talked quietly while the 'SAT was being completed.

"Mr. President, General Lacey is on the green line," Helen said.

"Thanks, Helen." The president switched on the 'SAT. "Abe, I've got you on speakerphone. Talk to me about that flying saucer. What have you been doing with it?"

"Mr. President, we first tried to establish contact with the owners of the spacecraft, then removed the communication system and installed it here on base at Chanute. That let us work on both the flying aspects of the spacecraft and, at the same time, the communications system. The scientists are going nuts trying to figure out if the communications system is faster-than-light, or if there is a mothership close to Earth. They reported the response time for 2-way communications with the aliens is a constant 10 seconds."

"Faster than light? That can't be possible." sputtered the science member on the committee. "They must have a ship in far orbit around the earth."

"Wait a minute! Wait a minute! Wait just a cotton pickin' minute here!" the president thundered. "Did I hear you correctly, Abe? Do you mean to tell me. . .you are already in two-way contact with the aliens?" The president was clearly taken by surprise with this information.

General Lacey continued. "Why. . .yes, sir! Dr. Foster also told me communications are so good that they changed the timetable on when to teach the aliens English and have already started the program."

"You're kidding!"

"What?"

"Already?"

"Preposterous!" Various members said at the same time.

"General Lacey, surely you understand. . .if the aliens ever learn English and are close to Earth, they can tap into our Tri-V broadcast system and understand us without our knowing anything about them?" This reply was from Ralph Zieba, the National Security Advisor.

"Yes sir, we know that," replied General Lacey.

"It's probably not an immediate problem, Ralph," added Secretary of State Marvin Westerling. "We all know it takes months to learn English, and that's with all the things humans already know. It might take years for the first meaningful communication to occur."

Over the 'SAT, General Lacey cleared his throat, "I'm sorry to disagree with you, Dr. Westerling, but that turns out not to be the case."

"What did he say?" Dr. Westerling asked in surprise.

"He said 'You're wrong, Marv!'" translated the president. "Tell us more, Abe. What do you mean, he's wrong?"

"I mean, Dr. Foster decided to give the aliens the first 30-minute segment of the language program, and then wait an hour, and repeat the same segment. That would give the aliens two time intervals, 30 minutes and 60 minutes that are useful to us. He planned to continue this pattern until he got some different type of response, then go to the second segment."

"And?"

"Mr. President, 60 seconds after the first half-hour presentation was completed, the aliens radioed the message "MORE," in English. They repeated this message every 60 seconds until we sent back a voice communication, "WAIT." Since then, because we were not really prepared to run the second segment, they repeated their message every 30 minutes until we sent the second segment."

There was a stunned silence from around the table.

"General Lacey, how much. . ." started Ralph Zieba, only to be interrupted by President Ericsson.

"Abe, have you received any other communication from the aliens?"

"Yes, Mr. President. After the second segment, they radioed "FASTER." We increased the transmission speed of the DVD by a factor of two and broadcast the third segment. After the third segment, they again radioed "FASTER," so we sped it up to four times normal."

"Oh, my word!"

"Maybe they are smarter than we are!" one fearful voice said out loud.

"Of course they are smarter than we are!" the president said forcefully. "They have spaceships and faster-than-light radios, and we don't! That's why that saucer is so darn important."

Ralph Zieba started again, "General Lacey, how many segments have you sent?"

"Wait a minute and let me check with Dr. Foster," Lacey replied, and could then be heard talking to someone in the background.

"So far, gentlemen, Dr. Foster says we have sent the first 8 segments out of 120. We have not sent any segment more than once, and we are still sending them at 4 times normal speed. The last message was "CONTINUE," to which we replied, "Wait 1 turn of the planet." Since then, there have been no other messages."

Instantly conversations and arguments broke out around the conference table, while President Ericsson sat quietly and gathered his thoughts. Phrases like, "The greatest achievement of all time!" and "A historic day in history" and "We still need to know about their military capability!" were said.

Finally, the president spoke over all the other voices.

"General Lacey, are you still with us?"

"Yes, Mr. President."

"Do you have any idea of their military capability? Have your people been able to fly the saucer at all?"

"Yes, Mr. President. The technicians took out the original controls and installed controls that fit humans. In fact, the controls were. . .uh. . .from a civilian floater, sir. Our test pilots say it is the easiest airship they have ever flown, but there is one serious problem. Something in the drive causes severe headaches, and the older the pilot, the worse the headache. Just today our best, and oldest, test pilot lost consciousness during a flight, but the younger co-pilot was able to take over and safely return the craft to the base."

"As to its military capability, it is far beyond anything we have in the air," General Lacey said flatly. "It's faster and more maneuverable than our best fighter."

"How do you know that Abe?" the president asked. "Who did the actual evaluation of the saucer?"

"Mr. President, do you remember that young Air Force Thunderbird Lieutenant you awarded a Silver Star for chasing and splashing a MIG fighter at Mach 3+ in his Raptor?"

The president smiled. "Yeah Abe, I remember that one very well. Johnson was his name, right? After your brass chewed him up one side and down the other about how stupid he was to push his Raptor that hard, I gave him the medal and a promotion to captain and told him how right his decision was! There are some advantages to being president, you know."

"Yes sir. Well, Captain Johnson was the co-pilot that saved our ship today. I asked him as a combat pilot if he thought he and three other Raptor pilots could take out the saucer he just flew if the saucer had equal missiles and a combat pilot aboard."

"And? Come on, Abe. Don't keep me waiting!"

"His face turned very pale, and he couldn't answer me, Mr. President," Abe said quietly. "He muttered he thought the Raptors wouldn't have a chance, sir."

At another meeting in Washington, sometime after the president's meeting, things started off well but ended in chaos.

"Gentlemen, the president has given us direct orders concerning the spacecraft our AI's captured."

"First," the chief of staff said, "we need to find out why the ship causes headaches in pilots. According to General Lacey, the older the pilot, the worse the headaches. Any ideas?"

"Sir, we could try shielding the pilot's head with different types of metal or ceramics to see if that blocks the headaches."

"Excellent idea, Colonel Brown! Take charge of that idea, and you head the team to try different helmet materials."

"Any other ideas?"

"General, I think we should also do a full spectrum scan on the craft to see if it is generating any unusual frequencies or radiations." This came from scientist Dr. Jeff Greenly.

"Yes, that's also very good. Colonel Brown, you do the full spectrum scan as well and include Dr. Greenly on your operating committee. Anyone else? Any other ideas?" No one else volunteered.

"OK, let's move on to the second directive. Based on General Lacey's comments, the president wants us to see if we can construct a duplicate ship or ships. Anyone want to take that one?"

There were several quick responses, and the chief of staff very carefully chose two individuals.

"Yuri, and Jacob, I think you two should combine efforts and see what you can do. Where will you work?"

Yuri and Jacob exchanged looks and grins, then Jacob said in broken English, "St. Louie, McDonnell-Douglas place. Is owing us big times for helping with wings on sick plane."

"I agree with Jacob," Yuri added smoothly. "I also think they will help us simply because it means they get to build the first flying saucer on our planet. That's a huge claim in history, my friends. A huge claim!"

"I think you're right about that, Yuri. Remember, Jacob," the general said pointedly, "we want to duplicate what already works, not redesign it. At least, not change anything yet. Okay?"

"Is good, General! We copy their socks off! Boy oh boy!"

"Okay, Jacob. Good luck." The chief glanced at Yuri and Yuri nodded his head as if to say *"Yes, General. I'll keep a very close eye on Jacob!"*

"The third directive is to determine what armaments we can use from the saucer. Evidently the defensive screen blocks both energy weapons and projectiles, so if we add offense, the craft will be a very potent weapons system. Ideas? Yes, Sam?"

"I think guns would be too difficult to mount and lasers would take too much power, so I think we should use missiles like we use on the Raptors. Two Ferret's for short range, two AMMRAM's for medium and two of the new Longbow's for long range." Sam Moffet had spent 15 years developing missiles before he ran for Congress and was elected.

"Good idea, Congressman. Anyone else?" The chief waited. "Any other ideas?"

There were no other answers.

"Do you want to run with that one Congressman, or should I appoint someone to use your idea?"

"Better go ahead and appoint someone, General." He paused and then changed his mind. "No, wait. I've got a real hot dog in my office that might be just the right person. He helped me develop the Longbow and came up with the simplest, easiest yet most secure missile mounting system I've ever seen. Let me bring him up to speed, and I'll send him to your people. Will that be acceptable?"

"Certainly, Mr. Congressman. If you vouch for him, he must be good."

"Thank you, General. I appreciate the chance to work with the military, again," he said with a grin.

"You are welcome, sir."

"Now," the chief of staff again addressed the committee.

"The fourth directive from the president is one that might cause some hard feelings and encroach on some people's turf." He paused to make sure he had everyone's attention. "Since age is a serious factor in who can fly the saucer or not, and since everyone can drive a floater, the president has directed us to find two of the youngest officers in non-critical fields in any of the branches to be assigned permanently to flying the saucer. There were several parameters these officers needed to meet, and I listed them all for a computer search. The absolute most critical parameter was their age." The committee members checked their computer screens.

After a short time, the chief of staff asked, "Does anyone see any problems with the selection parameters?"

There were several negative answers or nods.

"Okay, good. Does anyone else see any other type of problem for the search? Understand, gentlemen, the president specifically stated that branch of service was not, I repeat not, to be used as a criterion. We have been directed to accept the results of the computer search without variation." He looked at the members seated around the table.

"Well, Gentlemen? Do I hear acceptance of the computer search, or not?"

One by one, the senior Army, Navy, Marine, and Space Force officers present agreed to the results on behalf of their Branch. The Marine colonel said it best when he said "We're all professionals here, General. No matter how much we fight between ourselves, and no matter how much we disagree at times, we are all still Americans, and we are all on the same side."

"Here, here!"

"Well said, Colonel."

"Couldn't have put it better myself!" were the responses

from the other service representatives.

"Very well, gentlemen, I accept your professional assurances and your acceptance of the computer results. Let me direct the data to be sent to our terminals. I remind you, I haven't seen this data before either, so. . .I. . ."

The chief of staff read the data about the two officers selected by the computer, then looked at the committee in disbelief.

"What?"

"Outrageous!"

"This can't be true!"

"Preposterous!"

"Is this somebody's idea of a joke?"

"I've never heard of such a thing!"

"Ridiculous!"

"It's insane! The computer's insane!"

"How could something like this happen?"

Everyone was shouting at the same time, and the meeting dissolved into chaos.

The chief of staff 'SATed the president with the results of that meeting.

"Mr. President, we have the results of the computer search for two officers for permanent assignment to the Saucer Project and faxed a copy to your office. Everyone in the Joint Chiefs of Staff was unanimous. . ."

"Glad to hear that General." The president commented happily.

". . . in their condemnation of the idiotic results of this search! You can't possibly be serious about this, Mr. President! We beg you to reconsider! Please?"

President Ericsson stared at the general in surprise and then said, "Let me see those results." He put on his reading glasses. "If the computer picked officers you all agree are wrong, then they are probably the two very best people. . .and. . ." the president read the data on the two officers selected, then looked at the names, and threw back his head and laughed uproariously for almost a full minute.

"Oh, my word!" The president was laughing so hard he had tears in his eyes and a stitch in his side. "This is priceless! I can understand why none of you like this solution, but I think it is perfect!" Wiping the tears from his eyes, the president continued. "Absolutely Perfect! These are EXACTLY the officers I want for the saucer project! Make it happen, General, and I mean make it happen right now!" the president said firmly.

"Yes, Mr. President," the general said glumly and went to give the bad news to the others.

The chief of staff gave the president's orders to the Space Force 4-star general, who in turn 'SATed General Lacey to inform him about the directive.

General Lacey met with four other people, informed them of the president's decision, and convinced them it was the best thing that could happen. All four were visibly reluctant, but two of the four were also secretly pleased. They just couldn't let their wives know how pleased they were!

CHAPTER 22
"WHY ARE YOU STILL HERE?"

The musical performances of WOLFSTOCK had been over for a week, and Dan and Jolene were still getting used to having some free time again. As usual, they met in the school diner after band class, enjoyed a typical teenager's lunch, and spent the time talking with friends. Both had learned a great deal about the theater in general and musicals in particular, but they were still glad it was over. Neither one had anticipated how much time, energy and commitment it took to participate in a musical theater production. Granted, it was a marvelous experience, but not something they wanted to do for a living or repeat too soon in the future.

Principal Williams was a frequent and welcome visitor in the school diner almost every day. Unlike other adults in the building, he ate many of his meals with the students and made a point to be available to just talk or help with problems.

Today he wandered around a while, chatted with a number of students, and then went over to Dan and Jolene's table.

"Hello, Dan, Jolene. Do you mind if I sit down a while?"

"Not at all, Mr. Williams. Grab a chair." Dan told him.

"I trust you are both rested after the musical?" Mr.

Williams asked after he sat down and stretched his legs.

"We're just getting used to having our freedom back, Mr. Williams," admitted Jolene. "WOLFSTOCK took a lot more time than either one of us realized. More time even than playing on a sports team. It was much more fun, mind you, but it was a lot more intense!" She glanced at Dan and smiled, "Of course, it helps when you're working with people you like."

Mr. Williams saw the glance and knew what Jolene meant.

"You two did an outstanding job on stage, and I know Mr. Pierce was very grateful for all your help and dedication. I must say, that was probably the best production I have ever seen performed here at Ridgeway. I haven't laughed so hard in years!"

"Thanks, Mr. Williams. It was our pleasure, wasn't it Dan?"

"Oh, sure. I must admit I enjoyed it much more than I thought I would. It was even more fun than playing spaceball," Dan added.

"Speaking of dedication, I could use some help tomorrow morning. Are you both free at about 9 o'clock?

"Jolene, do you have anything? Dan asked, looking over at her. "I know we have a day off from band class."

Jolene shrugged her shoulders. "I don't have anything, Dan. How about you?"

"No. I guess we're both free, Mr. Williams. Where should we meet you?"

"How about stopping by my office? I'll see you tomorrow morning, then, at 9 AM. Thanks! I need to get up and move around some more." Mr. Williams got up and started wandering around the diner again.

After he left, Dan looked at Jolene and asked, "Do you

have any idea what he has in mind?"

"Not a clue, Dan. I guess we'll have to wait until tomorrow to find out. In the meantime," she handed her glass to Dan, "How about getting a girl a glass of soda pop?"

The next morning, Dan and Jolene reported to the principal's office just before nine o'clock. The secretary ushered them into the principal's conference room.

"Thanks for coming Dan, Jolene," Mr. Williams began. "Why don't we sit over at the table?" He waited until they were both seated.

"What I need help with is. . .finding the reason why you two are still in High School!" He opened two folders that were on the table. "I've reviewed your records, and you both have met all the requirements, earned enough credits, scored high enough on the mandatory testing, and passed the minimum age necessary for graduation."

Dan and Jolene were both shocked! They stared at Mr. Williams, and then looked at each other in amazement.

Mr. Williams continued. "So, tell me please, why are you still here when you both have better things to do, and the Space Academy to attend? Hmmm?" Mr. Williams was staring at them over the top of his glasses.

"Mr. Williams, that. . .that can't be right!" Jolene protested. We must have at least one more year, and. . ."

"The number of years in school doesn't count anymore Jolene, remember? Since the EdRev, quality of your education is more important than the quantity of time spent."

"Well, we haven't taken the Mandatory tests yet. . ." Dan added.

"Passed by Acclimation; both of you. It was a unanimous faculty decision, and it's marked right here in your folder." Mr. Williams tapped the folders with his finger. "That was the last thing you needed to complete for graduation. Actually, the faculty only waited until the musical was finished, then waived the tests by a unanimous vote."

"The counselors never said anything to us about that!" Dan protested.

Mr. Williams smiled and replied, "They weren't supposed to. It takes both faculty approval and direct approval from the principal before the mandatory tests can be waived."

"Then. . .then we don't have enough credits yet?" Jolene objected.

"Completed — Dan, you have 41. Jolene, you have 39. You only need 32."

"Well, aren't we still too young to graduate?" Dan offered hopefully.

"Age is not a deciding factor anymore. We've had several students younger than either of you graduate already."

"But, we can't be ready. . ." Jolene's voice tapered off.

"Yes, you are ready," Mr. Williams said with a smile.

"There must be something we haven't done yet!" Dan insisted.

"Everything that needs to be done, or passed, or taken is right here in your folders. You have completed all the requirements. Trust me."

Dan and Jolene looked to each other for help, then sighed and turned back to Mr. Williams.

"Now Dan, Jolene. Do either of you have any other questions or objections?"

"No sir. I guess. . ."

"Good! Let me present you with your High School Diplomas. Dan," and Mr. Williams stood up and shook Dan's hand as he handed him a Diploma "and Jolene," and he shook her hand and gave her a Diploma. "Congratulations!

There will be a ceremony where you walk across the stage and pretend to get your diploma, but that won't be for another three months. In addition, Jolene will be recorded as one of the top five scholars in her class, and you Dan, will be recorded as one of the top thirty scholars in your class. Congratulations again for an outstanding finish to your high school years!" As he was talking, Mr. Williams got up and opened the outside door to the conference room.

Jolene suddenly thought of another objection. "Wait a minute! I know why we can't do this. Our parents should be here to approve it!" She thought she had a valid objection.

"You are absolutely correct, Jolene," Mr. Williams agreed. He called out through the doorway, "Folks, would you come in please?"

Dan and Jolene's parents came into the office and congratulated their children with handshakes and hugs. Mr. Williams let this go on for a few minutes and then cleared his throat.

"Thank you all for coming, but Dan and Jolene have some other people they need to meet. Would you parents like to stay and meet them as well?"

"Yes, in fact, we would." Dr. Jackson said.

Mr. Williams opened his office door, and two people wearing Space Force blue uniforms came into the conference room.

"Ladies and gentlemen, this is Captain Kim Lee and Lieutenant Barbara Kowalski. They have been tasked with transporting Dan and Jolene for testing at the Space Force Academy in Colorado Springs." He turned to the parents. "Did you remember to pack bags for them?"

"Yes," Both sets of parents answered. "Their bags are out in our floaters."

"Then I guess it's time." Mr. Williams turned to Dan and Jolene. "Dan, Jolene, you have been two of the most outstanding students Ridgeway High School has ever served. Not always the easiest students—I don't think Mrs. Thornberry will ever forget you and the snake you captured, Dan!—but certainly among our very best. I see bright things for you in the future. Use what you have learned here and make us proud to say you went to school at Ridgeway!"

"Thank you, Mr. Williams," Dan said, shaking the principal's hand once again. "You make Ridgeway a place where students want to be."

"Yes, thank you, Mr. Williams," Jolene added, then sighed as she looked around the school. "I'm really going to miss this place."

Communication with the "aliens" was going on at a breakneck speed. Understanding each other, however, was something else.

On the human side, the scientists did not realize they were talking to a planetary computer, with all that implies. They thought they were communicating with the first alien species man had ever found.

On the computer side, it was judging the new race as it judged the "Creators." The Creators had been a species with four legs, a caudal appendage (tail,) scales (like an alligator) and fangs (like a lion.)

The computer had one advantage since it had viewed video images of the new species and "knew" they were different. The humans also had one advantage since their brains were able to bring unrelated facts together better than any mechanical or electronic brain.

It was not at all surprising that neither side fully understood the other.

The latest communication from the aliens was simple if not grammatically correct.

SENDING FASTER PLEASE, YOU THANK.

This was another request from the aliens to speed up the English Language DVD-CD program.

"For cryin' out loud, Doc. We are already sending the DVD at eight times normal speed! How can they possibly absorb a new language at that rate? They must be recording it for playback." The technician was getting frustrated at being asked to speed up the English language DVD yet again.

"I don't know how they can possibly learn it this quickly, Bill." He thought about it for a minute.

"You know, we haven't asked them any questions yet. Why don't we make this our first question? Here, let me type it in."

HOW CAN YOU LEARN SO FAST? Dr. Foster typed into the computer.

"We'll see if they can actually understand English, or just are getting lucky with some of the words. Minimum return time is 10 seconds, so however much longer it takes will tell us. . ."

RECORD REPLAY ANALYSIS WANT SOUND OR PRINT QUESTION.

. . . how long it takes them to think about it. Bill, what was the reply time?"

Bill looked at the stopwatch in disbelief. "Fourteen seconds, Doc. That's only four seconds of thinking time."

"Hmmmm. Are they asking us a question in return? "WANT SOUND OR PRINT." I think we would much prefer print, so we have a hard copy, right?" Dr. Foster looked around the room. "Anyone disagree?" He waited for a reply. "Okay."

WE WANT PRINT. CAN YOU DO THAT? He typed.

The stopwatch clicked again, and again it was fourteen seconds when the reply came over the speaker.

YES. SMALL WAIT.

WE WILL WAIT.

"Bill? Could we send the DVD program any faster?"

"No, Doc. Any faster than we have right now will cause some dropout of the video signal, and big pieces of the language program will not transmit. I'm really surprised that the DVD is holding up at 8 times normal. Sorry. It's just not physically possible."

Sarah was one of the other technicians working with Dr. Foster's team. She had been looking at the way the alien 'radio' was put together, and studying the actual container, it came in.

"Bill?" she said tentatively, "would you look at this, please?" Sarah pointed to something on the back of the alien radio.

"These holes on the back of the transmitter look a lot like IO (input-output) plugs. Do you suppose we could use the computer version of the language program? That would speed things up."

"Let me see those holes," Bill said as he looked at the back of the alien transmitter.

"Yeah, you're right," he added after a brief examination of the radio back. "They do look like IO plugs, Sarah." He turned back to Doctor Foster.

"Doc, if we could hook directly into their machine we could use the computer and transmit the whole blasted program in no time. They said "Record" and "Replay." Ask them if we could send the data electronically instead of visually."

Dr. Foster thought about that, but then remembered the concern of Ralph Zieba, the National Security Council Advisor. Dr. Zieba was worried that, if the aliens learned English, they could listen to our broadcasts and learn a lot we might not want them to know. Balancing this was the fact the president did not order him to stop sending the program or even slow it down.

And besides, the direct hook-up might not be possible anyway.

"Excellent suggestion, Bill. Sarah? Thanks for your sharp eyes."

"My pleasure, Doc," she replied with a smile.

"Well, I think it's time for a lunch break. We should probably go in shifts, so one crew remains here. Who wants to take a break and go eat lunch first?"

Everyone in the room looked around, but nobody volunteered.

"Oh, Come on now!" Doc asked in exasperation. "Somebody here must be hungry?"

Again, there were no takers.

"Doc?" Sarah started hesitantly; "I don't know about you, but I'd miss my next ten meals just to be here talking and listening to aliens!"

Others in the room muttered their agreement with Sarah.

Dr. Foster looked around the room, smiled, and shook his head. "You're nuts! All of you! You've still got to eat sometime." No one changed his or her mind, and he sighed.

"Okay. I give up. I confess I don't really want to leave either. Why don't we eat lunch here? Obviously, we are going to have time to. . ."

The printer connected to the computer starting printing as he spoke.

". . .eat between messages."

THIS IS TEST MESSAGE. CORRECTLY DID YOU IT RECEIVE?

"Wow! What was the time of the 'small delay' Bill?"

"Twenty-one minutes, Dr. Foster. Look how much better their English is this time."

"I noticed that. They must be quick learners."

"They also solved a major problem in only 20 minutes, ladies and gentlemen. That speaks highly of their organization."

"Okay, let's confirm we received their message and ask our own questions."

WE RECEIVED YOUR MESSAGE CORRECTLY. WE HAVE FOUND ROUND HOLES IN THE BACK OF YOUR RADIO. ARE THE HOLES FOR ELECTRONIC INPUT?

10 seconds later.

CORRECT.

"Hey, that's great! Where is it?" Bill asked. Dr. Foster typed in the question.

10 seconds.

THE INPUT HOLE ON THE BACK.

"Now we are getting somewhere! Ask them which hole we should use, Doc." The message was sent.

10 seconds.

USE THE XXXXXX HOLE FROM THE XXXXXXX.

"What? Doc, it didn't print out right."

"I see that, Bill. What do you suggest?"

"Tell them the message was not received completely, then send back what they sent and explain we don't know what XXXXXX and XXXXXXX are."

"That sounds reasonable. Let's try it."

MESSAGE NOT RECEIVED COMPLETELY. WHAT WE RECEIVED WAS;

"CORRECT. USE THE XXXXXX HOLE FROM THE XXXXXXX."

DO NOT KNOW WHAT XXXXX AND XXXXXXX ARE. EXPLAIN?

10 seconds.

THE XXXXXX HOLE IS THE INPUT.

"That's pretty clear, but which one is the XXXXXX hole? Let's ask again."

HOW DO WE TELL WHICH HOLE IS THE XXXXXX HOLE?

10 seconds.

XXXXXX IS ON THE BACK.

"Sarah?" Dr. Foster asked, "how many holes are on the back panel?"

"I checked the whole thing, and there are nine holes are on the back panel."

"Okay, let's see if we can get them to count and tell us which hole the input is."

NUMBER THE HOLES 1, 2, 3, 4, 5, 6, 7, 8, 9 FROM THE LEFT. WHICH HOLE IS THE INPUT?

10 seconds.

YES.

"What do they mean, 'Yes'?" Bill said in frustration. "We didn't ask a Yes or No question! I don't think they understand English as well as they think they do."

"You mean 'as well as WE think they do, Bill,'" replied Dr. Foster. "We can only continue what we are doing and hope to ask the right questions." He then typed in the expected reply.

YES, WHAT? He typed.

10 seconds.

THAT IS INPUT. IT IS XXXXXX HOLE.

WHICH ONE IS THE XXXXXX HOLE?

10 seconds.

THE INPUT HOLE ON THE BACK.

"Oh, for crying out loud! We're going in circles here, Doc. He said the same thing earlier."

"Wait a minute. They gave us the exact same answer earlier?" Dr. Foster asked in surprise.

"Yeah, it was right about here on the printout, after we asked where it was."

"Let me see the printout, Bill." Dr. Foster studied the printout a while, then turned to the members of his team.

"I think we can try an experiment to see if they will change their answers, or just repeat the same thing," he explained. "Let me go back to this point, and we'll see what happens." He typed in a response.

HOW DO WE TELL WHICH HOLE IS THE XXXXXX HOLE?

10 seconds.

XXXXXX IS ON THE BACK.

"That's the exact same answer as before."

"Let's try another one."

WHICH ONE IS THE XXXXXX HOLE?

10 seconds.

THE INPUT HOLE ON THE BACK.

"It's exactly the same again, Doc. What's going on? How did you guess that?

"Let's just say. . .I'm beginning to learn something about the character we are talking to."

This discussion went 'round and 'round, on and on, back and forth until, finally, Dr. Foster sent a message to the aliens that it was time for their rest period, and they would resume talking in 12 hours. The aliens had no problem understanding that message, but everyone in the human lab was frustrated with the outcome and some left with a headache.

Clearly, talking and understanding were two different items.

CHAPTER 23
THE SPACE ACADEMY

The Space Academy in Colorado Springs, Colorado, grew out of the Air Force Academy that had been there since the mid-20th century. Like Military Academies all over the world, the Space Academy was rich with traditions designed to impart a sense of dignity, responsibility, and purpose to its cadets. The Space Academy had a dual function now since it still acted on behalf of the United States Air Force but also incorporated the newest and most elite of the Armed Forces, the Space Force. The Space Force would be the smallest of the military branches and was easily incorporated into the Air Force Academy Grounds

Traditions have always played an important role in the training of cadets, and most traditions are firmly set in stone. Many traditions have been in place for hundreds of years, like the hazing of freshman cadets and upperclassmen "questioning" underclassmen.

Dan and Jolene, however, were about to break some of those traditions.

Captain Lee and Lieutenant Kowalski transported Dan and Jolene to the Space Academy at the request of Space Force General Abe Lacey. General Lacey had been responsible for the Academy appointments for both Dan and Jolene because of the "Battle of Echo Canyon." It was the president of the United States, however, who awarded them commissions as officers in the military service of the United States "as soon as they pass the entrance exams."

Lee and Kowalski agreed to General Lacey's request that they wear civilian clothes while accompanying Dan and Jolene, at least until they arrived at the Space Academy. The general also provided special ID's for the officers "Just in case you need to get someone to do what they are supposed to do."

The special ID's proved to be a very good idea, as Captain Lee and Lieutenant Kowalski discovered almost immediately.

"I'm sorry, sir. The Academy is closed to civilians until tomorrow morning." The Space Force Sergeant had not raised the barrier preventing vehicles onto the campus.

"I understand that, Sergeant. If you check these papers, however, you'll note I am Captain Lee, and this is Lieutenant Kowalski. Our two passengers are about to enter the Academy for testing."

He smiled. "We are not civilians."

The sergeant read the papers.

"Yes, sir. I need to see your ID's please, Captain, Lieutenant, and the ID's for the others in your vehicle."

"Give him your ID, Kowalski. Dan, Jolene, hand me the papers you got from Mr. Williams."

The sergeant again read all the material, but still didn't raise the barrier.

"I'm sorry, Captain, but I'm not sure these papers are enough for me to let your passengers onto the campus."

"I appreciate your caution, Sergeant. Why don't you check with your officer and see what he thinks?"

"Yes, sir. I'll do that. Please stay in the vehicle and don't open any doors, Captain. Do you understand that, sir?"

Lee nodded. "I know about the lasers, Sergeant. We'll stay right here."

"Thank you, sir."

While the sergeant backed away from the floater and spoke into his microphone, Captain Lee turned to Dan and Jolene and explained.

"Although you can't see them, the base and road are protected by high-intensity lasers which are partly triggered by motion. It would not be a good idea to test them."

While Captain Lee was talking to Dan and Jolene, a tall officer with lieutenant's insignia left the guardhouse and came out to the car.

"Good evening, Captain," he said as he saluted. "What do you need on base that you have to enter this evening?"

"Some place to sleep tonight, Lieutenant," the captain replied with a smile. "These two civilians need to take the entrance exam for the Academy tomorrow. As soon as they pass the exam, the commissions awarded to them by the president as second lieutenant become active. General Lacey has made arrangement for the four of us to stay at the BOQ (basic officers' quarters) until their testing is complete."

The tall lieutenant replied as he looked at the paperwork.

"I hope you understand how irregular that sounds, Captain. I mean, most cadets actually take four years to be commissioned, not four days!" he said sarcastically. "What makes you think these two. . ." his voice tapered off as he read further in the paperwork.

"I've heard these names before, Captain, but I can't place when or why. Refresh my memory, please."

"As high school students, Dan and Jolene were involved in the Battle of Echo Canyon. It was Dan's sharpshooting skills that allowed the AI's to capture the flying saucer and

Jolene's skill as a pilot that saved Dan after he was wounded."

"Echo Canyon! Now I remember! Rumor has it Lacey got them merit appointments, but the president commissioned them without the Academy. Is that true, sir?"

"Yes, it is, Lieutenant. The AI's also insisted Dan get the CIB (Combat Infantry Badge)" Lee said as he showed his special ID to the captain of the guard.

"Thanks for the explanation, Captain Lee, and I hope they do a good job on the exams. As you know, the service can always use more good people, sir." He handed the ID's and papers back and saluted Captain Lee.

"Let them pass," the tall lieutenant told his sergeant.

As Captain Lee drove the floater towards the BOQ, Dan asked, "How many people know about what happened in Echo Canyon?"

"In civilian life, not many. In the military, I doubt if you will find anyone who hasn't at least heard the story." He glanced at Lieutenant Kowalski. "Barbara, why don't you explain to them what that really means."

"It means some people may resent your quick promotion despite what you did to earn it and may try to put up roadblocks to slow you down. On the other hand, most military people will regard you as real heroes, and the vast majority will want to help you in any way they can. That's why General Lacey wanted us to be with you during the entrance exams."

There was silence in the floater until just before they arrived at the BOQ. Jolene turned to Dan and spoke quietly for the first time since they stopped at the gate. "Now I'm beginning to wonder if this was really such a good idea."

The next morning, Dan and Jolene reported to the testing center after breakfast to begin their entrance exams. At least, that's what they thought they were doing.

"Okay, Dan, Jolene, this is as far as Barbara, and I can go. During the rest of today you need to follow the instructions and the procedures as best you can. Tradition has it that we can only give you one last piece of advice." Captain Lee looked at Lieutenant Kowalski. "Barbara, do you want to say it, or shall I?"

"I'd like to Captain if you don't mind," she said eagerly.

"Go ahead, then. I don't mind."

Lieutenant Kowalski made eye contact with both Dan and Jolene, then said slowly and distinctly,

"As I was told, so I tell you. Appearances can be deceiving. Remember, that you don't really know what is being tested."

". . .you don't really know what is being tested," Jolene repeated slowly.

"And, appearances can be deceiving," Dan stated.

"We'll meet you here after your testing. That should be about 3 o'clock. Good luck to you both, and remember what we said."

"Thanks for your help, Kim, Barbara. Dan and I appreciate it," Jolene admitted.

"And we will remember," Dan added, and they then climbed the stairs into the testing center.

"Should we have told them more?" Barbara asked as they watched Dan and Jolene enter the testing center. "I'd really hate for these two kids in particular to flunk the tests."

"They're both going to break enough traditions as it is without our help. All we can do is cross our fingers and hope they realize what's really happening!"

Over the next few days, Dan and Jolene were subjected to an amazing battery of tests. The physical agility tests they accomplished with ease, and the academic tests were hardly more difficult. Dan and Jolene didn't see each other during the day while testing so they couldn't compare notes until the evening.

Some of the tests were like nothing they had ever done before.

Take the simulator test. They were strapped into a moveable chair with hand controls on both sides. A light in the form of an "X" was aimed from the top of their chair at a blank wall in front of them. When the test started, a large and bright circle of light was displayed on the wall, and they were told to keep the "X" inside the circle.

It was easy, at first. The circle moved slowly to the left, then slowly to the right, then slowly up and down. As the test progressed, the circle moved faster and more erratically, then began to get smaller. The light in the room faded slowly to dark.

Suddenly, a loud explosion went off in the room, and the chair turned upside down with the operator hanging from the safety straps. Smoke began to fill the room, and it was harder and harder to see the circle.

Both Dan and Jolene started out thinking this was a fun test, but they were both very glad when that particular test was over.

Another test was the water balloon test.

It also started out as a fun test since they were given a mini-laser similar to a PerLaz and asked to shoot water balloons that were tossed at them. They were told to shoot the balloons before they got too close or they would get wet.

At first, it was very easy since the balloons were tossed one at a time and slowly, and only from the front of their bodies. As the test progressed, the speed of the balloons increased, and they started coming from the sides as well as the front. Then the light faded to twilight, and the balloons also started coming from above and in pairs.

By the time the test was finished, the area was almost dark and balloons were coming fast and from 360 degrees.

Both Dan and Jolene were completely soaked.

When the lights came back on, they were taken into a drying room with wind jets that dried their clothes in a few minutes and given towels for their face and hair. Jolene in particular thought that was a nasty test since it mussed up her hair more than Dan's.

What neither one of them realized, however, was some of the most important tests were not testing what was obvious.

Take the clothespin test.

"What I want you to do is drop the clothespins one at a time into the jar between your feet. If you hold the pin just right, it will go in straight. Aim the clothespins, drop them straight, and then turn in the jar with the clothespins to the sergeant outside the room. Good luck, kid. I have to go to another cubicle to start someone else."

When Dan was done, he was disappointed to find he only had 1 clothespin out of 20 in his jar. He walked slowly to the desk outside the room, hiding the bottom of his jar from view with his hand. No one was there, but a scruffy looking janitor was mopping the floor.

"How many did yah get, sonny?" the janitor cackled at him as he glanced at Dan's jar. "Only one? How're yah gonna pass with only one clothespin, kid?" Dan looked at the man but didn't reply.

"Tell ya what, sonny," the janitor dropped his voice to a whisper. "I won't tell if you wanna add some more 'pins.' Most of 'em do that just so's they pass the test."

Dan thought about doing that, but then he remembered "*. . .don't really know what is being tested*'" and shook his head, no.

The janitor went back to mopping. "It's your life, kid," he said as he mopped around the corner. The sergeant returned and took Dan's score.

Another unusual test was the pinball game test.

"Here are the scoring instructions printed on this sheet. You may take whatever time you need before you start, but the game only lasts 3 minutes from the time you start until the buzzer sounds. Don't ask me any questions, because I can't answer any. The higher the score, the better, so score as high as you can." The pinball game had six colored lights, four gates, four bumpers, two chutes, and one pop-up thing.

Jolene read and studied the sheet. She decided to concentrate only on possible scoring combinations. She got ready to make a list since she had the time and pencil and paper available.

Eight minutes later, Jolene realized she hadn't found a single combination that would score any points.

There must be something wrong here, she thought. She took the sheet back to the desk, but the tester didn't even look up when he said, "No questions, kid. I can't help you with this one."

"Yes sir, I understand that, but I think I may have the wrong sheet for this game. There aren't any scoring combinations using these instructions. I checked them all. There isn't any way to score."

The tester finally looked up, looked directly at Jolene then rolled his eyes and said slowly, "Kid, why would we have a game if you can't score any points? That's really stupid."

"There aren't any combinations that score points," Jolene repeated stubbornly. "I checked them all."

"If you say so. All right, gimme your sheet, and go through

the green door down the hall."

Jolene hesitated a moment, then handed him the sheet, turned and went to the green door.

The hardest tests were the ones that neither Dan nor Jolene realized were tests. For instance, during one break time, they were told to take one sandwich and one drink. The friendly janitor was cleaning in that area, and he insisted they eat more than one sandwich and tempted them both.

"Gotta keep your strength up, kid. These are really important tests, and one sandwich ain't enough! 'Sides, I don't wanna haul this stuff back just so's they can throw it away. Here, lemme help." He took an extra sandwich apiece and brought it over.

"Now ya kin honestly say YOU didn't take it!"

Neither Dan nor Jolene ate the extra sandwich even though they were both very hungry.

All in all, both Dan and Jolene did excellently on the testing. The results were sent to the very top as directed.

"Mr. President, will you take a 'SAT from the commandant at Colorado Springs?"

President Ericsson put down the report he was reading and said grumpily as he switched the speakerphone on, "Yeah, maybe I can get some good news for a change."

"Good to hear from you, Willy," the president spoke into the 'SAT. "Is it too much to hope you have good news for me today?"

"Good to talk to you again, Mr. President, and yes sir, I do have good news."

Commandant Collins had served as a corporal under Lieutenant Ericsson before Ericsson was wounded during 'The Troubles,' then went into politics and became president.

"Those two youngsters Lacey sent for testing both scored

at or near the 100 percent level on every test. That puts them both in the top two percent of everyone that ever took the test! I'll have to say I'm impressed."

"That's great news, Willy; great news. I've got plans for both those kids, and I need them in uniform, in service ASAP."

"That leads me to the reason for my call, Mr. President. Tradition has it cadets go through Hell Week even if they have a commission already. Do you want us to. . ."?

"No! Absolutely not! Not for these two kids, Willy! These two are going directly to the Saucer Project, and we need them there immediately. We have problems with older pilots getting severe headaches while flying, so we wanted the two youngest officers available."

"Yes, sir. How would you like me to handle this, sir?"

The president thought about that question for a moment. "Let them know they passed, get them all their uniforms, but keep them at the Academy for the next week or so. Not your initiation week, mind you. They need to learn basic military courtesy, chain of command and the like from those two escorts Lacey sent with them. Brief those two officers personally and have them conduct a crash course for the kids in everything they really need to know. I know it's a lot to ask, but they need to have some kind of background, so they understand how to relate to others in uniform." The president concluded.

"Yes, Mr. President. Wow! Four years of learning in one week! I'm glad it's someone else that has to teach it."

"Just make it happen, Willy, and then give those kids a party or something."

"Yes, Mr. President."

"And no initiation week! I want you to be clear on that

Willy," the president said firmly. "They had their initiation when they fought those robots in Echo Canyon and allowed us to capture that flying saucer!"

"That will break some traditions, Mr. President, but I can deal with that." He hesitated, then asked, "Boss, since you commissioned them already, why did they need to take the test for the Academy?" (Corporal Willy always called Lt. Ericsson "Boss.")

"All right, Corporal, since yah asked me, I'll tell yah." The president paused and then continued, "I hope these two will become leaders in our military ten or fifteen years down the road. In order for them to relate with others in the Officer Corps, they need the Academy. Even if they only attend every once in a while, they can still receive the college degree they need. More importantly, they won't be regarded as 'Mustangs' after about five or six years in service if they graduate from the Academy." A Mustang was a "wild" officer who wasn't commissioned the regular way, and sometimes didn't know proper procedures.

The commandant thought about that a moment then answered, "You know, I think you're right about that, Boss. It's brilliant, actually. Of course, you were the only lieutenant I ever worked for that had any brains or could find his butt with both hands at the same time."

"Coming from a hard-nosed corporal like you, that's quite a compliment, Willy. Thanks! I know I can count on you to do what I need to be done. Have a great weekend."

"Thanks, Boss. You too, Mr. President."

Salvation and solutions to difficult problems often come in a manner or form that is least expected or not planned for. Take the case of the chimpanzee given a choice of escaping from his cage in one of four carefully selected ways. The research scientists eagerly watched to see which of the four ways the chimp would choose.

The ape escaped a fifth way.

The communication adventure with the aliens was not going well at the site where Dr. Foster's team was trying to get information from them.

"We've been over this a number of times, Doc! If we can find the input, we can speed up the communications. If we speed up the communications, we can ask them which one is the input. If we choose the wrong connection, we could lose our only communication. It's a circular problem with no solution." Bill, the technician, was clearly reaching his frustration point.

"I know that, Bill. Does anyone have any other ideas?" Dr. Foster asked of his team. "Anyone at all? Anything, no matter how crazy?"

His comments were met with a glum silence.

"Well then, let's take a break and eat. Suzy, would you. . ."

"Already ahead of you on that one, Doc. I ordered pizza from the new place on base. They said they would bring a couple different varieties over. That way none of us has to leave here." As she was speaking, they all heard a car pull up. "In fact, that may be them right now."

As the team set up some tables and the deliveryman carried the pizzas in, he looked around and asked why everyone looked so unhappy.

"We are communicating with someone," Dr. Foster said carefully, "but they don't understand enough English to give us the information we need. We need them to tell us which hole on this box is the input hole."

The delivery man looked at the box and shrugged his shoulders. "I see a camera there. Does it work?"

"It does," Suzy replied.

"Can you send them pictures?"

"Sure. Actually, we started out sending them pictures from a DVD language program."

The man looked at the box, then walked around the table to view it from all angles.

"Well, when I'm teaching my little boy, I point to things, say the name and wait for him to repeat it. Why don't you aim the camera at the box, point to each hole one at a time, and wait for the people to tell you which hole is the right one? They don't need to know a lot about English to do that," he shrugged. "It seems simple enough to me."

A bomb exploding could not have had more of an effect than his words.

Suddenly everyone in the room was moving in all different directions at the same time, the pizzas forgotten on the table.

"I'll get the camera set up!"

"I've got the transmitter!"

"Suzy, you type the message and explain what we are doing. Let's hope we don't catch them sleeping!"

"Bill you get. . ."

"I'll get the recording system working, so we have backup in case the printer goes down!"

"Good. What else do we need?" Dr. Foster asked then waited.

"I'll see if I can breadboard a switchable circuit so we can vary the impedance and voltage on the I/O circuit if needed."

"Great idea, Jim. That way we can tune and maximize the signal."

"We also need to record this entire event as we do it. Is there another camera so we can record us as we work this thing?"

"Yeah, Doc, but it's in the storeroom. I'll get it and get it going. Don't anybody do anything big until it's ready," he shouted to the room. The technician ran to get the camera.

"I'll get the DVD Language Program ready so we can cross-feed it into the input. That way we don't lose any time."

"Thanks, Vitold. I almost forgot about that."

"Anybody think of anything else?" Dr. Foster asked. "Did we forget anything else, anything at all?"

"Uh. . ." the deliveryman said timidly into the silence. "Do you suppose. . .somebody could pay me for the pizzas?" He had watched with amazement the results of his suggestion.

"I'll get it," Dr. Foster said and paid for the pizza plus an extra-large tip for the driver.

"Thank you very much for the idea about the camera," Foster added. "That was great! You may never know how much you helped us tonight."

"Wow! Thanks for the tip, sir! I'm glad I could help." And the driver left smiling at a tip that was almost as large as his normal pay for all evening.

"Okay people," Dr. Foster said, rubbing his hands together in anticipation. "Let's see how quickly we can get this up and running!"

CHAPTER 24
FLYING IN HAL

Once Dan and Jolene left the Academy in Colorado Springs, they were taken to Chanute Space Force Base to begin their work on the flying saucer HAL. They were still getting used to the idea of wearing a uniform, and especially receiving salutes from airmen and women who were two and three times their age.

As luck would have it, Dr. Ludwig von Gregheim was available to tutor the couple as they started testing the flying capabilities of HAL. Dr. von Gregheim was the foremost expert on space propulsion and was also a very personable mentor who didn't look down on people as young as Dan and Jolene. He began their experience by explaining everything they knew or guessed at how the saucer HAL worked.

". . .so we were able to determine what the aliens were like physically by the size and configuration of seating equipment and console arrangement in HAL. Also, what frequency range their eyes see as well as what sounds they hear."

Dr. von Gregheim chuckled and then continued. "Apparently, they are much, much larger than we are as this ship only had room for one alien. They appear to be about the size and shape of either a 1500-pound polar bear or Komodo dragon with claws instead of digits or fingers. Their body must be much longer than it is tall. Clearly, they have four controllable limbs as we do, they see about the same range in colors as do we, but they may not be able to hear sounds above 10,000 cycles per second. Humans theoretically can hear up to 20,000 cycles per second although most people have trouble hearing above 18,000."

Dan and Jolene had been listening intently while Dr. von Gregheim explained how and why the spacecraft HAL had been modified.

"As far as the new controls go, we. . .uh. . .borrowed them from a disabled floater in the parking lot." He neglected to add that since they could not get permission to dismantle the government-owned floater, a technician "crashed" it accidentally on purpose so they could salvage the controls. "The controls work exactly the same as a floater since they are from a floater, but we added a second set as a backup. It's a good thing we did because one of the test pilots became unconscious while flying and the co-pilot had to take over."

Jolene looked sharply at Dan, then asked the professor, "Became unconscious how Professor? This is the first time we've heard about that."

"Yeah," Dan added, "If there's a problem with HAL, we need to know about it before we go flying off somewhere."

The professor looked at Dan and Jolene. They reminded him of his own children, Hans, and Trudi who both died 15 years earlier in a commercial floater accident. He definitely wanted to keep these two "kids" safe and wondered what was the best way to approach the subject.

"Dan, Jolene," he started slowly, "did you ever wonder why you two were selected to fly HAL? I mean, the military services have thousands of experienced pilots."

"We did talk about that, Professor," Jolene admitted, "and

decided it was for one of two reasons. First, either because we captured the saucer in the first place. . .in other words, a political decision, or second because we are probably the youngest officers in the service. We thought it must be one of those two reasons."

"I'm impressed!" the professor said in surprise. "In fact, you were both chosen by a computer search because you were the youngest two officers available."

"Let me guess, Professor. The pilot who passed out was probably the oldest of all the pilots who flew HAL, right?" Dan asked shrewdly.

"Right."

"And he probably had the most hours flying HAL, true?" Jolene added.

"True."

"So, it's a problem with age and duration . . ." Dan began.

". . .and Dan and I could probably fly HAL the longest before we feel the effects of whatever is happening," Jolene concluded. "That's logical."

"Ach, du lieber!" (Oh, my dear) Professor Gregheim exclaimed. "You see things so clearly!" He smiled at them both fondly. "There are some committees working on the problem from different angles. One is thinking it might be due to high or ultra-low-frequency we feel but can't hear. They are getting ready to try varied materials to shield the crew's ears. Another committee is setting up tests to do a full spectrum analysis of HAL to see just what radiation is being generated." He paused for a minute.

"Neither committee can do anything while you are flying HAL. How soon do you think you might be ready to take a test flight?"

"Well, I have to check our schedules just to be sure, Dr.

Gregheim, but I think we can be ready in about, say, ten minutes? Is that okay with you, Jolene?"

"What? Ten minutes? Absolutely not, Dan! What are you thinking?" she replied indignantly. "I need at least twenty to thirty minutes to use the restroom, tie my hair back and change into pants!"

"Okay, okay! Twenty to thirty minutes it is." Dan turned back to the professor and shrugged. "Sorry for the delay, Professor, but we'll be ready in about thirty minutes."

Professor von Gregheim tried very hard not to smile at this horseplay.

"Fine. I'll meet you both outside. . .uh. . .in about 30 minutes."

"I suppose we trust the vision screens on this thing, right?" Jolene asked.

"They have been 100 percent reliable, at least so far," the professor replied. "As a spacecraft, you can't have windows like we do for atmosphere flyers. The windows would break under the cold of space."

"These controls look familiar, but what else has been added that wasn't here before?" Dan was clearly suspicious of the changes done to HAL.

"First, we put in a recycling life support system. Except for the heating and cooling function, it will be needed only on space flights. Second, we added seats for the pilot and co-pilot plus two additional seats for the crew. Third, we adjusted the brightness but not the color on the view screen to better suit our eyes. The aliens apparently see the same color range we do, but we think their eyes adjust to dim light better than ours. Fourth, we installed our own radio communications system for talking to base."

"Come on, Professor. There has to be more you did than

just that."

"Well," Professor von Gregheim replied with a straight face, "We did change the labels to English so they would be easier to read."

Jolene looked sharply at the professor, saw the twinkle in his eyes, and realized he was pulling Dan's leg. She tried not to snicker out loud since the joke went right over Dan's head.

"You must also understand, however, that while this ship uses floater controls, it is many, many, many times more powerful than your student floaters. You must exercise caution until you adjust to the power."

"Okay, enough about the changes," Jolene said impatiently. "Let's see how HAL flies." She checked the vicinity for other aircraft as best she could using the viewscreen, then said: "What's our call sign for HAL?"

"We've been using X64", but the tower operators also recognize 'HAL,'" the professor explained.

"Chanute Tower, this is X64 HAL." Dan, as co-pilot, worked the radio.

"Go ahead, X64."

"Tower, permission to take off for an exploratory VFR flight?"

"X64, you are cleared for takeoff at 17 past the hour, VFR. Do you have an ETR?"

"Tower, estimate one-hour to return."

"Tower understands one-hour ETR. Good luck, HAL."

"Roger, and thanks," Dan said. Jolene released the lock controls, lifted to the minimum height required, and then used the accelerator like she usually did in her floater.

The results were frightening.

HAL took off in a straight line with a force that exceeded seven times the pull of gravity, or 7 G's. All three passengers were thrust back into their seats with seven times their own weight. Dan and Jolene, though startled, were able to remain conscious, but Professor von Gregheim blacked out immediately. Jolene quickly eased up on the controls, but the damage had already been done.

"Oh, my stars, Jolene!" Dan groaned. "What were you thinking?" He shook his head to clear it.

"I'm sorry, Dan, I'm Sorry! I'm Sorry! I didn't realize how much stronger this thing is than a floater." She turned to look at the professor.

"Professor? Professor!" Dan turned around also.

"He's unconscious and bleeding from the mouth." Dan started unbuckling his safety harness. "Be very gentle with the controls until I can get back to him." Dan undid his safety harness and climbed into the back seat next to Professor von Gregheim.

"Professor, can you hear me?" Dan asked. The professor rolled his head slowly from side to side, groaned, and started blinking his eyes.

"Professor, are you okay? Are you with us yet? Professor?"

"Ach, mein kopf!" Dr. von Gregheim muttered in German. "Was ist los?"

"Professor, I'm Sorry! I'm Sorry!" Jolene wailed from the pilot's seat. "I didn't realize how fast this thing was!"

"Are you okay, Professor?" Dan asked again.

The professor shook his head slowly from side to side, they licked his lips as if to get rid of a bad taste. "I thought I warned you about the power in this ship. Did I forget, or weren't you listening?"

"Professor, you are bleeding from the corner of your mouth," Dan said to cover Jolene's embarrassment.

Professor von Gregheim licked his lips again. "I bit the

inside of my cheek is all." He smiled wickedly. "I bet the blood may have scared you, no?" The professor got a handkerchief from his pocket and dabbed at his mouth.

"It scared me, yes!" Jolene said, calmer now that she knew the professor was okay.

"Why don't you go back up to your seat, Dan? I'm okay back here, but I'd feel more comfortable knowing there was someone else who could fly the ship if something happens to Jolene." Dr. von Gregheim realized he needed to act calm if he was to help Dan and particularly Jolene settle down.

As Dan strapped back into his seat, he quietly asked Jolene, "Are you okay now?"

"Yes, Dan," she took a deep breath and continued, "I'm fine now. I just wish I had taken it easier when we started."

"Live and learn or crash and burn." Dan quoted Mr. Kissinger's favorite band saying. (Mr. Kissinger had been a military pilot during 'The Troubles.') "Where are we headed now?"

"We were headed to the base infirmary, but right now we're headed due north. I figured we would do a box loop, north then east then south then west back to base."

"Good idea, Jolene." The professor agreed. "Are you both okay? Either one of you have a headache?"

"I have a huge headache, Professor, but it has nothing to do with HAL," Dan replied sarcastically as he glared over at Jolene.

"Now Dan, Jolene couldn't possibly have known how much stronger HAL is than her floater." The professor said, then added shrewdly, "I bet it's a problem that won't happen again. Right, Jolene?"

"Oh, you're so right about that, Professor," Jolene answered contritely.

"Okay, then, let's continue with the test flight."

"Chanute Tower, X64," Dan said over the radio.

"X64, go ahead."

"Tower, X64 requesting permission to land outside our lab building," the professor whispered quickly to Dan, "Tell them Code Jericho."

"Code Jericho, Tower," Dan added.

"X64, stand by."

A few seconds later, the tower replied.

"X64, you are cleared to land off the normal runway at the Developmental Lab Building."

"Roger, Tower. We are beginning our descent now."

The tower operator increased the power of his transmitter. "All aircraft operating in this vicinity, be advised spacecraft X64 will be landing outside the normal landing zone on the northeast corner of the base."

Jolene brought HAL into to a safe, slow and smooth landing in the spot the scientists designated for it. As they left the spacecraft, Professor von Gregheim complimented Jolene on her handling of the craft.

"Now that you know the power of HAL, you did an excellent job flying the pattern and landing, Jolene. I'm impressed." He continued, "I seem to have developed a headache, though. Do either of you have a headache or pain anywhere. Anything at all?"

Dan looked at Jolene before replying with a frown. "Not really a pain, Professor, but my ears are ringing slightly from the high pitch whine I heard in HAL."

"I heard something like that too, Professor," Jolene agreed. "It seemed to get more intense the faster we went. It sounded like one of those hearing tests where the pitch gets higher until you can't hear it anymore."

"Yeah, you're right, Jolene," Dan agreed. "That's exactly what it sounded like."

"Interesting. Very interesting. I'll pass that along to the committees working on the problem."

"Now, tomorrow we need to fly again. Since you both still need practice with the claw, it will be Dan's turn to pilot and Jolene's turn to use the arm." The claw was attached to a maneuverable arm that could be used to pick items off the ground. "Can you both be ready by 8 AM?"

"Professor, we're both scheduled for a 'Military Courtesy' lesson from oh-eight hundred to ten-hundred tomorrow. Could we fly at 11 instead of 8?"

The professor smiled. "I forgot about your other mentors. 11 o'clock will be fine. I'll see you then."

"Thanks, Professor. We'll be here on time and ready to fly," Dan added.

As Dan and Jolene left Professor Gregheim, they were unaware that sharp eyes were watching them through powerful binoculars. The person watching had seen the flight of HAL, and had a much different idea on what could be done with the saucer. The most powerful airship on the planet could be used so much better than as a flying kindergarten!

The observer made notes about the flight, and the two pilots with the aged professor obviously helping them fly the craft.

What a prize!

Now, if he could only find some way to approach the pilots without anyone knowing! *I know at least two countries that would pay me several million dollars if I deliver that flying saucer to them! he thought. Or, either one or both of those two kids!*

CHAPTER 25
WHICH HOLE IS IT?

D r. Fosters' teams quickly set up the cameras to transmit live video to the aliens. The basic premise was sound, but the execution proved to be very frustrating.

"Do they understand what we are doing, Sarah?" Dr. Foster wanted to make sure everything was in order before starting the camera.

"Yes, Dr. Foster. They will tell us "Yes" or "No" as we point to each hole."

"Good! Okay, let's begin." The video camera was turned on and pointed at the communicator. "Bill, take your pencil and point to the far-left hole." Bill did as he was asked, and the team waited for a reply.

10 seconds later, it came. "No."

"This is gonna work. I just know it!"

"I'm sure it will, but let's proceed in order. Bill, next hole please."

That one was also a "No." And the next one and the next one until there was only one hole left.

"That's gotta be the right one, then, Doc. Naturally, it would be the last one in the series! Should we ask anyway?" Bill was getting a little impatient.

"Yes, please, Bill. We need to be systematic about this."

Bill pointed to the last hole but muttered something that sounded like ". . .waste of time" to Sarah.

The excitement turned to disappointment, then anger, as the answer also came back, "No."

"What the heck? There aren't any holes left. Doc, we pointed to all the holes on the back, and it didn't say yes to any one of them!"

Dr. Foster thought about that a moment, then asked Sarah to type in a message.

Was one of the holes we pointed to the input hole?

10 seconds later, the reply came back "No."

Where is the input hole? was sent.

On the Back.

We showed you all the holes on the back panel.

No. That was the side.

"What! Of course. Of course! Turn the box over so we can see the underneath. Carefully, now!" The box was tilted to one side and then set down flat.

And there it was; a hole stamped with markings that looked like writing. "Quick, show this hole to the camera. Sarah, ask the question."

Is this the input hole?

"YES," came the reply. The team erupted with cheers and shouts and whistles.

"Now we're getting somewhere. Bill, can you and Alan jury-rig a connector from the DVD output and. . .? Oh. Never mind." Alan was already bringing a cable with loose wires and handing it to Bill, who carefully inserted the wires into the hole.

"Okay, Sarah. Tell them we will send a test feed in about five minutes."

We have found the input hole and will send a test message in about five minutes. Tell us if you can understand it.

"YES," came the response, but nobody was looking at it.

The first try was not successful, but the second one was. The DVD feed from the computer started at normal speed then was increased to 16 times over speed at the request of the aliens. In a matter of about eight hours, the entire 120-hour English Language program was transmitted. At the conclusion, the aliens requested a delay of three days before contact was made again. The team agreed, but most of them thought privately the aliens would need a lot more than three days to digest and understand all the data.

In the meantime, Dr. Foster needed to make a 'SAT.

"Mr. President, General Lacey on line 3. He says he has good news."

"That will be a change," the president grumbled. He poked at the speaker button.

"Good news, huh? I could use all of that I can get, Abe. What's up?"

"Mr. President, Dr. Fosters' team has completed a direct hookup to the alien communicator, and they were able to transmit the entire English Language DVD program during the past eight hours. Dr. Foster says the aliens have requested three days to study the program, but they are already understandable in English."

"The whole program? How in the world can they understand the whole program in just three days? English still gives me fits sometimes, and I grew up with it."

"Yes, sir. Dr. Foster believes they are using a computer, like we would, to organize the material for them. Either that or they are very gifted beings, sir."

"Gifted or not, they might be monsters, or worse! How are we coming with replication of the flying saucer and the control of HAL?" The president was clearly concerned.

"That's more good news, sir. Dan and Jolene have both become so proficient in flying HAL that they skunked a pair of planes sent to play "tag" as the professor called it. Neither plane could keep them in camera sights, but Dan and Jolene both had multiple camera shots of the planes." General Lacey hesitated and then asked the question Dr. Foster wanted him to ask. "Mr. President, Dr. Foster asked if Lieutenants Jackson and Fisher could play "tag" with a couple of F-22 Raptors to see how they fare against our best fighter and pilots."

President Ericsson was silent long enough that the general almost asked the question again. "Go ahead, Abe, but start with one Raptor, then two, then a combat configuration of four." He snorted. "If two wet-behind-the-ears lieutenants can outfly our best pilots, or even stay with them, we have a lot of work to do."

"Yes, Mr. President. I do have more good news. The team in St. Louis has almost completed the first HAL replica, with one more in the works. They will need to borrow the real HAL sometime soon. Should that happen before or after Dan and Jolene play tag?"

"After. Abe, I want to know the results immediately after this laser tag game is done, you hear me? Immediately."

"Yes, Mr. President. I'll 'SAT you immediately. Anything else I can do for you today, sir?"

"Yeah. Next time you come by, sneak in an old-fashioned hot pastrami sandwich for me. The cooks here in the White House are great, but somehow they can't make a good hot pastrami sandwich for nothing!"

General Lacey tried not to laugh as he replied, "Yes sir, Mr. President, sir! I'll find some good Kosher pastrami sandwiches and sneak them in for you, sir! Goodbye."

"Smart aleck General. Kosher Pastrami indeed!" but he

was smiling as he said that.

The meeting was being held in the pilot's ready room. Present were four F-22 Raptor pilots, including Captain "Speedy" Johnson and his three wingmates, "Baldy" in Two, "Bronco" in Three, and "Madcat" in Four. Also present were Lieutenants Fisher and Jackson and Dr. von Gregheim.

"Let's begin with a word about safety." Dr. von Gregheim was determined not to lose either HAL, Dan or Jolene, or any of the pilots or planes. "The point of this entire exercise is to determine how effective HAL is first in a defensive mode, then as a weapons platform. To that end, Lieutenants Fisher and Jackson will alternate as pilots in HAL, and engage first one Raptor, then two, then three and finally all four." He looked at the fighter pilots. "You four have all flown as a team, and you know each other's tactics as well as what your aircraft can do. These two lieutenants have only been flying the spacecraft for two weeks, and still do not fully understand its capabilities. They also have no real combat flying experience."

"Dan, Jolene—HAL is capable of much more than your bodies can stand. This little game is not worth you hurting yourselves or tempting the other pilots into something dangerous for them. If at any time any of you, or me for that matter, feel things are getting out of hand, the termination code is 'ABORT, ABORT, ABORT.' Does everyone understand?"

There were nods of agreement from everyone, and one of the Raptor pilots asked, "What altitudes will we use as our envelope for this game of laser tag, Professor?"

"Good question. Captain Johnson, since you've flown both aircraft, I'll defer to your judgment."

"Thanks, Professor. I think nothing lower than fifteen thousand feet for safety, and nothing higher than sixty thousand feet. That's a good range for the Raptor, and I know darn well HAL works great at those altitudes."

"Very well, then. I'll be in the control tower watching. Good luck to you all, and let's see how HAL fares against the Raptor."

What followed in this game of "laser tag" was very surprising. Given that neither Dan nor Jolene had any real "combat" air experience, they made several mistakes that rookies always make when flying against an experienced fighter pilot. Speedy had decided he would be the one to fly solo against them since he actually had combat experience flying the Raptor.

Despite their obvious mistakes (like flying straight and level at the same speed too long), the super capabilities of the saucer allowed them to correct and evade every attempt Speedy made to keep them in his gun cameras.

One of the most effective moves Jolene made as pilot almost resulted in a collision when she slowed the saucer to a near standstill while Speedy was accelerating towards them.

"WHOA," Speedy called as he lifted up and over HAL just in the nick of time.

"Jolene, you gotta check your six (directly behind position) before you slam on the brakes like that! I almost hit you!" Speedy's heart was racing after the near collision.

Dan radioed back. "Roger that, Speedy, but the problem is we can't see our six, or our three or nine. All we can see is straight ahead."

"You can't see?" Speedy asked in disbelief. "You can't see me, and I still can't get a good shot off at your ship? That's unbelievable."

"Roger that, Speedy. We need to get a wrap-around viewscreen so we can see other than just straight ahead."

"Wow! Okay, let's try it with two fighters. Bronco, you

heard they can't see behind or to the side?"

"Roger. That should make them easy meat, Speedy," he replied happily.

"Don't count on it, hotshot!" Jolene muttered to herself.

"Hunter 1 from Control," professor von Gregheim radioed. "Is it getting too dangerous to continue the fight?"

"Negative, Control. We just didn't realize how limited HAL's visibility was. Now that we know, we can adjust."

"HAL from Control, do you agree with Hunter 1?"

"Affirmative, Control. We're not ready to quit already. Besides, we haven't had our chance to shoot back yet."

"Okay, Control says to continue the pattern. Just be careful."

"Roger, Control," Speedy replied for them all. "Bronco, remember about their visibility problem."

"Roger, that One. Wouldn't that make them a cripple kill?" Bronco asked.

"Ordinarily it would, but I still haven't been able to get a good shot at them, even when they can't see me."

"Roger."

"HAL, we're going to add Bronco to the mix. Try not to use your instant stopping power unless you must. I don't want either of us to run into you," Speedy radioed.

"Roger," Dan replied.

With the primitive radar in HAL, Dan decided he needed to watch it more carefully since they were blind in most quarters. That way he could warn Jolene not to stop too quickly if a Raptor was close behind.

Jolene, of course, had other ideas.

She was learning to zigzag much better than when she started and accelerate quickly to get away from the Raptors. She discovered she could climb and dive faster than the fighters, but she couldn't throw HAL around as much because the seats installed in HAL did not provide enough support for the sudden attitude changes. More than once she thought she hurt Dan with a sudden change, but Dan, the big lump, wouldn't say anything about it.

The Raptors finally started scoring hits only when all four of them worked together, and Dan couldn't relay quickly enough to Jolene where they were. Speedy decided that it was time to let HAL take the offense.

"Okay, break! Let's switch positions and let HAL take the offensive against me," Speedy called.

Inside HAL, Dan asked Jolene if she wanted to switch positions and let him fly.

"Not on your life, Daniel. They've been chasing me all over the sky, and now," she paused, turning to look at Dan with a wicked smile, "It's payback time!"

The camera footage would tell the tale conclusively, but Dan and Jolene in HAL were able to prevent any laser gun "hits" by one or two Raptors, took one "possible" hit against three, and only received solid hits when all four Raptors worked as a highly-coordinated team.

Against simulated missiles, HAL was almost as effective. In real life when they could have "seen" the missiles, HAL's ability to move in unexpected directions would make it a difficult target.

On offense, HAL did even better. They scored multiple hits against one, two or three Raptors, and hits against three of the four against four.

"Pretty impressive, HAL," Captain Johnson radioed at the end of the game. "Time to go home and watch the gun films. And" he continued, "get something to eat and drink."

Unfortunately, that's when the trouble started.

CHAPTER 26
A FALLING HUNTER

"Hunter Lead to Flock. Let's go home."

"Two." "Four."

Three did not answer.

"Hunter Three from Lead."

No answer. Captain Johnson tried again.

"Hunter Three from Lead! Bronco, where are you?"

"Lead from Four! Three is at our five o'clock, drifting into a spin!"

"Four, stay with your wingman! Get close and check his vital signs! Two, start Mayday procedure while I close for override!"

One of the F-22 safety systems allowed another F-22 pilot to check vital signs on the pilot, but only if the two planes were within a few hundred yards. A more advanced system also allowed the flight leader to "sync" his controls with the disabled plane's controls and fly both planes. This would allow one pilot to land both planes safely.

"Lead from four! Hypoxia! He's not getting enough oxygen to stay conscious!"

"Roger four. Let me get close enough. . .a little more. . .a little more. . . Okay! Three is synched to one, and we are heading for the deck so he can breathe!"

As Captain Johnson put both planes into an emergency descent, Bronco, the pilot in Three, roused enough to make a noise into his mike. No words, just a noise by which he showed he was still alive.

"Hands off the controls, Bronco! Hands off the controls! One more minute, Bronco, and we'll be down where there's enough oxygen for you to breathe!" The captain explained to the others; "I can fly us down quicker than having him bailout."

". . . Copy. . .bailout. . ." the pilot in Three haltingly replied.

"No, Bronco! Do NOT, I repeat, DO NOT BAILOUT! STAY IN THE PLANE!! STAY IN THE PLANE, BRONCO!! STAY . . . IN . . . THE . . . PLANE!!!"

It was too late.

Bronco, semi-conscious from a lack of oxygen, heard what he thought was an order to bailout, and pulled the eject lever before he could be dissuaded.

"Canopy away clean! I say again; Canopy away clean!" Madcat reported.

"Escape pod away clean! I say again; escape pod away clean!" Baldy added.

"Two and Four! I've got to stay with the Bronco's plane to land it! Two, take charge and stay with Bronco! Four, Stay with Two! Good luck!"

"Roger that, One. Two has the lead," came the terse reply from Baldy.

"Two from Four. The pod has a bad spin going. I lost Bronco's vitals when he punched out. He didn't separate from the Pod, did he?"

"Negative, Four. He's still with it."

"Roger Two. When does the drogue chute come out?"

"Supposed to be at twenty-five thousand. Maybe another ten seconds."

They waited.

Dan and Jolene in HAL had stayed out of the way while this drama was taking place. Dan had started thinking about how they could use HAL to help. He thought about grabbing the pilot with the claw and catching him in mid-air but realized not only was that far-fetched but probably unnecessary. Still, it wouldn't hurt to practice in his mind using the claw to save a pilot.

"Okay, there goes the drogue chute. Pod separation should occur at about eighteen thousand," Madcat reported.

Two and Four waited for Bronco to separate from the pod.

"Four, call out the altitude for me. I'll keep my eyes on the pod. Stay outside my orbit, but stay close."

"Roger Two. Twenty-Two thousand." Both Two and Four were descending more rapidly than normal just to stay with the falling pilot.

"Twenty-thousand."

The escape pod was designed to prevent a pilot from freezing to death or suffocating until he reached safe air. It was set to separate from the pilot at about eighteen thousand feet.

"Eighteen-thousand. Separation should occur soon."

After pod separation, the pilot's own drag chute should appear pulling the main parachute itself open at about ten thousand feet.

"Sixteen-thousand. No separation yet."

Four knew the separation should occur between eighteen and sixteen thousand feet. It was not unusual, however, for separation not to happen until fifteen-thousand feet.

"Fourteen-thousand. Still no separation!"

Terminal speed on a falling object was between 130 and 140 miles per hour, and that meant the pod was falling over 200 feet every second. It doesn't take long to lose altitude at that speed.

"Twelve-thousand! No separation! I repeat; No separation! Crap! We're going to lose him!" Madcat exclaimed in despair.

"Eleven-thousand! Still no separation!"

Dan decided it was time to help.

"Jolene, get ready to match speeds with the pod while I grab the harness!" He radioed to the two fighters.

"Two from HAL! Two from HAL! We're going to try a rescue! Back off and give us space!"

"Ten-thousand!"

"What? What can you do?"

"We've got a controllable arm and a gripper. I can grab the drogue cable and slow it down."

"Nine-thousand!"

Two didn't hesitate. "HAL from Two! Go for it! There's nothing we can do to help! Four, break off and stay out of the way but keep calling the altitude!"

"Roger, Two. Good luck, HAL!"

"Okay, Jolene, get above him and drop down." As Jolene piloted HAL, Dan got the arm extended and the gripper ready.

"Eight-thousand!"

Jolene zoomed towards the Pod. At the last second, she backed off sharply, causing them both to be thrown hard against their shoulder harnesses. Dan reached for the cable, but it swerved to the left. He tried a second time and got the drogue chute cable in the gripper.

"Seven-thousand!"

"Start applying back pressure, Jolene!" he yelled.

Jolene did just that, gently at first, then harder and harder.

"Six-thousand!" The ground still seemed to be coming up very fast.

"Harder, Jolene." Dan urged. "It's heavier than I thought!"

"Five-thousand!"

"I can't go any harder, and it's not enough, Dan! Hold on tight! I'm gonna zoom forward instead!" Jolene disengaged the reverse drive and pushed the throttle forward. Their downward plummet changed into a forward motion and started to flatten out.

"Four-thousand! Four is breaking off. I can't spiral down too much lower! Ground level is fifteen hundred feet HAL!"

"Roger fifteen hundred feet, Four," Dan replied.

As their speed progressed forward, the downward motion slowed then almost stopped. Jolene gradually increased their speed until they were flying parallel to the ground.

"Okay, Jolene, slow down and set us down." Jolene looked ahead and saw no clear landing area and nothing but trees except inside a large warehouse fence. "I'll put us down there, Dan. How's the gripper?"

"Better hurry. The cables are sliding again."

Jolene touched down with the pod, then backed away to land HAL. Almost immediately HAL was surrounded by armed men.

"What's this? Who are these people?" Dan said angrily. "Jolene, I'll go talk to them and see if the pilot's breathing. You stay here and get ready to run if things get rough."

Not on your life will I run away! We've got a bigger stick! Jolene thought, but she was learning not to say things like that, at least not out loud to Dan. After Dan left, she radioed Two.

"Two from HAL. He's down safe, but we're surrounded by armed men. We need help quickly. How about a low pass just short of supersonic to let them know you're here?"

"Roger, and thanks HAL! Rescue is on the way."

"Four from Two; Daisy Chain and flip. Show some teeth. I'll do East-West, you do North-South. Copy?"

"Roger. We'll show 'em a good time, Two!"

'Show some teeth' meant taking the rockets, missiles, and guns normally concealed inside the belly of each Raptor, and rotating them to the outside where they can be seen. It was a visual signal, like an animal showing its teeth, that the Raptor wasn't something to mess with!

Dan was having a tough time convincing the men to let him check the pilot. They seemed to not understand English and kept him covered with their weapons at all times.

"Space Force! United States Space Force!" Dan shouted and pointed to the American Flag patch on his coveralls.

Jolene spoke over the intercom to Dan.

"Dan, stop shouting at them and point up into the sky to the east and hold that pose!"

Frustrated, Dan did as Jolene asked, and several of the men turned and looked where he was pointing. Two seconds later, Hunter Two came zooming overhead about 200 feet above the ground at almost 500 miles per hour.

Everyone except Dan hit the dirt, but even Dan flinched from the sound.

Ten seconds later, Hunter Four did the same thing from the north.

When Dan looked around, everyone but him was flat on the ground holding their hands over their ears.

"Dan," Jolene called on the speaker, "MedVac is about two minutes away and homing in on HAL. They say take off his. . ." Jolene's voice was lost as Two came back from the west in a repeat low-level, high-speed Passover. ". . .until they arrive."

"What did you say?" Dan asked.

"I said. . ." again, the sound was lost as Four repeated his Pass, but Jolene waited to continue. ". . .I said the MedVac people said to take off his mask and let him breathe on his own until they arrive." Jolene shouted.

"Gotcha." Dan could hear the MedVac coming and moved slowly towards the pod and pilot while watching the armed guards. He looked in and saw the pilot already had his mask off and was breathing very heavy. His eyes were wide open, however, and he looked up at Dan and gasped out, "Thanks!"

Dan's "You're welcome" was drowned out by Two passing overhead again.

In the meantime, Hunter One had landed both his Raptor and Broncos on base. Landing two planes was difficult but taxiing them both together was all but impossible due to irregularities in the pavement. Hunter One had been listening to the radio traffic between Two and Four, then from HAL. He fumed and fretted waiting for the base crew to get to his location and take charge of the other plane. Protocol required him to wait with the other plane until the ground crew arrived.

Dan's report of armed men surrounding Bronco and HAL, however, and Jolene's call for help were too much for him to ignore. He shut down the engines on Three, disengaged his controls, went to full military power and lifted off en route to the site. He accelerated quickly and stayed just below supersonic speed, arriving at the warehouse site in six minutes.

The MedVac had arrived but didn't land because Jolene warned them the site was hot.

"Roger, HAL, copy the site is hot. The Marines will be here shortly."

When Two had called "Mayday," a number of systems begin to function automatically at the airbase.

The MedVac was rolled out of its hanger, and the maintenance crew started the power-up procedure. The MedVac carried a flying crew of two and a medical crew of two paramedics and one flight nurse. Since they knew about the diagnosis of hypoxia, they immediately made ready the portable oxygen container as well as various drugs that could be used to help a hypoxia victim. They lifted and went to emergency power to reach the site.

The base hospital emergency room went on alert, and an emergency alert went out to medical staff by radio and pager.

At the fire station, firefighters suited up and rolled their equipment outside to wait for directions.

The ready platoon of Marines stationed at the air base buttoned up their augmented armor suits, and the first squad boarded the ready alert assault floater. Unlike the MedVac, they lifted off under normal speed since there was no immediate threat. The Marines would be used as the rescue personnel if needed due to their suits and strength. The second squad suited up and boarded the back-up floater, but stayed on the ground.

Jolene's call for help to Hunter Two about the armed men changed that situation dramatically.

The airborne Marine floater went to maximum military power and homed in on the MedVac beacon while the AM's (Augmented Marines) prepared to deal with the "armed men." The second squad lifted off, went immediately to full military power and also homed on the MedVac beacon. Although they started eight minutes behind squad one, they would arrive only 2 minutes later.

"Two from One, I've got the lead again."

"Roger. How'd you get back here so quickly, Speedy?"

"I pedaled real hard, Two. Two and Four, change to triangle orbit left at 1000 above the ground. Backpedal to about 150 or so."

"Two." "Four." came the reply, and the three planes shifted into a triangle orbit (each plane 1/3 of the way around a circle moving counterclockwise) around the warehouse site.

The first Marine squad floater dove towards the ground, tilted back abruptly in the "cobra hood" move, and the AM's jumped out at about 15 feet above the ground. They hit the ground running and deployed with lightning speed around the armed men while two AM's went directly to the escape pod. The floater then backed away and hovered in a covering position to allow its guns and rockets to back up the Marines. The MedVac floated forward and touched down by the pod, and the paramedics raced towards the pod.

The armed guards were still on the ground from the noise of the Raptor's passes and made no attempt to either get up or resist.

The Second Marine floater made its approach 90 degrees from the first, deployed in the same manner, and also hovered in backup mode. So far, neither side had fired any weapons, and Jolene decided the Raptors could safely back off.

"Hunter Lead from HAL."

"Hunter Lead."

"The Marines have landed, Bronco is safe and alive, and I think you can back off a little."

"Roger, HAL. Hunter flight, let's form up and orbit left

on my wing."

"Two." "Four. Lead, did she say Bronco was OK?"

"Roger, but without HAL it would have been a different story."

"Roger the different story, Lead. We owe them big time!"

As it turned out, the "armed men" were guards in training for a multi-national corporation. They were expecting a simulated test today as part of their security training and thought the pod and HAL was that test. None of their weapons were loaded, and everything was cleared up once communication (in Polish, Russian, German, French, and Spanish as well as English) was established.

Bronco (Lt. Matthew Dillon) was med-vac'd back to the base and would spend the evening in the infirmary, flirting with the nurses.

Dan and Jolene, however, had to explain in detail what happened first to Professor von Gregheim, then to the communications people, then to Colonel Evergreen, the Airbase Commander and so on. By the time they went back to the recreation room at the hanger, they had told the story at least six times.

It wasn't until they actually sat down that they realized supper was long over, and they were both very tired and very hungry. Dan was insisting they go find something to eat when the three pilots from Hunter flight plus the base commander entered bearing several pizzas and cold drinks.

"Look! It's Beauty and the Beast; I mean, Jolene and Dan! To the victor, belong the spoils. I don't think these pizzas are spoiled yet, but I think we should eat them quickly just to be sure." Colonel Evergreen was clearly pleased with the nicknames he had just given Dan and Jolene.

"Wow! Thanks!" Dan said. "We were just going to try to

find something to eat ourselves."

"Well, pizzas and sodas are not a very large reward for saving Bronco's butt today, but it was the best we could do on short notice. Besides, we never get to order the "garbage" pizzas because Bronco is such a fussy eater."

"Garbage pizzas?" Jolene asked.

"Yeah. Garbage pizzas come with everything on them; sausage, pepperoni, mushrooms, black and green olives, and other good stuff. We get so tired of the 'cheese pizzas with no meat' that Bronco likes."

The base commander, Colonel Evergreen said, "I'm sure we'll find some way to reward you two officially for your quick action today besides just giving you nicknames, but for right now, I'm hungry enough to eat Bronco's Raptor. Dig in."

Jolene asked Dan, "What's this thing about nicknames?"

Dan shrugged his shoulders, but Colonel Evergreen answered "All the pilots get nicknames. Some nicknames are opposites, like 'Tiny' for a tall, big person. Some names are after events like Captain Johnson is 'Speedy' due to his almost Mach 4 run after a MIG fighter jet. It's 'Baldy' because of his thick hair, 'Bronco' because he can't fly in a straight line and 'Madcat' for those stupid wild cats he raises and feeds. You two are obviously a pair, so 'Beauty' fits exactly how Jolene looks, but 'The Beast' is just the opposite for Dan. Nicknames make for quicker identification in the air, but they must be earned."

"That's right," Speedy said. "The commanding officer gives the nickname. Since you were flying with us today, Colonel Evergreen gets the honor."

The four officers and commander then introduced Dan and Jolene to that famous military forum entitled the "bull session," and the soda and pizzas disappeared as quickly as the stories appeared. The events of Bronco's rescue were rehashed over and over again. After a short time, more pizzas and more sodas were ordered, and the bull session continued.

"You know, 'Beauty' fits Jolene to a T" Speedy said, "but I'm not sure about 'The Beast' for Dan."

"Beauty is perfect for Jolene," Madcat said enthusiastically. "Why, if she wasn't attached to the Beast here, I'd be more than glad to give her a tour of the base." Madcat was clearly taken with Jolene.

"Sorry, Madcat," Speedy said. "The president himself assigned these two to the Saucer Project. 'Sides, you wouldn't want to tempt the Beast here into using his shooting iron."

"Oh? Why not? I'm pretty good myself, you know."

"Yeah, wearing a Raptor, you aren't bad, son. The AI's that rescued these two after the Battle of Echo Canyon, however, were impressed enough with Dan's pistol shooting that they awarded him the CIB. That's Combat Infantryman's Badge. For ground pounders, that is 'The Award.' Luckily, they don't use nicknames, so we get to name them."

Naturally, they all wanted to hear every detail of the Battle of Echo Canyon.

Dan was always reluctant to talk about the battle, but Jolene was eager to tell the story to such an appreciative audience. Clearly, 'Beauty' fit right in with the Bull Session group.

All in all, it was a wonderfully warm ending to what could have been a very bad day.

Chapter 27
"HELLO? HELLO?"

Doctor von Gregheim was briefing Dan and Jolene after the excitement of the previous day was ended.

"The committee that's trying to find a solution for the sound or radiation problem with HAL has a number of suggestions for us to try. Before we get into that, why haven't you told me whenever you start to get a headache when flying HAL? I'll confess, I've forgotten to ask you every time, but you haven't mentioned headaches for a while either." Professor von Gregheim was clearly worried that Dan and Jolene were hiding a problem.

Dan looked guilty, and Jolene just crossed her arms with a smug look on her face.

"Well, Dan? What aren't you telling me? Hmmmm?"

"Well, you see Professor, it's like this. I'm not having headaches anymore, and I don't think Jolene is either. That's why we haven't said anything." Dan and the professor both looked at Jolene.

"I'm not having headaches anymore either, Professor," Jolene replied smugly.

Professor von Gregheim looked at them both and realized they weren't telling him everything. "And why not, do you suppose?"

"Uh, well, Jolene got a little chilly on one flight because I forgot to turn on the heater and so we wore warmer clothing the next trip. She also wore a pair of earmuffs to keep her ears warm."

"Ear muffs? What do you mean, ear muffs?" the professor asked in surprise.

Without a word, Dan went over to his duffel bag and pulled out a set of black ear muffs. These were the kind with an adjustable plastic band that went across the top of the head and fuzzy fake fur to keep the ears warm.

"These, Professor." He handed them to Professor von Gregheim.

"These?"

"Yes these, Professor," Jolene confirmed. "I thought they would keep my ears warm while we fixed the temperature in HAL, and I flew several hours without any headache or hearing that high pitch sound at all. At least, I didn't have a headache." Jolene looked at Dan with satisfaction.

"And you, Dan? Did you get a headache, or did you not try them?"

"My ear muffs are pink, Professor," Jolene interrupted before Dan could reply, "and Dan said it was the stupidest thing possible to think simple ear muffs would make a difference, and he'd die before he wore pink ear muffs! He wouldn't try them because they were pink, even when his head started to hurt!"

"Aha! So, you did get a headache, and you didn't tell me? Wasn't I clear about keeping me informed about this? Didn't you know how important this was?"

"Well. . ." Dan started to reply, but Jolene cut him off again.

"I insisted, absolutely insisted, he try them on, or I told

him I was going to abort the flight!" She giggled. "I'll have to admit, Dan looked pretty cute in pink ear muffs."

Dan was clearly embarrassed, and added, "But my headache started to fade as soon as I put them on. . ."

". . .while I began to hear that high-pitched sound from before, and my head started to ache soon after that. When we got back, we both went to the PX and bought more of the same type earmuffs. I got a second pair in white. . ."

". . .and I bought this pair in black and another pair in navy. We've been using them ever since, and neither of us has had a headache at all." He frowned as he glanced at Jolene. "Well, at least not a headache caused by that high-pitched sound."

"So! You two solve a major problem, a problem we have dozens of people and several laboratories working on, and you didn't even think to tell me? You let us spend money and waste time on a problem that was already solved?" He glared at both Dan and Jolene. They couldn't tell he was really tickled they solved the problem and was only pretending to be angry.

"We're sorry Professor, but. . .well," she hesitated. "You tell him, Dan."

"Tell me what, Dan?" von Gregheim asked crossing his arms impatiently.

Dan was silent for a few seconds and then started slowly. "Professor, Jolene and I were afraid to tell you because we might lose the assignment of flying HAL if you knew the solution was as simple as this. There would be no reason to use the two "youngest" officers, meaning Jolene and me, if a simple pair of ear muffs solved the problem."

Professor von Gregheim took a deep breath and sighed. "Okay, I understand now why you didn't say anything. I must pass this information along anyway, however. I hope you realize that, but I don't think you will be pulled off HAL. First, there is no guarantee the ear muffs will work on older ears. Second, the president himself thought you two were perfect for this assignment, and nobody, but NOBODY, wants to upset the president by changing your assignment! Third. . .I think I'll go buy some earmuffs myself and send them to the committee in Washington. We'll let them study it and figure out why they work."

"Professor," Dan suggested, "Why don't you wear my black ear muffs, and let's all go for a ride to see if they work for you. If they work for someone your age, then they should work for the regular pilots."

"Someone my age, huh? I'll try not to take my afternoon nap while we're flying!" the professor retorted sarcastically.

"Now Professor, Dan didn't mean it the way he said it, did. . .you. . .Dan?" Jolene asked dangerously with her hands on her hips.

"Oh! Uh . . . no! I just meant . . ."

"I know what you meant, Dan, and it's an excellent idea. Let me get my coat, and we'll go flying."

During a short but high-speed trip, Professor Gregheim wore the earmuffs and did not get a headache. He concluded the ear muff solution was indeed a simple one. They returned to the base, and he immediately went to report his findings to General Lacey.

"Now," the old professor said, "Since I've got a lot to do, thanks to you two, I want you to find something productive to do while I do the paperwork. Ear muffs, indeed." He muttered.

"Thanks, Professor! We really appreciate this, and we're sorry we didn't tell you."

"Do you have any suggestions for something new that we can try, Professor?" Jolene asked hopefully in an attempt to distract Dr. Gregheim.

The professor thought about it a minute, then said, "Make sure the oxygen system is working first, and then see how HAL operates at high altitude. Sooner or later we need to take it up to orbit height."

"All right!" Dan said. "That sounds like fun."

Jolene added. "How high can we go?" she asked.

"Well, don't go to Mars or Venus just yet!" the professor replied absentmindedly, his mind already composing the information for a 'SAT.

"Yes sir, and this time we'll tell you how it works right away," Jolene promised.

"Thank you. I would appreciate that." He smiled at both of them. "Now, get out of here and go play. Shoo!" and he waved his hands at them.

Dan and Jolene smiled at each other. Jolene took Dan by the hand, and they left quickly to go back to HAL.

"General Lacey, it's Professor von Gregheim on line two."

"Okay, I've got it." The general pushed the speakerphone button.

"Professor, good to hear from you. I just got done talking to Colonel Evergreen, and he told me about the excitement during your war-game. I trust Dan and Jolene and HAL are okay?"

"Oh, yes, they are fine, but they've handed me a headache I need to share with you."

"Wonderful. I love headaches." Lacey replied dryly.

"I'm sure you remember the problem about real headaches your test pilots suffered when flying HAL?"

"Yes."

"And you know the president set up a committee to solve the problem by trying different shielding for the pilot's ears?"

"Yes, I know about that."

"And another committee was going to measure for radiation or sound to see if that was the same problem?"

"Yes, yes, I know all about that. What's your point, Professor?" General Lacey asked impatiently.

"The point is. . .Dan and Jolene solved both those problems, so we don't need those committees anymore. Do you want to call the president and tell him, or should I?"

"What? Wait a minute, wait a minute! What do you mean they solved the problems?"

"Jolene bought a pair of ear muffs because her ears were cold." The professor was smiling as he said this.

"Ear muffs? What do you mean when you say. . .ear muffs?"

"I mean, the kind you wear with a plastic strap that fits over your head and furry things that rest on your ears. Evidently, Jolene wore a pair in HAL, and her headaches disappeared. Dan didn't have any, and he was still getting mild headaches."

"How do we know it was the ear muffs that prevented the headaches? Did Dan try them?"

"He told me he'd rather die first because Jolene's ear muffs were pink! Evidently, Jolene can be very persuasive, since he eventually did try them."

"And?"

"And Dan's headache started to fade while Jolene's started to grow."

"Unbelievable! Here we set up two committees to work on this problem, and they solve it because their ears were cold! Do you know where Jolene got the ear muffs?"

"Yes, General. She said she got them at the PX here on

base. After the flight, she bought another pair in white, and Dan bought a black pair and a blue pair of the same style and make. I went to the PX and bought several pair in different colors to send to the committee. They are only a couple dollars each; not even the expensive kind."

"Ear muffs!" the general snorted. "I wonder if we should test them on someone else?"

"We did that already. Dan loaned me his extra pair, and I flew in HAL for about two hours without getting a headache, when before my head hurt after only ten minutes. I concluded they really work." The professor decided he also needed to tell the general about why Dan and Jolene didn't report this immediately. "General Lacey, they didn't tell me about the ear muffs at first because they thought they might not get to stay with HAL if anyone could wear ear muffs and fly. I told them there was no danger they would be removed. Was I right?" Clearly, Professor von Gregheim was concerned.

"Oh yes, you're exactly right about that! The president himself put them there after that computer search, Professor, and was positively delighted the computer chose Dan and Jolene! I would hate to be the one to tell him we moved them somewhere else! I'm thinking he would have an eruption of temper the likes of which I never hope to see! Speaking of telling him things, though, I need to make a 'SAT. Thanks for the information, Professor."

"Your welcome, General. I'm glad I shared this 'headache' with you."

"You know, our test pilots all wore helmets when they flew, but the helmets all had hollow space for headphones," General Lacey muttered. "I wonder if that's why the ear muffs worked, and the helmets didn't."

"I think that's a very good possibility, General," the

professor agreed. "That something so simple as ear muffs. . ." and he just shook his head.

"Okay, Thanks! Just in case the president asks about Dan and Jolene, what are they doing now?"

"I asked them to see how HAL handles at high altitude, General."

"Good idea, Professor. That should be safe enough," General Lacey said with satisfaction.

If ever a person were to "eat his words," it would be General Lacey for that statement.

"Chanute Tower from HAL" Dan radioed.

"Tower"

"Request permission to take off?"

"HAL, you are cleared to take off at 28 past the hour. Do you have an ETR?"

"Tower, we think about three hours. We will be doing some high-altitude testing."

"Copy about three hours, HAL. Good luck."

"Roger Tower, and thanks."

Aviation radio frequencies are open for anyone to monitor, and the people outside the base were listening intently anytime Dan and Jolene were flying. They were trying to discover a pattern that they could exploit to get closer to Dan or Jolene. What they wanted, of course, was HAL.

Once they made sure the oxygen and heating systems were working, Dan and Jolene increased their altitude until they reached about 90,000 feet. This was much higher than any aircraft, even fighter jets could reach. The thinness of the atmosphere at that level meant they needed more power to do simple turns, and many of the moves took longer since there was no air to push against.

Things were going well, and they were about to head back

to base when the unexpected happened.

"Hello? Hello?" The voice seemed to come out of mid-air.

Dan and Jolene looked at each other. Who was talking?

"Hello? Hello? Can you hear me do me you understand?"

Dan took the lead. "Yes, we can hear you, and yes, we understand you. Who are you, and how are you talking to us?"

"The spacecraft you are flying is from my planet, and there is a back-up. . .radio in it so if the primary stops. . .work I can still. . .communicate."

Jolene gasped. "Your planet! You mean. . .this spacecraft is yours? Who are you?"

"I am . . . your language does not . . . in my language my title is, Computer High-end Awareness Robotic Linguistic Integrator. I received the English . . . language program you sent and spent. . .one rotates of your planet. . .learning it. Do you correctly understand what I speak?"

"Yes, yes we can understand you. Did you say, you learned the whole English language in one Day?" Dan asked in amazement.

"One rotate. . .one day is what it time." The voice replied.

"What it 'took,'" Jolene corrected automatically.

"Yes, what it took," the voice replied. "Are you control in the. . .95484736 and are you part of the race human?"

"Yes, we are part of the human race. Are you an alien or are you a computer? I mean, are you alive, or are you a machine?" Dan asked.

"Thank you. I am. . .the central machine left in charge of. . .planet Saurian? I was made by the. . .Creators. . .to manage Saurian lives so they. . .could work? Play? Do something else. Are you in control of the 95484736 are?"

Dan and Jolene looked at each other in amazement. They

were actually talking to an alien computer! *What a wonderful opportunity*, Dan thought.

"I'm not sure what you mean, 'Are you in control of whatever-you-said.' We have named this spacecraft HAL, and we are in control of HAL. Is that what you wanted to know?"

"Thank you. I accept you call 95484736 'HAL,' and I will say it also. Question. Do. . .humans make names everything for?"

"For everything," Dan corrected. "Yes, I guess we do make names for many things we make, and all intelligent beings have a name."

"Thank you. Notice I names are. . .short? . . .and my title is. . .extended? Long? How can I make it shortening?"

"You mean, 'shorter.' Would you please say your name, I mean your title again?"

"Thank you. Computer High-end Awareness Robotic Linguistic Integrator. That is as close as I can talk my Title English in." Dan was writing the words down as they were spoken.

"In English, not English in. Jolene!" he said excitedly, "look at this!" Dan showed the words to Jolene. They smiled at each other and said, "Charlie! Computer, we are going to call you Charlie."

"Thank you. How is Charlie name for me?"

Dan replied, "I used the first letter of each word in your title. C,H,A,R,L,I and then we added a silent E on the end to make a regular name. Charlie, we are glad to talk to you."

"Thank you. I accept Charlie as my short name."

"You're welcome, Charlie. My name is Dan. . ." Jolene interrupted ". . . and my name is Jolene. Is there anything else we can do to help you?"

"Thank you. Dan. Jolene. Yes, I need massive. . .big. . .helps with a major problem. Are you able to make a decides to help, or do other humans need to make a decides you with?"

"Decision, Charlie, not 'decides,' and it's 'with you,' not 'you with.' Aren't you talking to the people who taught you English?"

"Thank you. Decision. No talking to other humans. They will not be ready for one more. . .day. . .to talk. Charlie monitored. . .HAL. . .and listened to Dan and Jolene. I decision talk with you was easier. Is HAL not on the ground but out in. . .airlessness?"

"Out in space, Charlie. We call it space. And 'decide' would be correct this time. We're not quite out into space. We are at 90,000 feet above the planet, and space starts a little higher than that."

"Thank you. Question. Why are you. . .not on the ground. . .but not out in space?"

Dan looked over at Jolene with a question on his face. Jolene looked back, and mouthed the words, "be honest." "Charlie, we are still learning how to fly in HAL. The original controls were much too large for us, so our technicians put in controls for human size people. This is the first time we have flown this high."

"Thank you. Do you need help flying in. . .space?"

"Yes, Charlie, yes we do!" Dan said excitedly. "Boy, Jolene, what a break! To get to learn from the person. . .I mean, computer, that made HAL in the first place."

"Now wait a minute, Dan. I'm not sure if this is a good idea. Shouldn't we call Professor von Gregheim first?"

"We should definitely call him, Jolene. It's just that I'm not sure how far our radio will reach." Dan replied. "Charlie, may we call the other humans to tell them what we are doing?"

"Thank you. Yes, that is an idea good."

"You mean, a 'good idea,' Charlie. Okay, let's see if we can get the tower on the radio." Dan picked up the microphone.

"Chanute Tower from HAL, Chanute Tower from HAL. Do you copy?"

"Chanute Tower. Go ahead, HAL." The sound was clear but weak.

"Tower, we have discovered an. . .uh. . .on-board tutoring program and we are going to use it to fly out into space. Would you notify Professor von Gregheim for us?"

"HAL from Tower. An on-board tutoring program?"

"Affirmative, Tower." The two tower operators looked at each other in surprise.

"HAL from Tower. Check to make sure your IFF Mode 3 is set to 10, and Mode 4 is turned on."

"I have it, Dan," Jolene said. "Mode 3 is set to 10. . .and Mode 4 is turned on. Ask if they have us, Dan."

"Tower from HAL. Modes 3 and 4 are set. Are. . .receiving our IFF?"

"Roger HAL. We have your IFF." The operator looked closer at the data being received. The altitude registered 80,000 feet plus. "HAL from Tower; how high are you?"

"About 90,000. . .Tower."

The tower operators looked at each other again.

"HAL, repeat. Did you say 90,000 feet?"

"Roger, Tower. Flight. . .niner-zero thousand. This is a spacecraft, you know."

About this time, the ATC supervisor came over and asked what was going on.

"Sir, X64 HAL is at 90,000 feet. The pilot says they found an onboard tutorial that will show them how to fly in space. They asked us to contact Professor von Gregheim to let him know what they are doing."

It was most unfortunate that this supervisor, Barry Munson, was a political appointee and had no idea what HAL was or anything about HAL's capabilities. "They must mean 9,000 feet, not 90,000. Tell them to have a good time, and then call this Professor von whatever to let him know."

"But sir. . ."

"Now Frank, do as I say, please. I don't want to write any negative reports this shift."

Seething inside, Frank had no choice but to follow his supervisor's orders.

"Psst." A sound from the other operator caught his attention. The other operator pointed to a flashing red light that showed the video and audio tapes were recording. That meant everything from the time the supervisor came over was being recorded. Frank shook his head. He knew he was off the hook, but he was worried about Dan and Jolene.

"HAL from Tower."

"Tower, your signal. . .fading, but go ahead." Hal was getting out of range.

"HAL, message from the supervisor is 'Have a good time.' I'll phone the professor immediately. I suggest, I mean presume, you want to wait for his approval?"

"Negative. . .but th. . ."

"I do not copy, HAL. Where are you heading? I repeat, where are you heading?"

"Chanute Tower, you're. . .you still have. . .I think. . .try for the moon first. . .us luck."

The supervisor heard the transmission from HAL about going to the moon and laughed. Other people in the tower reacted very differently.

"Oh, my God!"

"HAL from Tower, HAL from Tower!" No answer.

Frank increased the power to his transmitter to emergency maximum and tried again.

"HAL from Chanute Tower, HAL from Chanute Tower, do you copy?" Still no answer.

"Frank!" the other operator said urgently, "They don't know about the military bases on the moon or the defenses there!"

Frank felt the blood drain from his face and he reached out, flipped up the protective cover over a red button and pushed the button.

"Okay, Charlie, they told us to have a good time. Jolene, what do you think about going to the moon?"

Jolene frowned. "Honestly, I don't have a good feeling about this at all, Dan. A trip like this should be planned out with backups and contingencies. This is not a flight for two rookies, even if we do have Charlie to help us."

"Jolene," Dan said quietly, "this may be the only time we ever have a chance to go to the moon. That is something I have wanted to do ever since I was a little boy! Are you suggesting we don't take advantage of this situation?"

Jolene knew Dan was at his most intense when his voice got quiet, and his speech slowed down. *I'd better have a good argument for this*, she thought. She reached over to hold Dan's hand.

"Ask yourself this, Dan. Would Professor von Gregheim, or General Lacey, or even President Ericsson approve if they knew what we intend to do without asking them?"

Dan stared bleakly at Jolene as he wrestled with that question in his mind. Finally, he took a deep breath, shook his head and said, "No, they probably wouldn't."

"Then maybe we should wait and go another time, don't you think Dan?" Jolene knew this was a time to be gentle and persuasive with Dan, not bossy or sarcastic. She stroked his hand with her thumb.

"Okay." Dan took another big breath and let it out slowly. "Okay. Darn it! Charlie, are you still there?"

"Thank you. I am still here." The computer replied.

"I guess we need to wait before flying into space. Will you show us and help us on another day?"

"Yes. You can help me not with my problem until you fly in space. I will help you another day."

"Thanks, Charlie. It's 'not help me,' instead of 'help me not.' You said you had a major problem. Can you tell us what your problem is and how you think we can help?"

"Yes Dan, Jolene, I will tell you." Charlie then told them about the tragedy on planet Saurian.

In the meantime, General Lacey 'SATed the president.

"Mr. President, do you want to disband the committee on the headache problem in HAL, or would you like them to examine the solution that Dan and Jolene discovered first?"

"What? What do you mean, the solution they discovered? They weren't part of that committee. How did this happen, Abe?"

"They weren't part of the committee, Mr. President, but they are flying in HAL every day. Jolene got cold, so the next time they flew, she wore earmuffs to keep her ears warm. Evidently, the earmuffs also blocked whatever sets off the headaches. Dan didn't have any, and he was starting to get headaches."

"Ear muffs! For cryin' out loud. Ear muffs?" The president was silent a couple of seconds, then asked, "How do they know it was the ear muffs? Did Dan try them too?"

General Lacey chuckled, "He wouldn't try them at first because Jolene's ear muffs were pink. Jolene had to threaten him with something before he would put them on. When he finally did, his headache started fading, and Jolene's started growing. They told Professor von Gregheim about it, loaned him a pair of ear muffs and took him flying, and he didn't get a headache either."

"Ear muffs! All right, get a couple of samples and send them here. Pink ear muffs, indeed!"

"Mr. President, Dan bought the same kind of muffs in black and navy blue. Neither of them has had a problem since, but they didn't want to say anything because they were afraid they would be taken off the HAL assignment and moved somewhere else."

"Not on your life, Abe! Those two are on that project for good! Sooner or later they will find out how to do things that no one else even thinks about! Mark my words on that one." The president chuckled, and then added, "Those are two very talented kids, Abe. The best way to handle them is to give them all the support we can, and let them experiment with HAL."

"Yes, sir, I agree with you about that."

"And pass this along, so they get it. "Well done," on solving the headache problem. Do you know what they are doing now, Abe?"

"Yes, sir. Professor von Gregheim has them working on flying at high altitudes. Sooner or later, we will need to see how HAL maneuvers in space."

"With those two, I wouldn't be surprised if it wasn't sooner than later," The president chuckled. "Thanks, Abe, and pass my congratulations on to Dan and Jolene."

How prophetic his words were, the president would learn only too soon.

CHAPTER 28
SCRAMBLE! SCRAMBLE!

Ever since the terrorist attacks on the United States in the early 21ˢᵗ century, every airbase with fighter jets had kept at least two planes on ready alert status. This status meant there were pilots in a waiting room already dressed, planes ready to launch immediately, and automatic priority clearance for takeoff. The planes were also armed with missiles and guns. These planes were always called the "scramble" flight.

When the tower operator Frank pressed the "scramble" button, Lieutenants Wood ("Woody") and Stevenson ("Cardshark") were halfway through their alert period. They immediately sprinted for the Ready Raptors and got them rolling before the canopies closed.

"Scramble 1 is rolling," Woody radioed.

"Scramble 2 is rolling," Cardshark echoed a second later.

Scramble aircraft do not stop on the threshold of the runway but turn and take off immediately. The tower quickly suspends all other takeoffs and warns all aircraft still in the air.

"Roger Scramble 1 and 2. Heading is 93 degrees, distance 320 miles, and opening, altitude ninety thousand feet; repeat, altitude angels ninety-zero. Go max, repeat, go max."

Scramble aircraft always took off on afterburner, but the "go max" signal told them to continue on burner (maximum thrust) until contact.

The target time for a scramble liftoff was 120 seconds. Woody and Cardshark beat that time easily, their wheels leaving the ground 93 seconds after the alert buzzer sounded.

"Chanute Tower, Scramble 1. Roger. We are go max, heading 93 degrees. Be advised, we can zoom-climb to about 85,000 feet. Nature of target and capabilities?"

"Scramble 1, Chanute Tower. Roger 85,000 feet. Target is unarmed spacecraft X64 HAL. Repeat, unarmed spacecraft X64 HAL. Do Not, repeat, Do Not show teeth. Message relay as follows: 'Missiles on moon. Stay at least 100 miles away from surface.' Repeat. 'Missiles on moon. Stay at least 100 miles away from surface.' Do you copy?"

"Tower, Scramble 1. Roger. Unarmed spacecraft. Show no teeth. Message relay only."

"Scramble 1, they are out of my radio range, and the last signal from HAL was, they found a tutorial program that will show them how to fly in space. They said they were headed for the moon, but they don't know about our defenses there. Copy?"

"Copy, tower. Those are the kids in the saucer that saved Bronco, correct?" Word of Bronco's rescue by Dan and Jolene in HAL had rapidly spread throughout the services. Egotistical as they are, fighter pilots were very loyal to each other, and saving Bronco's life was a debt they all felt they owed.

"Affirmative. You bird pilots owe them."

"Chanute Tower, Scramble 1. Roger, we owe them. We are passing 20,000 feet and will max out in two minutes. Message relay will begin then. Repeat, Message relay will begin then."

Dan and Jolene were stunned by what Charlie had told them. It was difficult to believe that a whole race, a whole world of intelligent beings could be extinct. It was also difficult to believe that Charlie was not a real live person, but rather a self-aware computer.

"Not the whole race, Charlie! Not all of them! Your people can't all be gone!" Jolene, in particular, was having difficulty accepting the extinction.

"There have been no live Creators on the planet Saurian in the last . . . 35.372 Earth years. My prime directive is to notify the Creators if intelligent life we found. The only Creators who might be alive are at the two colony planets or the expedition ship."

"Charlie," Dan asked, "With spaceships like HAL, why haven't you tried to contact the colony planets?" It was an obvious question.

"Nine ships have I sent. There is a magnetic field or something else that disrupts digital beings between Saurian and the colonies. All nine ships did I lose contact with and could not resume. I surmise that biologic people such as humans would not be affected. You could see if any Creators still life and I can do my Prime Objective and tell them we found you."

"'Live,' Charlie, not 'life.'" Dan corrected automatically. "And that's your major problem? The one you need our help to solve? Finding out if any of your Creators. . .are still alive?"

"Yes, and telling them about you race."

"Your race, Charlie, not you," Dan corrected absently.

Both humans fell silent, then looked at each other and blurted, "We've got to help Charlie with this!" at the same time. They smiled at their identical outburst, though neither one felt like smiling about the situation. They were still having difficulty accepting it.

"Jolene, this puts a whole different light on our going

to the moon today. It's not playtime. We need to see if it is feasible before we relay Charlie's request to our bosses."

"I hate to say it, but you're right, Dan. Charlie, how long will it take us to go to our moon and back, and will it be safe for us? Will we have enough air to last?"

"How long it takes depends on how much the shielding protects you. At maximum velocity, you will arrive at your moon in. . .38.412 minutes. At the slowest with no shielding, 3.755 days there and 3.755 days back."

"38 minutes! I can't believe that!" Jolene exclaimed.

"Charlie, can we increase speed and shielding as we go along, or must we start out and stay at the maximum?" Dan found the time easier to accept than Jolene.

"Gradual is the increase, and you can tailor made it to your own comfort."

"Tailor 'make,' Charlie, not 'made.' Jolene, we have permission. Are you ready to do this?"

Jolene frowned. "I'm still having trouble with that 'have a good time' message. I'm not sure why, but it still doesn't feel right. However," she sighed, "I'm ready. We need to do this."

"Good! You pilot HAL, and I'll command this time." This was a pattern Dan and Jolene had fallen into, and it worked very well for them.

"Okay, Charlie, how do we do this?"

"First, aim you viewscreen at the moon."

"Aim 'your' viewscreen, Charlie, not 'you' viewscreen."

"Thank you. Now increase power gradually."

"How do we turn on the shielding?"

"Automatic function when airlessness. . .space. . .is detected."

"Charlie, don't we have to calculate our course through space?"

"No. Your moon is too close."

"Too close?" Dan and Jolene exchanged glances.

"Yes. Too close. Did I not say it correctly?"

"No, Charlie, it sounds correct, but humans have never regarded our moon as being too close." *I guess we have a lot of unlearning to do*, Dan thought.

"Okay, Jolene, start easy, and then we'll see how we feel."

Just before Jolene started adding power, the regular radio burst into life.

"X64 HAL, X64 HAL, do you copy?"

Dan picked up the microphone. "X64 HAL copies. Go ahead."

"X64 HAL from Scramble Lead. Emergency message as follows. 'Missiles on moon. Stay at least 100 miles above surface.' Repeat, 'Missiles on moon. Stay at least 100 miles above surface.'"

"Copy, Scramble Lead. 'Missiles on moon, stay at least 100 miles from surface.'"

"Affirmative, HAL. Thanks for saving Bronco, Lieutenant. He's ugly, but he's ours. Be careful out there. Wish I was going!"

"Roger on the careful, Scramble lead, and thanks for the warning. HAL out."

Scramble 1 and 2 had zoomed to 87,000 feet, a new record for the Raptor. After they delivered the message, they pointed back towards Earth and began a long glide down to where they could restart their engines.

"It's a long way down, Lead. Think we'll have problems?"

"Negative, Two. We've done this before, just not so high. Keep separation, and we'll check in every minute or so." Woody looked around at the blackness of space. "A shame we can't stay, Two. It's beautiful up here."

"Roger the beautiful. It sure is, Lead."

Barry, the tower supervisor, was furious. First, there was that loud noise, and now, nobody would talk to him. It was a situation he could not tolerate.

"Frank, I don't know what you did, but you need to stop it and explain this instant exactly why you didn't do as I told you! I demand you talk to me, or you're going to be in big trouble!"

Frank, as primary operator, was directing not only scramble flight but tanker support vehicles for airborne refueling.

"SERGEANT!!" Frank shouted loud enough the Marines downstairs heard it. All three came racing up the stairs into the control part of the tower.

"Sergeant, we have scramble aircraft aloft, and this civilian is bothering me. Take him where I can't hear him."

The sergeant snapped a salute and replied, "Yes sir!" He looked at the two Marines and said, "Grab him."

Barry, already upset and scared by what was happening, protested loudly and tried to get the Marines to arrest Frank instead. The Marines didn't respond to his demands. Each grabbed one of his arms, and they carried him down the stairs. There the supervisor was placed in a small conference room with the two Marines guarding the door. The door shut and locked, and Barry just stared at it. Finally, he sat down.

Some hours later, that same conference door opened, and Congressman Melvin Montgomery entered the room.

"Mel! Boy, am I glad to see you!" Barry quickly got to his feet.

"Hello, Barry. Looks like you got yourself in a pickle here," the congressman replied mildly as he entered the room and sat down.

"It wouldn't have happened if that stupid air traffic controller had done what I told him! I gave him specific instructions, and he ignored me. Several times, he ignored me!"

"Okay, Barry, settle down. Settle down. Why don't you sit down and tell me everything that happened, and I'll see what I can do to fix it. We've worked through things before, and we can work through this. Now, can you tell me what happened?"

"I'll be glad to tell you what happened!"

Congressman Montgomery listened to Barry explain the events of the day as Barry understood them. The congressman soon realized, however, that Barry was placing the blame entirely on other people, and not accepting any blame himself.

When Barry was through, Congressman Montgomery replied, "Okay, I think I see a way we can solve this problem. I need to ask you some questions first." He said as he got out a small pad he always carried and got ready to take notes.

"Barry, when I appointed you to this position, I told you about the supervisory school. How many sessions of that school did you attend?"

"I thought there was only one session, Mel. I didn't know it was going to be longer than that. I had conflicts with other things I already had scheduled."

"So? How many sessions did you actually attend?" the congressman asked again.

"Just the one session, Mel, but I had to leave early to get to another appointment. After I missed several other sessions, it didn't seem worthwhile to go back."

"I see." Mel wrote in his notepad. "There is also a monthly meeting to review new developments, like new aircraft and their capabilities. Have you attended any of those?"

"I didn't know anything about those meetings, Mel."

Mel wrote some more.

"Okay, what about the Emergency Manual and Scramble Procedures. Did you read through that and become familiar with it?"

"I figured my job would be to supervise the other people, and I didn't really need to know that stuff, Mel."

The congressman finished making his notes.

"Okay, Barry. I need to talk with some other people, but I think I can solve this quickly. Let's play their game, and you stay here until I get back. I'll see you in a little bit." Congressman Montgomery got up and left the room.

"But. . .Mel?" Clearly, Barry was not satisfied with the response he got. He knew Mel would fix things for him, however, so he sat down to wait.

Congressman Montgomery talked to the controllers in the tower, then listened to the tape of the incident. "Unbelievable. Do you want to press charges, Captain?" the congressman asked Frank. "You obviously have grounds for several charges."

"Congressman, if you leave him here as supervisor, then yes, I will press charges. I'll have to! It's not fair to let him endanger the lives of other people and get away with it."

"And if he's not here, then what?"

"Sir, I'd gladly drop all charges just to get rid of him. We need a supervisor that knows what they are doing, sir. Not one who. . ." he quickly decided to say out loud what he was thinking, ". . .wants a paycheck but does absolutely nothing to earn it."

"Thank you, Captain. It's painfully obvious Barry is the wrong person for this job. By the way, did you say you lived close to the base here? Is that right?"

"Yes sir. When I'm not assigned somewhere else, my wife and I have our permanent home about two blocks from the main entrance." He chuckled. "It means I get called in a lot to work if someone is sick. Luckily, we have a batch of new controllers available next week. I'm finally scheduled to take two weeks' vacation."

"Good luck. Listen. . .I'll take care of this situation, and I must say I'm proud of the way you handled this incident. Any word on HAL yet?"

"No, sir. The Scramble flight delivered the emergency message about the defensive missiles on the moon and warned HAL to stay at least 100 miles away. The Scramble Flight Leader said HAL acknowledged the warning. They thought they had permission to go to the moon because of that. . .that person downstairs! I'm really angry about that, Congressman."

"Captain, I guarantee you will get along just fine with the new supervisor I appoint."

"Okay, Barry," the congressman said, sitting down again at the table. "I think I can solve this today."

"Is that controller going to lose his job?"

"Yes, he is, Barry, but not in the way you think. First, what do you know about Spacecraft X64 HAL?"

"Nothing, Mel. We don't do spacecraft here."

"Yes, you do. If you had gone to the update meetings, you would have known that. You would also have known that a spacecraft at 90,000 feet, not 9,000 feet, is not unusual. You would also have known that the spacecraft X64 HAL has the two youngest officers in the country as pilots."

"When they said they were going to the moon and you told them, 'have a good time,' they thought they had official permission for the trip. They are somewhere between Earth and the moon with the only working spacecraft this world has, Barry. All because you didn't do your job."

"But, Mel. . ."

"As of this moment, I accept your immediate resignation as supervisor. I hope that will be enough to convince the captain upstairs to drop the charges for your interference, but if something happens to those kids or HAL, I will be bringing additional charges myself."

"Resignation? But, Mel, you need a supervisor here, and. . ."

"I've got just the person in mind to take your place, Barry. He just doesn't know it yet." Congressman Montgomery got up to leave. "Oh, and by the way? When you see my sister, your wife? Tell her I said she married a bum."

Jolene had centered the moon in HAL's viewscreen and gradually increased the power throttle. There had not been any instrumentation put into HAL, so they could only fly by the seat of their pants. The GPS system and digital compass were good on Earth but not in space, so they had no help navigating from either instrument.

"Charlie, that radio message warned us to stay at least 100 miles above the surface. I guess there are missiles there to defend whatever we've built. How can we determine how far 100 miles is?"

"I can set the altitude if this communicator is still connected. Watch the panel above where the old controls were and see if anything changes."

"Okay, Charlie, I'm watching it." Dan looked where Charlie said, and suddenly there were many lights blinking on and off and changing color.

"Charlie, I see lights going on and off, and it seems some are changing color. Is that good news?"

"Yes, Dan. I can help you. I am still connected to the controls."

"Dan," Jolene interrupted, "look at the viewscreen."

Dan looked, and said, "The moon is definitely getting bigger. We must really be going fast. Can you guess the percent of power we are using, Jolene?"

"I'm about halfway on the throttle, Dan. Charlie, can you tell us how close we are to full power?"

"Yes, Jolene. Right now you are at. . .61.3526% of maximum, and will get to the moon in 2.1008 hours at this velocity."

"Charlie, should we keep increasing the power to see how it affects us?"

Charlie was silent for a few seconds and then answered, "I cannot tell how the shielding will affect or protect humans. The Creators never used more than 75% because it caused them pain. Are you willing to risk pain?"

Dan looked at Jolene, but asked Charlie, "Will the pain come suddenly or gradually?"

"On the Creators, it started at 74% and built rapidly to 78%."

"Thank you, Charlie. Jolene. . ." Dan started, but she interrupted him; "I think we should go for it, Dan. Charlie?" she asked, "can you monitor and tell us exactly what percent of power we are at? There's no instrument here I can read."

"My prime directive is to never hurt intelligent life. I will tell you, but you must . . . pledge . . . promise, to stop if you feel pain."

"'Promise' is correct, Charlie. We promise to tell you if we feel pain. Do you agree, Jolene?" Dan said formally.

"Yes, Dan, I agree."

"Okay, Jolene, then let's go power-up. Call it out for us,

please Charlie."

"Agreed. 61.3571, 61.3665, 61.3799, 61.3909. . ."

"Uh, Charlie?" Dan broke in, "could you just tell us whole numbers, like 61 percent, 62 percent, 63 and so on?"

"Yes, but Jolene asked if I would tell her exactly, Dan. Whole numbers would not be exactly."

Jolene giggled. "That's okay, Charlie. Humans approximate numbers by saying the word 'about.' We can increase the speed faster that way."

"Programmed."

"I'll watch the viewscreen, Jolene, and you watch the control."

"Dan, how about if I mark the percentage on the column here?"

"Great idea, Jolene. I should have thought of that one," Dan grumbled.

"Hey! I can have great ideas too!" Jolene complained out loud.

"Okay, let's start again. Charlie? Call it out please."

"Agreed. You are at about 61%."

"Go ahead, Jolene."

Jolene concentrated on moving the lever smoothly and continuously.

"62%." "63%." "64%."

Charlie continued calling out the power as Jolene continued to increase the throttle.

"71%." "73%."

"Let's stop when we hit 75%, Jolene."

"Agreed." Jolene didn't realize it, but she and Dan were beginning to imitate Charlie.

"We're getting close, Jolene. Get ready to stop if you feel anything."

"75%." Jolene made a mark and stopped moving the throttle.

"Dan, Jolene, do you feel pain yet?" Charlie asked.

"No, Charlie. I don't feel anything different. How about you, Dan?"

"I'm fine, Jolene. Let's keep going but stop every 5 percent."

Charlie started again. "76%, 77%, 78%, 79%, 80%. Dan? Jolene?"

"I'm fine, Charlie. How about you, Jolene?"

"Perfectly normal, Dan. Let me mark 80%. Should I keep going?"

"Yes, we should keep going." Dan decided.

"81%, 82%, 83%, 84%, 85%."

"Hold it at 85, Jolene. How are you feeling?"

"Dan, I don't feel any different than before we started."

"I don't either. Charlie, are you sure of your numbers?"

"Yes, Dan. Does it truly not cause you pain?"

"Neither one of us feel anything wrong, Charlie. Let's keep going."

They moved the throttle to 90 percent, then 95 percent and finally at full throttle.

"We must be different from your Creators, Charlie."

"Yes, Dan. Dan, Jolene, look out the viewscreen."

The moon was approaching at incredible speed. At least, that's what it looked like. They both knew they were the ones really moving, but it was hard to believe what they were seeing.

"Charlie, we won't go too close, will we?"

"No, Jolene. I calculated a course that will keep us 207.6352 miles above the surface."

"Mr. President, we have an urgent radio signal from

General Lacey." President Ericsson was in Marine One, the floater used to ferry him to and from local places.

"Okay, give me the headphones." The president took them from the flight sergeant.

"Abe, what's wrong?"

"Mr. President, HAL with Dan and Jolene aboard, is heading to the moon."

"What did you say? Heading to the moon? You mean. . .our moon? THE moon?"

"Yes, sir."

"HOW IN THE BLUE BLAZES DID THAT HAPPEN?" the president yelled angrily.

"From what I have pieced together, they were doing high altitude experiments."

"Yes, I know that! You already told me that."

"Yes, sir. They radioed Chanute Tower about some kind of tutorial program they discovered on HAL. They asked the Tower to notify von Gregheim that they were going to the moon."

"And the Tower gave them permission? You've got to be kidding!"

"Evidently the tower supervisor laughed at the idea and told them to have a good time. When the air traffic controllers tried to intervene, he refused to listen to them."

"Good Lord! Abe, I just realized something. Dan and Jolene probably don't know about our military bases on the moon or the defenses we have there!"

"Yes, sir. The ATC on duty scrambled two Raptors. The Raptors zoomed to 87,000 feet and relayed the message 'Missiles on moon. Stay 100 miles from surface.' Both Raptor pilots confirm that Dan received, acknowledged and repeated the message back to them."

"Thank heavens for that! At least somebody was on the ball."

"Yes, sir."

"Okay, Abe. Warn our bases on the moon. Make sure they don't shoot at HAL."

"Yes, sir."

"And Abe? Make sure somebody tells that idiot supervisor that if anything happens to Dan or Jolene or HAL, I will personally have a session with him with my bare hands!"

CHAPTER 29
MAN IN THE MOON

The United States in conjunction with the United Nations had established a large scientific research base on the moon. It was named Galileo in honor of the famous astronomer Galileo Galilei. There were other bases on the moon doing research of a military nature, and these were treated as military posts and defended by various means. One of the weaknesses of the military mindset, however, was the strict adherence to following an identical pattern or structure even when that pattern makes no sense.

As in any military base, security was an issue taken seriously. A perimeter was established just like bases on Earth even though there is no life on the moon. The bases also had the expected air defenses. The foolishness of guards "walking" a perimeter on the airless moon finally gave way to a single observation tower in the center of the base for both air and ground defense. From this observation point, the "guard" could see the entire perimeter and observe all space traffic.

Like guard duties all over the earth, guard duty on the moon soon became a chore, not a pleasure. There was no ground traffic except the base dune buggies going to the antenna array and back. Space traffic was also sparse, and the bi-weekly supply vessel was about the only vehicle to visit.

As is usual when highly trained technical people are given boring, menial and repetitive tasks, the guards soon found a way to automate their watch. Simple motion detectors at opposite ends of the perimeter coupled with closed circuit viewscreens took care of ground movement, and the search radar was connected to a buzzer alarm that went off anytime a moving object was in range. This freed the guards for more serious work, like using the Internet, writing e-mails home, and doing 'simulated air defenses' (i.e. Games) on the computer.

One very real danger was meteors. Tyco base had already had one meteor near collision, and the base survived only because of the automatic response of its missiles. Meteors could be distinguished from manned vehicles, however, because of their high velocity. At least, the two could be distinguished until HAL visited the moon.

The Copernicus Communications Center had a bell that rang when an incoming message was received. It rang one time for routine messages, two times for important messages and continuously for the highest priority.

Master Sergeant Sharokina Pazano was on duty when the bell sounded and kept sounding. She read the priority, "Operational Immediate," and immediately pushed the alarm for the duty officer. She then waited until the entire message had printed once and tore it off the printer. "Operational Immediate" was the highest priority, so she picked up the phone and dialed the base commander's 'SAT.

He answered within ten seconds.

"Kirk here, what's up?"

"Sir, you have an 'Operational Immediate' message. Shall I read it, or do you want to come here?"

"Read it, Sharky."

"Yes sir. 'Operational Immediate. Friendly ultra-high speed manned X64 en route to the moon. Immediately disarm all missile and meteor defenses until it passes.' It's signed 'By order of the president.'"

"Ultra-high speed, Sharky?"

"Yes sir. 'Friendly ultra-high speed manned X64' is what it reads.

"Call the guard tower. Order them to disarm all missiles and lasers immediately, by my order. Read them the message, and tell them I'll be en route to confirm, but shut down immediately. Specifically, tell them not to wait until I arrive!"

"Yes sir."

As Sgt. Pazano was dialing, the meteor alarm went off in the guard tower. Both operators noted the direction and speed of the meteor.

"Man, that things going fast! It's not going to impact anywhere near here, Lieutenant. Should we override the firing system?"

The lieutenant was thinking about the cost of each missile, and said, "I think the lasers would be a better, or at least a cheaper, choice."

"I've never seen the lasers fire before, Lieutenant. Can we get away with it? I mean, how much does it cost to fire them?"

"Only a couple of bucks worth of electricity every second. Why don't we. . ."

The communicator started ringing.

". . .get the laser ready to fire. I'll answer the 'SAT, and you ready the laser." He went to answer the 'SAT.

"Guard Post, Lt. Jones speaking." He answered the 'SAT.

"Lt. Jones, Sgt. Pazano in Communications. I have an "Operational Immediate" message, sir. "'Friendly ultra-high speed manned X64 en route to the moon. Immediately disarm all missile and meteor defenses until it passes.' It's signed, 'By order of the president.' Colonel Kirk ordered me to read it to you and confirm our weapons are safe. He's on the way to verify personally, but he said to shut everything down immediately."

"Holly Molly, Sergeant! Stand by." The lieutenant turned and shouted to his guard sergeant. "Bruce! Shut off the missile detector and laser immediately! That 'meteor' might be a spaceship!" He picked up the 'SAT again. "It's a good thing you called right now. We were just about to fire the laser at an extremely fast meteor. That might be what we have on the meteor screen."

While they were talking, Colonel Kirk entered the Guard Tower.

"Are we safe, Lieutenant? All weapon systems down?"

"Yes sir, but it was close. We were just about to fire the lasers at an extremely fast meteor. I'll bet any amount of money it's not a meteor, but that spacecraft."

"I'm glad I had communications call you directly with the message, then! You would have checked with me before you fired anything, right Lieutenant?"

"Oh absolutely, Colonel. Unless it is heading directly for us, there's no way we would have wasted several bucks worth of electricity without your approval, sir." The Lieutenant said this with a straight face, but there was a twinkle in his eye.

"Hmmmm, I'll just bet you wouldn't! I'm getting too close to retirement to let some wet behind the ear Lieutenant blow my career out of the water!"

"Yes sir."

"By the way, Jones, when the Inspector General came through here last week, did they find the computer games your people are using to stay awake during their duty shifts?

They didn't say anything to me about it."

"Sir, I showed them everything we have on the computer system as required."

"Why do I think that's not the truth, the whole truth, and nothing but the truth, Lieutenant?"

"I don't know, sir."

"How did you hide them, Jones? I'm not mad about it, but I'm really curious how you managed to hide them."

"Yes sir. All that software is saved in a folder marked "Defensive Contingency Simulations." That particular folder is under seven other folders. The IG people only opened three folders deep, but they did examine all the folder names."

"Hmmm. Pretty sneaky, Jones, but well done. I know how hard it is staying awake when nothing is happening. Keep up the good work, son, and maybe I'll get to retire before you blow up something important!"

"Yes sir," the lieutenant said with a grin.

Congressman Mel Montgomery slowly put the 'SAT down. The message relayed to him by General Lacey from the president was pretty clear. He thought about Barry, waiting downstairs. *That rotten, no-good. . .!* he broke his thoughts off. *I haven't told my sister that jerk she married is cheating on her as well as not doing his job. This is the last straw!*

Mel went slowly down the stairs until he stood outside the door guarded by Marines. He spoke quietly to the Marines.

"Gentlemen, I've just spoken with General Lacey. He said, make sure this prisoner doesn't escape since the president might want to deal with him. . .personally."

The Marines exchanged glances. "Sir. Yes sir!" They both knew very well what "deal with him personally" meant when the president said it. They were very much aware of the president's background in the military.

Mel pushed open the door, entered, and sat at the table. He ignored Barry's greetings and pleadings to get him out of here and stared at Barry for several seconds until Barry was quiet. After a few moments, the congressman began speaking slowly.

"Barry, what do you know about President Ericsson?"

"What? President Ericsson? I don't know. He got elected president. What else am I supposed to know about him?"

"What did he do before he was president, Barry?" the congressman asked quietly.

"I don't know. What a minute! Wasn't he in the military, doing something? I remember reading something about behind-the-enemy-lines interrogation, right?"

"Very good, Barry. He was in the Service doing something very dangerous, got wounded in the War, and then became president. I'm told he is a master at physical and psychological interrogation, Barry. An absolute master." Mel got up and started towards the door.

"Mel? Wait a minute! Mel? What does any of that have to do with me? And when are you getting me out of here?"

The congressman paused, turned, and smiled at Barry. "I'm not getting you out of here, Barry. As to what that has to do with you, the president is extremely angry about your failure today. Extremely angry. He is so angry in fact, he said if anything bad happens to those kids or our only spacecraft because of your stupidity, he's going to come and 'talk' to you, personally."

"Talk to me? Like he 'talked' to those other people I read about?" Barry almost screamed.

"Goodbye, Barry. Maybe, just maybe, I won't ever see you again. . .alive or in one piece." As the door closed behind the congressman, he heard Barry's body hit the floor. Barry had fainted.

Colonel Kirk made his way into the Communications Center. Sgt. Pazano was watching the passage of what she believed to be the friendly spacecraft from Earth.

"Sharky, any idea who they are or what it is?"

"Yes sir. I believe it is X64 HAL, the flying saucer the AI's captured after two high school kids disabled it. I guess they got it working again, Colonel."

"Hmmmm. Have you tried calling them?"

"No sir. Do you want me to try?"

"Why not? I've never spoken to a flying saucer before."

The sergeant switched to the universal band frequency used by most space traveling craft and increased the power of her transmitter. "X64 HAL from Copernicus Base, X64 HAL from Copernicus Base, do you copy?"

There was a brief wait, then, "Copernicus Base from X64 HAL. Roger. We copy."

"HAL from C-Base, Welcome to the moon. Who do you have on board, and how long did it take you to get to the moon from Earth?"

"C-Base from HAL. Thanks! This is Lt. Jackson commanding and Lt. Fisher is piloting. If we had gone full throttle, it would have taken 38 minutes from Earth to the moon, 5 minutes around the moon, and 38 minutes back to Earth. We are still learning about this craft, so we didn't use full throttle except for a short run. Our actual time was about 90 minutes one way."

Colonel Kirk looked at the sergeant, "I think my ears are going bad, Sharky. I thought he said 38 minutes from Earth to the moon. What did you hear?"

"Colonel, that's exactly what I heard. 38 minutes. Let me confirm."

"Copy HAL, would you confirm 38 minutes from Earth to moon?"

"C-Base, that's affirmative for full throttle. We're going to try it on the way back to see if Charlie is right about the time." The sound was fading due to HAL's speed around the moon.

"HAL from C-Base. Good luck. Make sure your brakes are working before you hit the Earth's atmosphere."

"C-Ba. . .om HAL. Copy the. . .. Next time. . .try to. . .and show. . .inside of HAL. . ."

"They're out of range, Colonel. Do you want to reply to the president?"

Colonel Kirk thought about that and then replied, "Yes, let's do that. Sharky, Make it an 'Immediate Attention,' for President Ericsson. 'HAL with Dan, Jolene and Charlie aboard passed safely by the moon. Estimated return time at full throttle is 38 minutes. Can we borrow HAL and come home for Christmas?' Put it over my signature, Sergeant."

"Yes sir. Colonel, do you really think we could get home at Christmas? 38 minutes is a whole lot faster than the 5 days it takes us now."

"Let's wait and see. When they get our message, I guarantee the president will be happy enough to give us all leave home for Christmas!"

The president was aboard Air Force One, the traditional mode of travel for presidents since the mid-20th Century. He was scheduled for a speech at the McDonnell-Douglas Plant in St. Louis and then planned on inspecting the site where the other saucers were being built.

"Mr. President, we have a reply to your 'Operational Immediate' to the moon."

"It's probably confirmation they got it, and they already

want to know how long to leave the defenses off," the president said dryly.

"Actually, no sir. It's better news than that." The lieutenant handed the hard copy to the president.

President Ericsson read the message in growing disbelief. "Safely passed the moon? Already? And who is this Charlie? Wait a minute, wait a minute! They estimate 38 minutes from the moon back to Earth? 38 minutes? I can't believe this!" He raised his voice and shouted. "Abe? Abe! Get in here and talk to me!"

General Abraham Lacey came running into the president's Air Force One office. "Here, Mr. President. I'm here."

"Read this," the president said gruffly, handing him the message form, "and tell me my eyes are not reading it correctly. 38 minutes indeed!"

General Lacey read the message form, then read it again.

"It's signed by Colonel Kirk, sir. The part about 'home for Christmas' is one of his trademark questions, Mr. President. Unless they have the time wrong, I have to believe it is an accurate message." Abe looked up at the president. "If I remember correctly, sir, you did predict Dan and Jolene would maneuver in space sooner than later? Did you have any idea they were going to do something like this?"

"No, Abe," the president said glumly. "What I meant was, they're too young to appreciate the dangers in space. Wait a minute. If that 38 minutes is correct, they'll be arriving back here pretty soon, right?"

"Yes sir. Should I get the communications officer for you?" Abe was reading his president's mind and guessed correctly the reason for his question.

"Yeah, Abe. If we can call HAL from here, let's have them land at St. Louis at the plant. Think they can find it?"

"I'm sure we can talk them in by landmarks, Mr. President. I mean, the Gulf of Mexico is pretty distinctive, and the Mississippi River would be impossible to miss."

"Okay, go get the COM people, Abe."

Before General Lacey could leave, the communications officer appeared at the door. "Did you need me, Mr. President?"

"Yes, Major. Can we contact spacecraft HAL from this plane? I want them to not land at their base but come to St. Louis instead."

"We have full capability from here, Mr. President. Should I send them your message?"

"Better do it quickly, son," the president said dryly. "Evidently they set a new speed record for here to the moon and back."

"X64 HAL from Air Force One. X64 HAL from Air Force One. Do you copy? Over." They waited a short time for an answer, then tried again.

"X64 HAL from Air Force One. X64 HAL from Air Force One. Do you copy? Over." The reply came as a surprise.

"Air Force One, Standby. We've got problems."

The communications operators looked at each other. Stand by? Nobody ever told them to standby. This was Air Force One, the president's own plane. Standby? They decided to wait rather than tell the president someone told him he had to wait.

As soon as they cleared the moon and had the earth in view, Dan and Jolene decided to try full throttle for the return trip. According to Charlie, traditional navigation was not necessary if the two bodies were in sight of each other.

Jolene went to full throttle much quicker this time

than she had the first, and the results of her quickness were terrifying.

Dan and Jolene both experienced queasy stomachs and distortion in their vision. They both had instant earaches, and both cried out in pain.

"Reduce the speed! Reduce the speed, Jolene!" Charlie said louder than normal.

"Oh, my ears!" Jolene cried out as she pressed her hands over the earmuffs. Dan was doing the same, only he took one hand off and pulled the throttle back slowly. About the time he was back to 75%, the pain in his ears subsided although his stomach still felt like it was rolling.

"Jolene?" Dan asked, "Are you okay?" Jolene still had her hands pressed tightly over her ears, and she was rocking forward and backward in her seat, obviously in pain.

"Reduce the speed to 50%, Dan," Charlie said. Dan pulled the throttle back until it was about where Jolene had marked 50%.

"Are you feeling pain?" Charlie asked.

"Yes, Charlie, yes I did! Boy, did I feel pain! I'm better now, Charlie, but my eyes still hurt, and my ears really hurt, and I thought I was going to throw up for a while."

"Throw up? Is that like toss up? What does that mean, Dan?" Charlie, being a computer, had no idea what Dan meant.

"Charlie, humans eat food which powers our bodies. When we eat something bad or have a bad physical experience, our stomach gets rid of whatever is inside. We call it, throwing up." Dan smiled grimly. "It's a very bad feeling, and a nasty experience, Charlie. Be glad you're made of metal and can't do that." He looked at Jolene. She had not said anything yet.

"Jolene, talk to me. Tell me you are all right."

Jolene still didn't say anything but shook her head 'yes' that she was okay.

"Is it your stomach?" Dan asked. Again, she shook her head 'yes.'

"X64 HAL from Air Force One. X64 HAL from Air Force One. Do you copy? Over."

"Charlie, can you suggest anything to help?"

"No, Dan. I am not familiar enough with humans except to suggest a reduction in speed. Are you in pain now, Dan?"

"Not now, Charlie, but it sure hurt for a time. Jolene, can you talk yet?"

"X64 HAL from Air Force One. X64 HAL from Air Force One. Do you copy? Over."

"Dan, people are calling you."

"Rats! They can wait. I want to make sure Jolene is okay, first."

"Dan, something you should tell them."

"Okay, Charlie. I'll tell them to wait." Dan picked up the microphone.

"Air Force One, Standby. We've got problems," Dan radioed.

Jolene straightened up for the first time, took a deep breath and let it out slowly. "Wow. I never want to feel like that again!"

"Are you going to be okay? Do you want me to pilot for a while?"

"I think I'm okay now, Dan, but now I know what Charlie meant when he said his Creators never went above 75%. Charlie, why did that happen this time, when the first time nothing happened at all?"

"I am not sure, Jolene. It may be you did it slowly the first time, and you did it quickly this time. Maybe the shielding takes time to adjust to the drive, or it did not stay synchronized to the drive."

"How close are we to Earth, Charlie? I've lost track of where we are."

"At this speed, 52.861%, you will reach Earth in 74.445 minutes."

"Charlie, would you please. . .

"Sorry, Dan. At ABOUT 53% you will reach Earth in ABOUT 74 minutes."

Dan smiled for the first time since feeling sick.

"That's better, Charlie. Thanks."

"Dan, didn't we get a radio call from someone?"

"Yeah, we did, Jolene. It was Air Force One. I think that's the president's plane, and I told them to wait."

"The president's plane? You kept the president waiting because I was sick? Dan, you're an idiot! Call them now, and I mean right now!"

Relieved that Jolene was feeling good enough to yell at him, Dan picked up the microphone.

"Air Force One from HAL. Air Force One from HAL. Do you copy?"

The communications people finally had to tell the president they were told to wait because HAL had a problem. Using language he knew better than to use in public, the president got up and went to the radio console.

"I told that so-and-so if anything happened to Dan, Jolene or HAL, I'd deal with him personally! Any word yet?"

"No, Mr. President. Should we try again?"

President Ericsson was thinking about this when Dan's call came in.

"Air Force One from HAL. Air Force One from HAL. Do you copy?"

"HAL from Air Force One. We copy. What is your status?"

"Air Force One from HAL. We're okay now, but it was touch and go for a while. We now know better than to go to full power too quickly. Both Jolene and I experienced intense ear pain, eye pain and we almost lost our cookies."

The president was listening in, and said, "Ask them if Charlie is okay, but don't let them know I asked."

"Yes sir."

"HAL from AF One. Is Charlie okay as well? Did he have the same problems you did?"

Jolene instantly said, "Don't answer that, Dan! How do they know about Charlie? I thought we weren't going to say anything about him yet?"

"We definitely don't want to say anything about Charlie until we know more about how they will react."

Jolene thought about that. "Okay, Dan. Let's not answer about Charlie."

"What should I say, then?" Dan wasn't sure at all how to answer this.

"Just tell them we're okay and then ask for permission to land at Chanute."

"AF One, HAL. We're all okay. Permission to go back and land at Chanute?"

President Ericsson and General Lacey exchanged looks, and the president said, "They're hiding something, Abe. It took them too long to answer. Who is Charlie, and why are they hiding him?"

"They must have a reason, Mr. President. Who in the world could they have smuggled aboard?" He told the radio operator, "Ask them again if Charlie had the same problems they did. Try to make it sound like we already know who Charlie is."

"Yes sir."

"HAL, AF One. We're glad your symptoms are better. Since Charlie is a different age, did he have an easier time or a worse time? I know the older pilots got severe headaches in HAL. How did Charlie do?"

"Dan, they think Charlie is a real person! Maybe we'd better confess that he is the name we gave the tutorial."

"That sounds like a good way out of this. We still don't want them to know what Charlie really is, do we?"

"No, we don't Dan. We also want to make sure they will let us help Charlie find his Creators, and not say no to his request."

"Absolutely. Charlie, do you understand about lying?"

"No, Dan. What is lying?"

"It is when a person, or a computer, says a deliberate untruth."

"Why would a person ever do that? I cannot think of a reason a computer would do that." Charlie asked.

"Charlie, if we tell them who you are, they may never let us go find your Creators. If we don't tell them, if we lie about you, then we can probably help you with your problem. Do you understand?"

"Dan, I. . .I am having trouble with the concept."

"Okay, Charlie, let's make it simple. Until I tell you it is all right, don't speak to anyone except Jolene or me. Is that easy enough?"

"Yes, Dan. Programmed."

"Call them back, Dan. Hurry."

"AF One from HAL. Jolene and I are the only two people in HAL. We started calling the tutorial program Charlie to make it seem friendlier."

"Abe, they are definitely hiding something. That answer

took too long and sounds too easy. Like they just made it up."

"I agree, Mr. President, but what can we do about it?" Clearly, General Lacey was concerned.

The president motioned to the communications officer. "Give me the mike, son. I didn't get to be president without learning how to fudge a little myself." He spoke into the microphone.

"Dan, Jolene? This is President Ericsson. Boy, am I glad you're both okay, but we were worried about you. I need a favor, kids. Can you help me?"

Dan and Jolene looked at each other. The president! They hadn't seen him since the awards ceremony.

"Yes sir, Mr. President," Dan answered immediately. "We'll be glad to help you. What can we do?"

"I'm giving a speech in about a half hour in St. Louis. Lambert International Airport is west and a little north of the Gateway Arch in downtown St. Louis. Can you find the airport, and then land on the north side of the McDonnell-Douglas plant? That's where they are making replicas of the. . .of HAL, and that's where I'm giving my speech. It would really be impressive for me to tell them you had just come back from the moon. Very impressive indeed!"

Glad they didn't have to explain any more about Charlie, Jolene nodded her head, and Dan told the president they would meet him there.

"Thanks, Dan, Jolene. I'll see you in a little while. Air Force One Out, Over, whatever it is I'm supposed to say!" The president was hamming it up a little to put the kids at ease.

General Lacey looked the president in awe! "My word, Mr. President, sir! What a devious, sneaky, underhanded way of getting what you want! My compliments on your storytelling ability."

The president smiled and stroked his chin. "Yes, I was pretty devious, wasn't I? Once they are on the ground, you and I will have a little chat with them and find out exactly what is going on."

"Yes sir. I must confess I'm looking forward to that chat."

"So am I, Abe," the president said rubbing his hands together. "So Am I."

CHAPTER 30
MEET ME IN ST. LOUIE

Unsuspectingly, Jolene navigated HAL safely through the atmosphere and into the Northern Hemisphere. For some reason, HAL didn't heat up as badly as traditional satellites and ships coming back to Earth. Dan asked Charlie why that was.

"Dan, I can only guess based on when the Creators used rockets instead of the anti-gravity drive. The rockets had to use the atmosphere braking to slow down, while HAL can slow down without the atmosphere. The force field shield is also a very good reason why there is very little heating."

Jolene found the Gulf of Mexico, then Lake Michigan, and that gave her a very good idea where St. Louis was. As they were coming down through 300,000 feet, Jolene had a thought.

"Dan, check to make sure our IFF is still on, would you?"

Dan looked over at the box and confirmed it was still operating. He told Jolene it was still on.

"Thanks, Dan. I'd hate to get blown up because we forgot to turn it on."

Jolene followed the Mississippi River upstream until she saw where the Ohio River merged near Cairo, Illinois. From there it was a short flight north to St. Louis, which was just south of where the Missouri and Illinois Rivers entered the Mississippi.

"Dan, how do we ask for permission to land?"

"It's Lambert International Airport, Jolene. Let me try to call them."

"Lambert International Tower, from spacecraft X64-HAL. Lambert International Tower from spacecraft X64-HAL. Do you copy? Over."

Nothing.

Dan called again with no results.

"I guess they're not on this frequency."

"Did you change from the moon frequency, Dan?"

"Oh. Uh. . .no, I didn't," he admitted sheepishly. "Let me try this one.

"Lambert International Tower from spacecraft X64-HAL. Do you copy? Over."

In the Tower, the supervisor heard the unusual call and told the regular ATC's he'd take this one.

"Unknown aircraft from Lambert Tower. Identify again, please."

"Lambert Tower, we are a USSF spacecraft designated X64-HAL. President Ericsson has directed us to land outside the McDonnell-Douglas area where he is giving a speech today. Request permission to descend and land."

All the ATC's were listening to this transmission, and one told the supervisor, "I don't show any unknowns on my radar."

"X64-HAL, we do not have you on the radar. State your direction of flight and altitude."

"Lambert Tower, we are northbound up the Mississippi River from the Gulf of Mexico, descending through about 200,000 feet at this time and passing over the Ohio-

Mississippi River junction. Estimated Time of Arrival to Lambert is about 12 minutes."

"Twelve minutes!"

"Is he kidding?"

"How high did he say?" Comments were flying fast and furious between the tower personnel.

"Uh, X64-HAL, where are you coming from? We have heavy traffic today, and I don't know what your landing requirements are. I take it you are a powered craft instead of a glider like the space shuttle?"

"Tower, that's affirmative. We are still learning how to fly this spacecraft, so we took HAL around the moon to check it out. Tower, HAL has hover capabilities. Why don't we stay at about 60,000 feet or so, and then drop straight down at the plant?"

There was dead silence in the tower after the 'around the moon' comment.

Clearly, the Tower supervisor wasn't sure about giving approval for Dan's suggestion, but he had to admit it was the least disruptive path on a busy day.

"X64-HAL, affirmative on the sixty thousand and drop. Do you have IFF?"

"Tower, affirmative. Mode 3 is set at 10, and Mode 4 is turned on."

It wasn't in the rulebook, but this supervisor knew when to go outside the box.

"X64-HAL, Tower clears you for, uh, the unusual approach to the McDonnell-Douglas plant." *Good luck, buddy. I hope you can pull it off!* The supervisor thought.

"Thanks, Lambert Tower. We'll watch out for other traffic."

In the tower, one of the air traffic controllers asked the

supervisor, "How in the world are you going to write this one up? I've never heard of anything remotely like it!"

The supervisor shook his head, agreeing with the ATC. "Tomorrow. After I have several stiff drinks tonight, I'll decide how to write it tomorrow."

Meanwhile, back at the Chanute Tower. . .

"Captain, I've accepted Barry's resignation. The question is, do you still want to press charges?"

"What I'd like to do, and what I should do, are two different things, Congressman," Frank said. "No sir, I won't press charges since you took him out of here, but Congressman, you've got to get us someone who knows what goes on in a tower and can actually help us!"

"You mean, someone that has actually worked in a control tower before?"

"Yes, sir. Someone with experience in a control tower. Someone who can make the right decisions when those decisions are difficult, and people's lives are on the line."

"Should they be in the military, do you suppose?" the congressman asked innocently.

"Sir, that would be a huge advantage."

"I understand the salary for a supervisor is pretty substantial, isn't it Captain?"

"Congressman, it's at least twice what we make as ATC's. I would definitely call that substantial."

"I would too, Captain. Thank you for all your help. I take it you can operate without a supervisor for a day or two?"

"Actually. . .and honestly. . .we've been without a real supervisor for several months, Congressman. I think we can manage a little longer."

"Okay. By the way, did you say you finally get to take a vacation, and it's scheduled the next two weeks?"

"Yes sir. One more day here at work, and I have two weeks off. My wife and I are just planning to stay home and relax instead of traveling anywhere or visiting anyone. I'm looking forward to it."

At the end of the shift the next day, the base commander came to talk to Frank.

"Frank, I have some good news for you, and I have some bad news. Which do you want first?"

"Give me the bad news first, sir. That way I can leave with the good news fresh in my mind."

"You only get one week of vacation right now."

Frank just stared at him. "Don't tell me. Somebody scheduled me for something else, right?"

"Yep."

He took a deep breath. "I don't suppose I can get out of it, can I?"

"Nope."

"Okay," Frank said with a sigh, "What's the good news?"

"The good news is, you are scheduled to take the one-week long Tower Supervisor Introductory Class instead of your second week of vacation."

Frank looked at the base commander in disbelief.

"What?" he stammered. "You can't be serious!"

"Oh, yes I am, Frank. Evidently, you impressed the heck out of the congressman with your professional attitude and knowledge, and since you live in his District, he chose you to be the next supervisor. Let's see now, a 100% increase in pay for the same hours, plus supervisors get six weeks' vacation a year, not just two. Congratulations, Frank. Welcome to your first supervisory position!" The base commander offered his hand in congratulations.

Stunned, Frank just stared at him, then shook the

commander's hand.

"Supervisor?" he asked.

"Supervisor Frank. My guess is, you will make the best supervisor this base has ever had. No one, but no one has the knowledge you have, Frank. Again, Congratulations."

Relations aboard HAL were getting a little heated to say the least. Jolene was clearly not pleased that Dan had negotiated a landing with a maneuver she had never done before.

"Nice of you to ask, you big lug! How do you know I can do that? 'Stay at 60,000 feet then drop straight down!' I've never done that before! What if I can't do it, Dan? Then what?"

"Jolene, this is a training exercise. If you can't do it, and I bet you can, we'll think of something else. Besides, we promised President Ericsson we'd be there."

"'I bet you can' is a fat lot of help, Dan! Charlie, do you understand what we need to do?"

"Yes, Jolene, I understand you need to go to a certain point at 60,000 feet, then descend straight down to the ground."

"Well? Can we do that?"

"Yes, Jolene, HAL is capable of that. Would you like me to help you?"

Jolene sighed and calmed down at Charlie's offer.

"Yes, Charlie, please. I would very much like you to help me. What do I need to do first?"

"First, keep descending to 60,000 feet. Are you on course to get above your landing place?"

"Yes."

"Then continue."

Jolene followed the instructions, and eight minutes later

announced they were at about 60,000 feet and she thought they were above the aircraft plant.

"Second, stop your forward motion."

Jolene did that. Of course, HAL started dropping immediately.

"Charlie, how do I stop it before we get to the ground?"

"Use the anti-gravity hover control mounted on the. . ."

"Mounted where Charlie?" she asked when Charlie stopped talking.

"Jolene, your technicians removed it when they put in the new controls."

"Oh Great! So, what do we do, Charlie? We're falling!"

"We need to have your technicians put the controls back into HAL."

"That's fine, Charlie, as long as we live long enough to get back on the ground! Charlie, what can I do now without those controls?"

"I'm exploring the possibilities, Jolene."

"Well, explore them quickly, Chuck. The ground's coming up fast!"

"Jolene," Dan said quickly, "remember when we caught the pod? You need to go forward as well as down. That'll give us control back."

"Jolene, Dan is correct. As long as you are moving forward or backward, the hover function will work automatically."

"Yeah, but it also takes us out of our approved flight path. 'Straight down, Jolene! You can do it, Jolene'! Dan, if we get out of this, I'm going to use you like a rug under my heels! I'm. . ." Jolene was interrupted by the radio.

"X64-HAL from Lambert Tower!"

"Go ahead Tower," Dan replied.

"X64-HAL, your rate of descent is setting off our alarms!

Could you slow your rate of decent?"

"Tower, when they took the original controls out of HAL, they took out what we need to slow down. Actually, we are not quite in control at this time. May we have permission to move out of our straight down flight path?"

"HAL, are you declaring an emergency?" came the quick reply.

"Negative, Tower, not just yet. If we can spiral down, I think we'll be okay. Do we have permission to try?"

"HAL, you have permission to move out of your flight path. Be advised, we are holding all outgoing flights until you land." The ATC's, listening as usual to HAL's traffic, started holding the flights ready to takeoff.

"Lambert Tower to all incoming flights. Lambert is declaring an Advisory for an aircraft. . .I mean spacecraft, in difficulty. Angle your approach radars to maximum height, and watch out from above."

"Okay, Jolene, see if you can slow our descent."

Jolene started the forward drive and then turned left sharply to stay in a spiral. The more the forward speed, the more control and a slower rate of descent.

"HAL from Tower. Status?"

"Tower, I think we'll be slow enough for safety by the time we get to the ground. What is the exact altitude at Lambert?"

The ATC's exchanged glances. *How can they fly without the proper charts,* they thought?

"HAL from Tower. Altitude is 425 feet above sea level."

"Roger 425 feet, Tower."

"HAL from Tower, your rate of descent is still too high."

"Tower, we are beginning to slow down as we spiral around the flight path."

"HAL, if a straight-line descent would be better, try due

west, 270 degrees. You're clear for about 17 miles that way."

"Roger, Tower. We'll try that." You heard him, Jolene. Straighten out to due west."

"That would be easier if we had a usable compass in HAL, Dan! Charlie, can you help us with compass readings?"

"Yes, Jolene. Straighten out when I say, 'Straighten out.'"

"Charlie, just say 'now' instead of straighten out. It's quicker."

"Programmed. Now, Jolene."

As Jolene straightened out, the spacecraft became responsive again, and they were able to both slow the descent and point the direction they were going.

"Lambert Tower, HAL. We are in full control again. Thank you for your assistance, and if we come back, we'll try to do things the normal way."

"HAL from Lambert Tower. You are welcome. Stop in some time when we can see your ship."

"Wilco, Tower. Tower, we see a large gathering outside a plant. Is that where the president is?"

"HAL, for security reasons, I can't confirm that."

"Wilco, Tower."

"Jolene, go ahead and set HAL down behind the platform."

Jolene did as she was asked, and finally, HAL was safe back on the ground.

Or was it?

Of course, the communications people on Air Force One had monitored all the radio traffic between HAL and the Tower and stopped just short of notifying the president when Dan didn't declare an emergency. What they didn't know was, the president and General Lacey were also listening in on a repeater in the AF One presidential office anyway.

"Abe, you play a pretty good hand of poker, right?"

"I always thought so, Mr. President."

"We're going to need that skill when we talk to Dan and Jolene. They haven't been in the service long enough to automatically answer questions without hesitation." He snorted. "That's the problem with really talented kids like these two. They don't always answer to us less talented adults fully, or they have a different agenda that they hold in higher esteem than ours!"

"Yes sir. Mr. President, I've been thinking about this situation, and I think I have an answer. Why don't we. . ." General Lacey went on to explain what he had in mind.

"Where should I put it down exactly, Dan? You're commander for this flight, sir." She added sarcastically.

"Thanks for asking, pilot. How about landing over there, between the stage and the building? We'll be out of the way yet close enough the president can show off HAL."

"Gotcha." Jolene carefully landed HAL where Dan said, and they both felt a sense of relief at finally being back on the ground.

"Jolene, do you realize that was the longest flight we ever made in HAL? Both the longest in distance and the longest in time."

"My bladder realizes it big time Dan. Mr. Commander, sir, may I leave my post to go to the bathroom?" Jolene said this in a teasing manner, but clearly, she was serious.

"That's affirmative, Pilot. I have the same need. Speaking of needs, Charlie, do you remember not to talk to anyone but us?"

"Programmed, Dan. I have. . .I don't know English well enough to say how much memory I still have available, but it is more than I will ever use."

Dan and Jolene started to leave HAL, and then Dan hesitated and went back in.

"Charlie, if Jolene and I come back in HAL with other people, don't answer unless one of us says, "Charlie, we need your help." Do you have that?

"Programmed. Is that called a 'secret code phrase' Dan?"

"Exactly. You catch on quick, Charlie."

Dan and Jolene found the bathrooms and then were corralled by the Secret Service.

"Hello. I'm Agent Kari Andrews. The president would like you to be close to the platform when he gives his speech." Agent Andrews looked more like a beauty queen than a Secret Service agent, and Jolene was not very pleased at the way Dan was looking at her.

Where in the world is she carrying her duty weapon? Jolene thought. *Certainly, not in an ankle holster, not with those high heels. Not under that blouse or in the small of her back, either. They're much too tight. Must be in her purse.*

"Mrs. Andrews, do you know why the president wants us there? We're both pretty tired. You know where we went, don't you?"

"Yes, we do, Dan. The president was very impressed but rather upset you went to the moon without asking." She smiled showing her dimples and looked into his eyes, "and it's Miss Andrews, Dan, not Mrs. If you want to, you can call me Kari."

"That doesn't answer the question, Kari," Jolene interrupted, "and we DID ask and got permission from the tower supervisor." Jolene was clearly annoyed at the interaction between the agent and Dan. "Why does the president want us there?"

"First, so we know where you are. Second, so he can call

you up to the platform if he wants to during his speech. And third," she said with frost in her voice, "so he can go with you and have a talk about Charlie."

Alarm bells went off in Dan's head. *Talk about Charlie, is that what she said? He wants to go and talk to Charlie? I'd better let Jolene know about the new password.*

"Thanks, Kari. Do you mind if Jolene and I get a soda from the machine over there?"

Kari looked at the vending machines, saw no exit and said, "I don't mind. You must be dry after a long flight like that."

"Oh, we are! Kari, would you like me to bring you a soda as well?" Dan asked.

"Why thank you Dan, but I really can't. Maybe, another time?"

"Sure thing." Dan took Jolene hand and said, "Let's go get that soda I promised you." Jolene was about to rip her hand out of Dan's when he squeezed it hard enough she couldn't. She looked up at him, realized he wasn't joking, and reluctantly played along.

While they were getting sodas out of the machine, Dan whispered the secret phrase 'Charlie, we need your help' to Jolene. Jolene giggled to cover up the exchange, then leaned on Dan's shoulder in a clearly possessive way. "Dan," she said sweetly "I can get higher heels than she has, and if you get too chummy with her, I'll use them on your body places I've never touched you before." All this was said with a smile of course, and while she was leaning very close to Dan. Jolene gave a sidelong glance to see if Kari was watching.

As it turned out, the president didn't call on them, but clearly made reference to the flight they had just taken. He promised the people at the plant would all get a good look at

HAL in the future. Just hearing him talk about that made both Dan and Jolene nervous. After the ceremonies were done and the president was through with the individual discussions, he turned and headed towards HAL with General Lacey at his side.

"You remember how we're going to play this, right Abe?"

"Yes sir. sir, I'm the one who thought it up, remember?"

"Good. Just checking. I get to be the good guy, Abe."

"You know, Mr. President? I figured that out myself."

"Smart aleck General! Stop here a minute, Abe. Let them see us talking. I want them to worry about what we are talking about."

"Smart psychology, Mr. President. We're going to need all the leverage we can get to convince them to give us the truth about this so-called tutorial."

"I realize that Abe, but they're both basically good kids, so make sure to let me sugar-coat your harsh treatment."

"Yes, sir. Sugar-coat away," the general replied with a smile. "I can be very sour!"

CHAPTER 31

"MR. PRESIDENT, I'D LIKE YOU TO MEET. . ."

"Dan. Jolene. Good to see you again." The president came up to and reached out as if to shake their hands.

"Lieutenant Jackson, Lieutenant Fisher; you come to attention and salute when the commander in chief approaches you!" General Lacey was obviously not pleased at the informal way Dan and Jolene were reacting to the president.

Startled, both lieutenants snapped to attention, then saluted.

"Now, General Lacey," the president protested, "it's just us."

"Mr. President, they still need to learn how to do things correctly. Once we cut up HAL, they will be assigned other duties, and they need to know how to do things the right way, sir."

Cut up HAL? Did I hear him correctly? Dan and Jolene had the same thought.

"Yes, now about cutting up HAL, General? You never explained to me why we need to take it apart. I mean, it works, and it's the only one we have that does work."

"Yes, Mr. President. You see, we cannot correctly manufacture the other saucers until we cut into HAL and see how it was constructed. Once we do that, I don't think it will be possible to put it back together."

"Well, General, I can't say I like that idea, but you do have a point. Okay, let's get these two to fly it into the hanger and let the plant people here start opening things up. That way. . ."

"Mr. President! That's not a good. . ." and before Dan could go further, General Lacey jumped all over him.

"Lieutenant! You don't EVER interrupt the president when he is speaking! Consider yourself under. . ."

"Now Abe, wait a minute," the president himself interrupted. "Before you say something you'll regret, why don't we let these two go back to HAL while you and I finish our discussion? Then they can show us around inside while HAL is still in one piece."

"I. . .Mr. President. . .Yes sir! Lieutenants, come to attention, salute your president, then . . .go do what he told you to do!" Clearly, General Lacey was so angry with them, he was stuttering.

Dan and Jolene saluted, then turned and jogged back to HAL. They kept silent until they were inside, then both vented their own anger.

"We can't let them cut up HAL! Why don't we. . ."

"Let's fire up HAL and take him away where. . ."

They both stopped in mid-sentence to stare at each other.

"Boy, Jolene, it makes me feel good to know you're as angry as I am!"

"Me too, Dan. But we can't do anything about it, and you know that! Besides," she added shrewdly, "something smells about the way General Lacey is acting. He's never done that before, and I wonder if he and the president are pulling some kind of scam?"

"Scam or not, Jolene, there has to be a way out of this. Charlie, they want to cut HAL apart to see how it works so they can make more saucers. What can we do?"

Silence.

"Charlie?" Jolene asked?

Nothing.

"Wait a minute! I forgot the password. Charlie, we need your help."

"Password accepted. Thank you, Dan. What is the problem?"

"The. . .our people have decided they need to make more spacecraft like HAL. They think they must cut HAL into pieces to figure out how he is built. If they do that, we won't be able to talk to you anymore."

"Why do they need more spacecraft?"

"More spacecraft means more people can go out into space. For humans, if one of something is a good thing, then ten is better. If ten is a good thing, then one hundred is better. What we need is a way to keep them from k. . ." Dan changed his mind in mid-word ". . .tearing HAL apart. Do you have any ideas, Charlie?"

"Several ideas come to mind, Dan. First, you must abandon this idea of. . .not truthfulness . . . and let the decision-makers know about this radio and me. Second, you must present my major problem to them and get permission for you to search for the Creators. Third, in exchange for your help, I can deliver nine spacecraft to your planet within eight days, and ten more every five days until you have enough. Would that be helpful?"

Dan and Jolene sat in stunned silence.

Finally, Jolene said, "Charlie, would you. . .I mean. . .can you really do that?"

"Yes, Jolene. It is not difficult for me to have my plants manufacture spacecraft like HAL. I have a further suggestion if you want?" Charlie then went on to flabbergast Dan and Jolene even further.

"If they were going to run, Abe, they would have done it by now. Want to bet they argued about that?"

"No bets, Mr. President. I agree with you. I'm just glad they didn't."

"Let's wander over to HAL and see what happens."

"Yes sir." The two men started towards HAL. Before they got there, Dan and Jolene came out and stood at parade rest outside HAL. When the president and general got close, Dan called 'attention' and he and Jolene snapped to and then saluted. General Lacey returned the salute.

"Well, Dan, Jolene, why don't you stand at ease? I'm sure General Lacey will allow that while you show us the inside of HAL."

"Yes sir. Would you both please come inside HAL?"

The four entered HAL and sat in the four seats that were available.

Dan began speaking. "Mr. President, General Lacey, I'm ashamed to admit we have not been completely truthful with you. We ourselves just discovered something so absolutely incredible that we decided we had to share it with you immediately. Unlike the story about the tutorial," he added sheepishly, "which is true, by the way . . . but not like what we pretended it was. What we just discovered is. . .literally. . .out of this world."

The president and general looked at each other as if to say, 'I told you so,' then turned to listen to Dan.

"I think the best way to start is to introduce everyone. Charlie, may I present President Ericsson, the highest decision-maker in our country, and General Lacey, one of the military leaders of our country. Mr. President, General, may I present Charlie, the supercomputer in charge of the planet Saurian, where this spaceship HAL is from. Charlie has been talking to us through the instantaneous radio in HAL."

The president and general both were too stunned to speak, so Charlie spoke first.

"Hello Mr. President, General. Dan and Jolene have given me the name Charlie based on the first letters of my official title. I have been helping them learn to fly in space with HAL because I have a major problem and need their help. Do you both understand that I am a computer and not a biological being?"

The president recovered first. "Forgive us for our shock, Charlie. Dan and Jolene may have been talking with you for some time, but we had no idea you even existed! Our race has been seeking other intelligent races since before we could fly. For me to actually sit here and talk to a non-human intelligent being is. . .difficult to believe."

"I understand and appreciate your position, Mr. President. When I explain my problem to you, I hope you will not think less of my Creators."

Charlie then went on to explain the tragedy on the planet Saurian, and that there were only three possible places any live Creators could be. Charlie also admitted its own inability to send ships of discovery.

"After reviewing everything about your race, including Dan and Jolene's ability to adjust to one hundred percent power, I believe they could pilot a ship where my robotic devices cannot. I would like them to look for the Creators and will be in constant contact to keep them safe. My prime directive is to not cause harm to any intelligent creatures.

Your race falls under the same guidelines that my Creators do as intelligent beings. Obviously, rescuing any of the Creators and returning them to their home planet would be the biggest gift your race could give to my Creators."

"May I speak, Mr. President?" General Lacey asked.

"Of course, Abe. I'm still trying to adjust to this situation. The loss of an entire intelligent race! That's a catastrophe beyond belief!"

"Charlie, how do you reconcile your prime directive with taking humans as samples who died in space?"

"General, at the time the samples. . .people. . .were taken, none of them were believed to be intelligent. Also, plant life was the primary goal for samples, not animal life. It is with a great deal of. . .shame. . .that I realize my ships ended the lives of some of your species. It was a mistake, and I cannot undo it. What I can do is make sure I never repeat the mistake and try to make amends."

"May I add something, Mr. President?" Dan asked for permission.

"Go ahead, son. I don't think I can blow any more circuits today!"

"Oh, I don't know about that, Mr. President. What convinced us to tell you the truth about Charlie was the thought of HAL being cut up. We asked Charlie how we could prevent it, and he reminded us he doesn't live in HAL but is talking by an instantaneous radio mounted here. Charlie has offered to pay for our services with something pretty incredible. Charlie, would you tell them what you will do in exchange for our help finding your Creators?"

"That is logical, Dan. Mr. President, General, Dan said you wanted to cut up HAL to see how to make more saucers. My factories can make as many saucers as you need. I can deliver nine spacecraft to your planet within eight days and ten more saucers every ten days until you have enough. Would that be helpful?"

The two older men were speechless. Dan answered 'yes' for them both.

"I can also teach your technicians the principles of the anti-gravity hyper-drive and the hyper-speed communicator. Would that be helpful?

The president and general could only nod their heads 'yes,' and again Dan accepted verbally for them.

"If you can wait until I can help your technicians restore some of the controls to HAL, I can build your saucers with human controls, so you don't need to rebuild them. Would that be helpful?"

Again, the president nodded his head yes.

"Finally, since communication is vital to all sentient beings, I will provide five additional radios with each saucer, and you may use them as you like. Would that be helpful?"

"I. . .yes. . .Good Lord! We accept your offer, Charlie." Visibly moved, the president said it more formally. "Speaking on behalf of the Government of the United States of America, I, President Ericsson, accept your offer." He sighed deeply and then continued.

"Charlie, Dan, and Jolene are young members of our race. We would like to give them additional training before sending them on a journey such as you need. Do we have time? Can you wait until they are ready for such a journey?"

"Yes, Mr. President, I can wait. As part of the maturing process, let me point out Dan was quick to abandon the. . .concept of un-truth he called lying. While I have difficulty with this concept, it seems to me that a return to truthfulness could be an indication of maturity."

"I agree, Charlie." The president looked at Dan and Jolene. "Kids, Abe and I were afraid you were hiding something from us. We deliberately set up what happened outside to shake you up and scare you into telling us what was going on." He shook his head ruefully. "We had no idea what you were really hiding!"

"What you have accomplished, this. . .bridge. . .you have established with Charlie, is nothing short of incredible. Let me state categorically, we will not, and never intended to cut up HAL for any reason. Nor did we have any intention of re-assigning you. That was something we dreamed up to shake you up. General Lacey is not really mad at you, are you Abe?"

Abe smiled. "No sir, but next time I get to play the good guy."

"Hah!" Jolene blurted. "I told Dan something was fishy about the way you were acting, General! You are much too much the gentleman to act the way you did."

"Thanks, Jolene," Abe said ruefully. "I didn't realize I was that transparent."

"Now," President Ericsson continued, "I probably don't have to ask this, but are you, Dan and Jolene, both willing to become emissaries and undertake this mission for Charlie?"

Dan looked over at Jolene. She nodded her head yes. Dan looked at the president and replied, "Mr. President, we would be honored to serve in that or any capacity you want."

"Thank you. Charlie, we must assume that your Creators are still alive somewhere. I promise you we will do everything we can to help you find them. Frankly, it is in our best interest, but we also have a strong desire to meet another intelligent race. Will you accept Dan and Jolene as our emissaries, even if they are a little young?"

"I will gladly accept them as emissaries to my Creators

through me. They have proven themselves worthy, Mr. President," Charlie replied.

"Then it's settled. Abe, they need at least two other crewmembers. . .maybe four . . . to go with them when they go. Better think about who you want. Oh, and by the way? They are both out of uniform. As of now, I am promoting them to first lieutenant. Any problems with that?"

"No sir, absolutely none, except you beat me to it again!"

"Good! I'm glad I can still beat you at something." The president noticed the gleam in Lacey's eye and asked, "By the way, Abe, how long do you think they need to be first lieutenants before they get promoted to captain?"

General Lacey smiled at Dan and Jolene, then at President Ericsson. "About one day, Mr. President. May I do it this time, Please?"

The president laughed. "I suppose. Okay, First Lieutenants Fisher and Jackson, would you please fly us into the hanger they have prepared? Not to cut up HAL, mind you, but so the people here can learn from HAL. I think the general and I both want to fly in something as advanced as HAL, even if it is just for a few feet."

"Yes sir, we can do that. Jolene, do we switch, or would you like to pilot?"

"I'll pilot this time, Dan. Okay, would you two put on your seatbelts please?"

The general and president grumbled about fussy flyers, but they both bucked their seatbelts.

"Charlie, we are going to move HAL into a big building where they make aircraft so the technicians here can learn how it works." She turned to General Lacey. "I take it this is the place where Charlie is going to teach our people what he knows and how to make the saucers they made work, Right?"

"That's correct, Jolene," the general replied.

Jolene lifted HAL off, turned and went gently around the building to where a large hangar door was open. "Is that the place?" she asked.

"Yes, Jolene. They said they would have a place. . .I think that cradle over there is where they want HAL."

Sure enough, some workers were directing them to land HAL in the cradle. Jolene expertly moved HAL over the cradle, and then set it down.

"Okay, Pilot, we've landed, and you may stand down."

"Thank you, Commander, sir," Jolene replied formally.

"Interesting. Very interesting," The president said. "I want to thank both of you not only for taking care of HAL but for all your work with Charlie."

"You're welcome, Mr. President. I presume you want us to stay here with HAL while they study it?"

"Absolutely! Will that be a problem for either one of you?"

"Other than we have no money, no clothes and no place to stay, I think we'll do just fine, sir!" Jolene added with a straight face.

All of a sudden, General Lacey had to turn his head and cough to hide a smile.

"Hmmm. I didn't think about that. Abe, do you suppose you can take care of the needs of two stranded first lieutenants in the wilds of St. Louis?"

Trying hard not to smile, the general replied, "I'm sure we can get these two captains some pay, some clothes, and I know the plant here has excellent guest facilities, sir. I have a feeling they might be living here for a while."

"General," Dan said with concern, "I just remembered; we need to let the professor know we are back safe and close out our flight with Chanute Tower."

"Good Idea, Dan. I think we should also call Dr. Foster and have him bring a few people here to study and talk to Charlie."

"I agree that would be very helpful, Mr. President," Abe said

"I think I'm also going to leave some of my people here with Dan and Jolene. They have both suddenly become 'hot' items with their relationship to Charlie, and I want to make sure no one with a higher rank messes with them."

"Now, that makes very good sense, Mr. President."

"I'm glad you agree, General. I'll leave Agents Andrews and Taylor in charge, and we can add some other agents later. For right now, however, let's go eat. It's been an exciting and very productive day, but I'm hungry."

EPILOGUE

Dan and Jolene spent several months at the McDonnell-Douglas plant in St. Louis helping "bridge" the gap between Charlie and a number of people. During that time, there were several interesting developments worth mentioning.

First, Dr. Foster and three of his team were immediately asked to visit. They were told the language program worked, but there was a better place they could talk.

"Dr. Foster, I'm Captain Dan Jackson, and this is Captain Jolene Fisher. We've been asked by President Ericsson to work with anyone who deals with HAL or Charlie."

"Thank you, Captain Jackson. I know HAL is the name of your spaceship, but who is Charlie?"

"Charlie is the computer that received the English Language DVD you sent."

"Computer?" Dr. Foster asked in surprise.

"Yes sir. Let me introduce you. Charlie, this is Dr. Foster. He was in charge of the team that broadcast the English language program to you. Dr. Foster, this is Charlie. Charlie is the name we gave him from his official Saurian Title "Computer, High-end, Aware, Robotic, Linguistic, Integrator. Charlie?"

"Dr. Foster. What a privilege to speak with you. Let me say thank you for the work and effort you put into teaching me how to speak English. Without your work, I would not have been able to communicate with Dan and Jolene or talk to your President Ericsson and General Lacey."

Dr. Foster just stared, his eyes and mouth wide open.

"Dr. Foster," Dan prompted as the silence grew longer, "wouldn't you like to say something to Charlie?"

"Uh. . .. Oh. . .yes. . .yes, I would. Charlie," he started again. "Charlie, did. . .did you say you were a computer?"

"That is correct, Dr. Foster."

"I thought there was something unusual when you gave us the same answer every time we asked the same question! We thought we were dealing with . . . uh, real live aliens."

"My Creators developed me to run the Planet Saurian so they could devote their personal time to research and exploration."

"So. . .YOU. . .actually run the whole planet? I must say. . .I like the attitude of your Creators if they thought research and exploration were more important than politics! Charlie, when can we actually meet your Creators?"

Dr. Foster and his team were then told about the tragedy on the planet Saurian.

Second, Jacob became an effective communicator in spite of his broken English on technical matters with Charlie. Jacob was not only fascinated with Charlie, but Charlie could understand what Jacob was saying when no one else could. It came as no surprise when Charlie started speaking Russian, although the Russian phrases Jacob used couldn't really be said in polite society.

Third, when Jolene decided she needed some real clothes, Agent Andrews insisted on going with her. Jolene soon discovered that Kari knew many of the good shops around and had excellent taste in clothes and shoes. Over lunch, Kari confided she deliberately used her looks and personality on men to give the impression she was just another ditsy blonde. "I don't always carry a gun, but my spike heels have been reinforced into lethal weapons. I've studied special moves that allow me to use them as a very effective close-in weapon." Jolene was fascinated with the stories Kari told her about combat moves using her spike heels. She pleaded with Kari for some instruction, and Kari broke down and helped her practice some simple moves. Afterward, Jolene decided she needed to be more careful when she next stepped on Dan, and keep her heels away from certain spots on his body. Not surprisingly, Jolene spent a lot more time with Kari after these events, and they soon became friends.

Fourth, Dan and Jolene were shopping in different stores at a big mall when they were both approached by men who offered them one million dollars if they would land the saucer HAL at a certain location. They both refused with such indignation that it drew the attention of Secret Service agents shadowing them. Both men were arrested immediately, and Dan and Jolene decided to shop together in the future.

Fifth, about six weeks after the work began in St. Louis, Charlie asked if Dan and Jolene could find some time to talk.

"Sure thing, Charlie. You must want us to help you with something. What can we do to help you?"

"Dan, Jolene, I have decided that HAL is not a suitable vehicle for you and four other humans to make a long journey. HAL is too small and doesn't offer the facilities I now know humans need. I've been studying the plans for different floaters and have decided to incorporate some of the best features into a new spacecraft for your journey. Would a larger craft with bathrooms and more privacy be helpful?

Dan and Jolene looked at each other. "You'll still be on the bigger ship, won't you?" Dan asked cautiously.

"Of course. Remember that I do not live in HAL. It is just where the radio is located."

"Then, yes! It would be nice to have toilets and a place to change clothes in private." Clearly, Jolene was pleased with Charlie's idea.

"I also put in a galley for food, the best communicators I could make, and duplicate controls so two people can help each other pilot."

"That's excellent, Charlie! May I ask what else you included?"

"Of course. The eating galley is big enough for six humans, and I also included six individual rooms for sleeping, clothes storage, and dressing, and two separate toilet and bathing facilities."

"Wow! That's great! Charlie, we may also need more water than your people do. Did you do anything about that?"

"Yes, Jolene. I have included about 500 gallons of water per person."

"500 gallons each? For four people? Charlie, that's a huge amount of water. Does it fit without taking up too much space?"

"Yes, Jolene, it fits. To correct you, I plan on 500 gallons for six humans, not four. I calculate with the recycling available, the water could last up to 19.117 years."

"Oh, Charlie, Thank you! How did you learn how to do all this? And how did you decide what we would need?"

"I studied the commercial floater planes manufactured here, as well as blueprints for your underwater submarine ships. Dan, Jolene, the trip you will make is the most important trip ever to be made for the benefit of my Creators. It will determine if any of them are still alive, or if I alone survive."

"Charlie," Dan said slowly, "You will never be alone. Never. Although I hope we find your people, you will always have a home with us. Humans do not forget their friends, and you have become the best friend Jolene, and I have ever had."

Charlie was silent for a while, then answered, "Thank you, Dan. Computer language has no word for friend, but English does. I accept your friendship and that of Jolene, and understand the sacrifice it will be for you to leave your world to help me with my quest."

"Actually, Charlie, it may not be quite the sacrifice you think it is. I think we are both looking forward to it, aren't we, Dan?"

"You bet! And if Charlie can actually improve what HAL offers, it might be more comfortable than our quarters here. I'm ready to leave here anytime!"

"I am glad you said that, Dan. Would you both please come outside?

"Sure, Charlie. Are you going to show us the plans for the new ship?"

"No. I just thought you might like to watch your new ship land for the first time. I built it a while ago, modified it extensively and sent it to your planet. Just about now it is landing outside the hanger. Would you like to see it?" Charlie teased.

Dan looked at Jolene, Jolene looked back at Dan, and they both broke into a dead run to get outside and view their new ship.

Author's Brief Biography

Dennis R. Durbin retired after teaching 38 years in Illinois Schools. He received his Bachelor's Degree from the University of Illinois Urbana Champaign and his Master's Degree from Northern Illinois University DeKalb and has an additional 32 hours towards a Master's Degree in Instructional Technology. He taught Band, Choir, Music Appreciation, Theater, AutoCAD 2000 and 14 modules of Technology in the Tech Lab. Dennis is married, and he and his wife have two children; a son and a daughter.

Dennis is also known as Officer Durbin and worked part-time as a Police Officer for six police departments over a span of 37 years. Dennis presently works as a Police Officer for a department in Northern Illinois. He worked as an Engineer-Announcer for three radio stations and Assistant Station Manager for a student Television Station. Dennis was also a Steelworker for Granite City Steel, Vilberg-Victor Steel Fabrications in St. Louis and Blaw-Knox Heavy Equipment in Mattoon. He also designed all the spaceships in this series and made the 3D models in AutoCAD 2000.

In 2003 Dennis and his partner were awarded the "2002-2003 Illinois High School 'Technology Program of the Year'" award by the International Technology Education Association.

The school flew Dennis and his partner to Nashville for the Awards Ceremony.

Dennis recently decided he might consider retiring from police work when he reaches 72 years of age in 2018. He plays 21 band instruments plus all the percussion toys available and has spent years and years teaching Color Guard, Marching Band and Drum & Bugle Corps in Illinois and Wisconsin.

www.dennisrdurbin.com

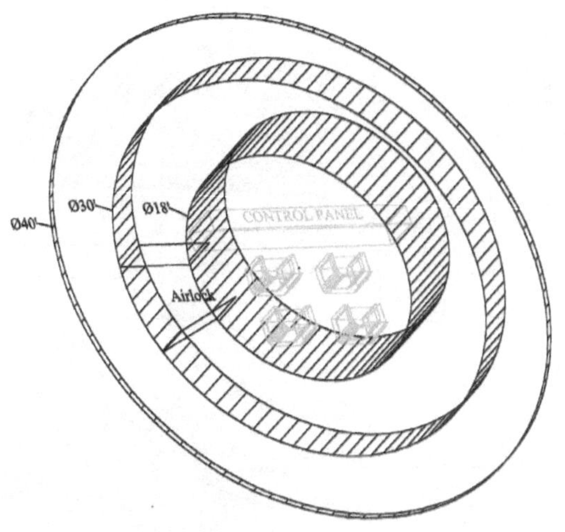

Ø40'
Ø30'
Ø18'
CONTROL PANEL
Airlock

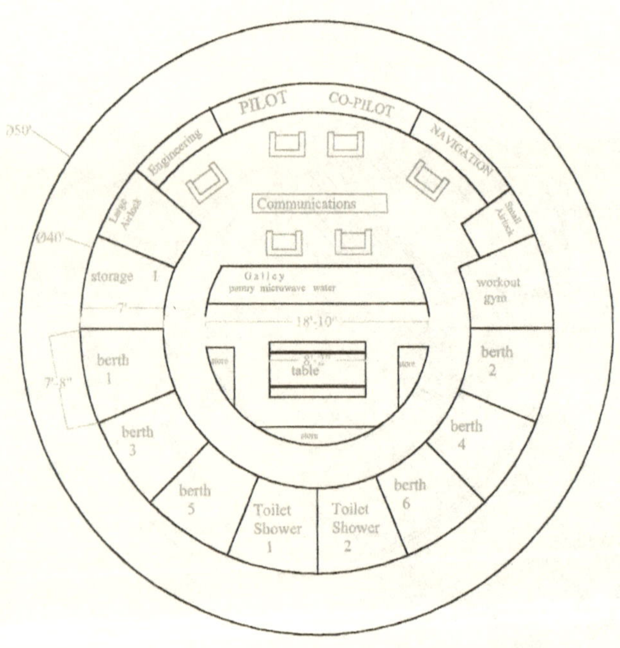

Ø50'
Ø40'
PILOT
CO-PILOT
Engineering
NAVIGATION
Large Airlock
Small Airlock
Communications
storage   1
workout gym
Galley
pantry   microwave   water
7'
18'-10"
berth 1
store
8'-6"
table
store
berth 2
7' 8"
store
berth 3
berth 4
berth 5
Toilet Shower 1
Toilet Shower 2
berth 6

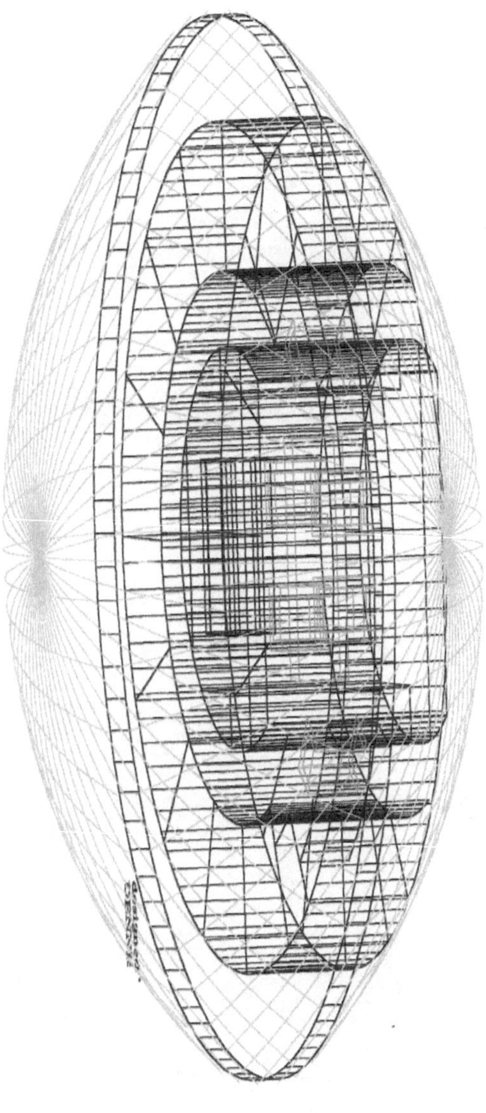